When Virginia... ages to fall asle... head to help pass the time while she was staring at the ceiling. As she got older the stories became more complicated—sometimes taking weeks to get to thei...

...li... ...with her wonderful husband and two teel... ...t still takes her for ever to fall asleep.

LILIAN AND THE
IRRESISTIBLE DUKE

Virginia Heath

MILLS & BOON

First Published in Great Britain 2020
by Mills & Boon, an imprint of HarperCollins*Publishers*
1 London Bridge Street, London, SE1 9GF

© 2020 Harlequin Books S.A.

Special thanks and acknowledgement are given to Virginia Heath
for her contribution to Secrets of a Victorian Household series.

ISBN: 978-0-263-27286-4

For all my writing friends
who help me climb every mountain.
You know who you are.

Chapter One

April 1843

Lilian huddled beneath her fancy new shawl, enjoying the bracing sea breeze almost as much as the soft heat of the early morning sunrise. Some things were simply too special to miss and her first sighting of Italy was one of them.

What a painting it would make! The wispy clouds peppering the orange-tinged sky, the shadows they cast on the green hills on the horizon, both framing the clusters of pale stone buildings as they trickled down into the town and the imposing high walls of the ancient port, standing tall and proud in the turquoise ocean.

She had seen Turner's beautiful depictions of Italy years ago, at an exhibition in Somerset House, and had fallen in love with his romantic landscapes, but now she realised even his talented brush had not done this magnificent vista justice. It was more beautiful than she could have ever imagined…not that she had imagined she would ever get to see it.

Hers had been a life of great responsibility and great purpose. Three children to bring up. A devoted wife to a wonderful and philanthropic man. Helping him to build his dream—the Fairclough Foundation—from the ground up so together they could help hundreds of unfortunate women forge better lives for themselves with new skills and a clean slate. Then continuing that dream and raising their family all alone after her beloved husband had been taken from her much too young. Life had been hard. At times, downright impossible. Only a few months ago it had all seemed likely to fall crashing about her ears.

Yet here she was.

Still standing and a little lost, truth be told, because the world seemed to be moving rapidly around her and she no longer knew her place in it. Her purpose had been diminished and she had allowed it to happen. And happily. It was only right that her children should forge ahead with their own lives. The natural order of things was for parents to step aside as they did so.

Yet it didn't make it any easier. Especially as in her mind she felt no different from the way she had two decades ago. At five and forty she was a long way off old, yet equally well past young. Neither ready to retire to a life of knitting or embroidery nor sure what she might do next. She felt as if she was standing at a crossroads and this unexpected trip to Rome a temporary reprieve from the indecision of which path to tread. An adventure.

A new adventure pursuing a lifelong passion. An adventure entirely for herself for a change. Finally going to see the great masterpieces she had always dreamed of and most particularly Michelangelo's spectacular ceiling in the Sistine Chapel. A painting she had wanted to see since she had viewed a tiny example of his work briefly on loan to the National Gallery. Art had always been her solace—not that she had any talent for drawing—but it had been a way for her to relax when life got too much. When the world got on top of her, stealing an hour looking at the beauty which others created with a simple brush and palette always rejuvenated her. Something about the Italian painters and landscapes always called to her, but she had never dreamed she would ever visit Italy to actually see it. After a quarter of a century devoting her life to others, she still couldn't quite believe it. Or get used to the new freedom she had not been ready to experience.

'I'll wager you are glad we all talked you into coming now, aren't you?' Beside her, Alexandra was grinning. She had seen this panorama many times before and had a whole host of friends here. 'We shall have a leisurely breakfast, drinking cappuccinos in Civitavecchia and be in Rome with Carlotta in time for dinner. Palazzo delle Santafano is just outside the city. Close enough to see it all and far enough away to escape when the city gets too much.'

Civitavecchia... Palazzo delle Santafano... *Cappuccino...* Every word in Italian was music to her ears, sounding sinfully mysterious and romantic. She had always been a romantic soul at heart. 'I cannot imagine it ever getting too much.' Lilian watched the walls of the port loom ever closer like an excited girl at her first assembly. 'It is so lovely.' And so unlike London she might as well be in a different world. But then she had practically crossed the world to get here. Trains, carriages, ships...so many days of travel she no longer knew which day of the week it was and really couldn't bring herself to care. Not when every day had suddenly seemed like a bold new adventure. She had never seen France, or even the white cliffs of Dover for that matter until she started this trip. Thanks to the Foundation and more than two decades of motherhood in her spartan home at the back of the institute, her life had been rooted in London on the dubious streets close to the Irish Rookery in the shadow of Westminster Abbey.

'Trust me—it will. The pace of life, the heat, the customs, the people… The Italians are very different from what you are used to. They are a passionate race.'

Lilian knew that. Or rather she suspected as much thanks to her lone encounter with her first and only Italian at Christmas. Pietro Venturi— Duca della Torizia… Another jumble of seductive Italian words.

He had been nothing like any man she had ever met. Dark, much too tall and exotic, he was more confident and considerably less reserved than the typical English male. He had looked boldly into her eyes, lingered over kissing her hand, flirted outrageously and his deep voice and seductive accent had quite taken her by surprise. She blamed that and, of course, the three glasses of wine she had consumed at Lady Fentree's soirée last Christmas for agreeing to travel back to Alexandra's house alone with just him in the carriage. And she blamed the alcohol, the shameless flirting, the accent, those intense sultry dark eyes and the intimacy of the carriage for allowing the Duca della Torizia to steal that kiss. And for kissing him so enthusiastically back.

Her first kiss in a decade. Although she still hadn't made her mind up if it was the unexpected surprise of a single kiss after so long without which made it so scandalously memorable, or the fact that he did it so well and so thoroughly. For its entire duration she quite forgot she was a middle-aged widow who had never shown any desire to be kissed again before he had stolen one.

'Mrs Fairclough...you have such beautiful eyes...'

He had stared deeply into them, tracing the pad of one finger gently down her cheek and making her skin tingle for the first time in a decade.

'For some reason they call to me...'

Then his lips had whispered over hers and everything—the carriage, the snow, all her myriad responsibilities, all her problems— everything but him disappeared as she lost herself in his kiss.

And as much as the incident was regrettable in the extreme and completely unlike her, against all her better judgements her mind had frequently wandered back to it since, reminding her body that, although it was older, it still had the capacity to crave a man's touch just as it always had.

But that brief, chance meeting had signalled the start of something and was perhaps one of the reasons she had agreed to this exciting holiday abroad. While she disagreed she had earned a break from her life as her children had insisted—because she was too selfless by half and they wanted to repay her for everything she had done—Lilian did agree she was due an adventure. She also needed to do something to get away from her children, not because she didn't love them all to distraction, because she did, but because they were all newly married and ready to start their own adventures. Since her daughter Lottie had taken over the running of the Foundation with her husband, Jasper, Lilian had felt redundant and a little in the way.

She had once been a besotted newlywed herself and knew how all-encompassing and thrilling that heady time was. Love, lust, longing… the sheer joy of one another's company. She had had that once. Except she had got to enjoy Henry on her own, without a well-meaning parent in the wings, and she wanted the same for them. Millie and Cassius were at Falconmore Hall. Silas and Mary, freshly returned from America, had rented a house close to the Foundation so they could spend some time in England. And Lottie and Jasper had moved in with Lilian. It was they who most needed their privacy. Even with the very best intentions, she had walked in on them too many times in the midst of an embrace and felt awful when they had guiltily pulled apart when they should be basking in the first flush of love. Just as Lilian had shamelessly and greedily basked in it with Henry all those years ago. She had always been a passionate romantic at heart, too.

Not one of her children needed her now. They would, when grandchildren inevitably came along, but for the time being she had no real purpose and didn't want to be underfoot as they all enjoyed those first precious months with their new spouses. As much as her children loved her in return, they had also been unsubtly keen to reward her for her years of selfless service by acting together to send her on this extended trip abroad. She was both grateful and philosophical about their generosity, but she certainly didn't intend to squander the opportunity and hoped two months of distance from her old life and purpose might give her some clarity on what to do with it next.

'What is Carlotta like?' Their hostess, the Contessa di Bagnoregio, was a great friend of Alexandra from her youth. As a duke's daughter, and the wife of a viscount who had loved to travel, she was used to mixing with the aristocracy of Europe.

'A great deal like us. A similar age. Children all grown and flown the nest. Widowed like you. She has a wicked sense of humour, too, and hates being idle. Since her husband died, she has thrown herself into the art world. Her brother deals in it and makes an absolute fortune selling Old Masters to new money. He charms them into buying and she enforces the prices once the remorse of agreeing to them inevitably sets in—believe me, some of them are eye-watering. But if anyone can squeeze blood out of a stone it is she. I would hate to have to do business with her, as she has the reputation of being terrifying. Only a brave few dared argue money with her, but it is always futile as they inevitably end up paying through the nose regardless. She is also hideously philanthropic. The pair of you will get on famously.'

Lilian hoped so. There was nothing worse than staying in the house of someone you felt awkward around and she put no stock in titles or the superiority of blue blood with hers being the common red variety and her link to the aristocracy only tenuous through marriage. Not that her husband had put any stock in his snobbish family. Henry had remained happily estranged from them all after they had cut him off when he had lowered himself to marry someone so indisputably from trade. The one member of his family Henry had tolerated was his cousin Alexandra, who had been the only aristocrat Lilian had had any real contact with until her eldest daughter Millie had married Cassius and become a marchioness. Rank had never held much stock in the Fairclough household where strength of character and deed were judged to be more important measures.

'Come—we are about to dock. Let us grab what we need from the cabin and eat.' Alexandra tugged her arm. 'After we've watched those burly men unload some of the cargo first. Nothing quite builds up an appetite like the sight of the rippling muscles of a shirtless sailor.'

'You are incorrigible.' As was Alexandra's beloved husband, George, who had lobbied hard for Lilian to go to Rome with his out-

rageous wife. Both of them were of the belief she was in dire need of some fun. And to
make sure she had it, George had declared it a
ladies-only holiday, citing that he had far too
many pressing business matters to attend to
when she knew he simply did not want her to
feel like a spare wheel. Which she was starting to feel quite a bit.

'One of us has to be—but I am hopeful some
of it might rub off on you in the next six weeks.
You have been upstanding and sensible for far
too long and you will need to be a little incorrigible to have a proper Italian adventure.'

The roads to Rome, although charming,
weren't quite as good as Lilian was used to.
Thanks to the incessant potholes and sedentary
speed of their driver, who seemed determined
to go into every one of them, they arrived at
the *palazzo* after dark. Not only did she get to
miss the sight of it in daylight, her smart new
travelling dress was a crumpled mess and she
ached from head to foot. From what she could
make out as they rattled up the long straight
drive, the building was huge and rectangular in
shape. Friendly lamps burned in several windows
framed in lacey foliage she didn't recognise, but
that seemed to grow with abandon up the high

walls. They passed through a grand archway and she realised the house was not a solid block, but more a villa built around a huge torchlit court-yard filled with a fountain, classical-looking statues and a profusion of shrubs in enormous terracotta pots.

They were greeted by their hostess, a petite, smiling woman who was not at all as Lilian had imagined her. She had expected to meet someone more formidable rather than this dark-haired, elfin creature who preferred to kiss Lilian noisily on both cheeks rather than incline her head or shake hands like strangers did when introduced at home.

'Darlings, you must be exhausted! I shall have baths drawn for you both immediately so that you can refresh yourselves and relax before dinner. Apart from the torturous drive from Civitavecchia, which seems to get worse with each passing year, I trust the rest of your long journey was pleasant?'

'It was indeed, Contessa.'

'Contessa! We do not need to adhere to for-mality. Alexandra has told me so much about you in her letters I feel we are friends already. You must call me Carlotta—I insist. And I shall call you Lilian and by tomorrow we shall know all of each other's secrets like the very best friends always do. We have much in common. I hear your daughters are recently married, exactly like mine, although I have been blessed with *bambini* already. Two grandsons. Twins. From my eldest daughter and another surprise on the way from my youngest.'

'I had twins! A boy and a girl. Silas and Millie. Both very recently married alongside my youngest daughter Lottie. But only in the last few months. My daughter-in-law is already expecting, but no sign of...' What was the lovely word Carlotta had used? '*bambini* yet for the girls. Although I hope it won't be long.'

'They married for *amore*, did they not? That always speeds things along.' She wiggled her dark eyebrows suggestively. 'Ah...to be young and in love. So much *passione*, yes? I miss it. My Gennaro was a vigorous man.'

That she said such things out loud was both shocking and refreshing. Lilian was no prude. She had fallen head over heels in love with her husband and had enjoyed the physical aspect of their marriage immensely, but working at the Foundation, surrounded by so many unfortunate women who had not been afforded the luxury of virtue or tenderness, she knew both sides of passion. Knew it, but had never discussed it openly with anyone.

'Don't frighten her yet, Carlotta. Poor Lilian is fresh off the boat and still shackled by her Englishness.'

'A good point, my friend. I forget how buttoned up you all are. We will feed her and fill her with wine and in a few days some of those buttons will come undone.' Her hostess grinned wickedly. 'And if she is lucky, we will find this pretty English rose a hot-blooded Italian lover to rip off the rest.'

'Oh, I am not here for that!' Lilian could feel her cheeks heating with a blush, when she never blushed any more and hadn't for a good fifteen years.

'Nobody ever is, darling…but it wouldn't hurt now, would it?'

'No, really. I have no interest in men any more.'

Of course she didn't. She was forty-five, for goodness sake. Much too old for flirting. Let alone courting.

'Why ever not? You are a long way off dead.'

'Er…' Although she did have a point. One Lilian had not really considered until the Duca della Torizia had reawakened it and she had begun to think about it again. Something about him had made her body hum.

'And it is not as if we are talking marriage.'

Carlotta shrugged. 'Who wants to give up their independence for that again? One of the great benefits of our age and situation is we can indulge our own passions without such enduring complications. Although if the right man came along to tempt me, I might consider it…but he would have to be exceptional.' She sighed wistfully. 'In case you haven't already guessed, I am a hopeless romantic at heart.' Something else they apparently had in common. 'But I am scaring you as Alexandra says.' Carlotta smiled and took her arm. 'Forgive my earthy Italian nature. I have a tendency to say whatever comes into my head before I consider if it is appropriate.'

'It is why I love you,' said Alexandra, linking her arm through her friend's, too. 'And why I keep coming back here. It is good to be less English for a while, Lilian. Liberating, in fact. I am rejuvenated each time I come to Rome. Or at least I will be once I have soaked these old bones in that bath you promised, Carlotta. And you are right, the road from Civitavecchia. It is atrocious…'

It took almost an hour for the old friends to catch up and for Lilian to finally see her bedchamber. Except it wasn't a simple bedchamber. The beautiful suite of rooms was situated on a long landing just around the corner from Lady Alexandra's and was comprised of a small sitting room, bedroom and separate dressing area complete with an exquisite copper claw-footed bathtub filled with steaming water. She dismissed the maid, using mostly hand gestures as the girl knew no English and her own Italian was non-existent, and unpinned her hair. Sighing, she massaged her aching scalp with her fingers before kicking off her boots and undoing the back of her travelling gown.

She was about to strip it off when she remembered the decadent bar of fine-milled French soap she had treated herself to during their overnight stop in Bordeaux. Such a fine bath deserved fine soap and so did she. This trip was her time to be selfish and self-indulgent after all. She had faithfully promised her children she would enjoy the whole experience the way she wanted to and put any guilt aside for its duration. That meant she would bathe with her fancy soap and revel in every minute of it. She turned and headed to her still-unpacked trunk to fetch it when she realised the trunk was not hers, but Alexandra's. The footmen must have mixed them up. She could hardly have a bath and have nothing clean to put on afterwards either.

She poked her head out into the hallway to call back her maid, but the girl was gone. She knew Alexandra—her maid would still be there even if her mistress was already soaking in her bath and Lilian selfishly wanted her soap. Rather than retying her dress, she wrapped her shawl tightly around the loose and gaping bodice and decided to make a dash for it before the water got cold. With one hand on the shawl and the other holding the full skirts and petticoats of her uncharacteristically fashionable new dress, she scurried down the hall, staying close to the wall. As she pivoted around the sharp corner, she hit him, her face connecting with the broad expanse of his chest.

'I am so sorry…' She had to crane her neck to look at his face and the apology died on her lips a split second before her face heated crimson.

Chapter Two

Pietro had been having a bad day. Or rather it was not so much that the day was any worse than any other, but that he had awoken feeling restless and that restlessness refused to go away no matter how much he tried to divert it with purpose.

The restlessness, as he called the odd mood which crept up on him without warning, had always plagued him since he was a young man. A sense of something not quite right, something missing, a peculiar feeling of dissatisfaction with his life. It predated his marriage and had bothered him throughout its short and turbulent duration. In his youth, he put it down to ambition and over-exuberance and had always assumed it would disappear with age. Except with each passing year, and despite his success and his significantly increased fortune, it seemed to plague him more now than it ever had. His usual method of distracting it with work, and if that failed to assuage it with a brief fling with a willing woman, no longer seemed to alleviate it for quite as long as it used to and he often found his mood soured because he was so very bored with it all. Although he could never quite pinpoint exactly what it was he was dissatisfied with because he had no earthly idea exactly what it was he wanted.

To make matters worse, despite actively looking, suitable distractions outside his punishing work schedule had been thin on the ground lately. The stalwarts he could always rely on held little appeal and he hadn't met a new woman in months who had seemed worth the effort.

Apart from one…

One whom he would have enjoyed thoroughly seducing just before Christmas. The troubled, proper, pretty one who had strangely intrigued him at Lady Fentree's festive gathering in England. The one who had just apparently walked straight into him.

'Hello…'

Her dark hair was loose about her shoulders, silky and wavy against her pale English skin as one of those creamy shoulders was exposed bare above the shawl she clutched tightly. Feline green eyes blinked up at him, the mouth he had thoroughly enjoyed kissing all those months before a startled O. And she was blushing. At her age. How…interesting.

All in all, the woman who had strangely intrigued him during that chilly English winter, because she wasn't his usual type at all, suddenly looked very much his type in his home town now. A petite, gloriously curvaceous, tousled and thoroughly intriguing armful of woman who looked wonderfully scandalised to have collided with him again. Her eyes were on his mouth and he realised in that second she was remembering their heated kiss in the carriage just as he was. It was a memory which he had often revisited since, which was not like him either as he was not one to reminisce. What was the point? The past usually only served to depress him and he enjoyed the here and now.

But she had surprised him that night. He still couldn't think of a reason why he had been initially drawn to her at the interminable house party he had been dragged to. But once they were alone in that dark carriage, thick fresh snowflakes falling outside under the moonlit sky and crunching beneath the wheels on that much-too-short journey, he had remembered clearly why he had kissed her.

Because in that moment, he had wanted to. It was that simple. And she had surprised him by kissing him back with barely contained passion and, for a few short minutes, the carriage, the snow and the entire world had disappeared the second his lips had touched hers.

Pietro could not remember the last time such a thing had happened because his head was always full of other things. His business, his wealthy clients. Brokering discreet deals with the many financially challenged aristocrats who needed to liquidate some of their assets, then creating enough excitement and intrigue about those paintings and sculptures so they not only found a welcoming new home, but he was paid a fortune for rehoming them. At least one of these things was always at the back of his mind at all times and usually more to the forefront than the recesses, yet in that carriage, on that short road between one house and another, it had only been him and her.

It had been a truly unforgettable kiss. One which, if he were honest with himself, had caught him off guard and left him decidedly off kilter. Enough to leave the area quickly in case he was tempted to do it again. Such an unexpected and unforeseen reaction was far too complicated to indulge further and Pietro avoided complications like the plague.

'What are you doing here!'

'I live here.'

'You do?' Her voice came out in a delightfully outraged squeak as she simultaneously realised her shawl wasn't entirely covering her modesty and wrestled with it ineffectually.

He nodded, his mouth curving into a smile for the first time that day. 'Which begs the obvious question, *cara*…what are *you* doing here?'

'I am here with my late husband's cousin… with Lady Alexandra…we've come to stay with Carlotta…'

'Ah…' Instinct told him this was no accident. It had the stamp of his sister all over it. She despaired of his quarter-century of bachelorhood, declaring it unnatural—especially as he had been widowed so young. 'And she put you in this room?' Conveniently located right next to his in the family wing. Much too coincidental to be coincidence.

'Do you know Carlotta? Silly question…of course you know Carlotta if you live in her house…'

'Actually, this is my house.'

'It is?' She didn't look very happy about this news, her dark eyebrows drawing together to create a charming wrinkle between them. 'Lady Alexandra led me to believe this is her friend's house. Carlotta's house.'

'Carlotta moved in here after her husband died three years ago. To bother me. Something she does very well. My little sister has always liked to meddle.' And matchmake. Although she was usually more subtle about it.

'Your sister?'

'They never told you?'

'No…neither she nor my *dear* cousin thought to tell me that my host was her brother… Or that we had met.' Her eyes flicked to his lips again before she caught herself and forced them to hold his gaze. He bothered her. The knowledge warmed him until he reminded himself he should probably be more wary than warmed. Mrs Fairclough was a widow. He was a widower. Carlotta and Alexandra had conspired to put her in the room next door to him, thrust directly in the path of temptation, when there were another twenty serviceable bedchambers in the *palazzo* well away from his.

'Clearly they both like to meddle, as I suspect you have been brought here on purpose, Mrs Fairclough.' It didn't take a genius to work

out what was going on. Alexandra must have
reported back straight after Christmas, eager
to tell his sister he had shown an interest in a
woman and Carlotta being Carlotta, she had
assumed it meant more than it did and had
thought to encourage it. 'To matchmake, perhaps?' Unless the woman before him was in
league with them. She wouldn't be the first to
assume he was in need of a wife and, as he had
instigated their kiss, she might well assume she
could be the one to tempt him to abandon his
bachelor ways...

'Well, if they did, I can assure you it has
nothing to do with me! I would have put them
straight and told them I wasn't the least bit interested in such nonsense.'

A vehement and convincing denial which
needed testing. In his experience, nobody manipulated better than a woman, especially a
woman with a mission. 'Yet here you are...
Right next door to my bedchamber...' His eyes
appreciatively travelled the length of her, set-
tling on the bare toes poking beneath the hem
of her dress and back up again to the blush
which now stained her delicate collarbone,
swanlike neck and the alabaster cheeks his
fingers suddenly ached to touch—despite all

his rampant suspicions. 'Looking decidedly interesting.'

'I was about to get into the bath.' In her embarrassment, her teeth worried her plump bottom lip, drawing his eyes there as she clutched at her shawl like a shield. 'Your servants brought me the wrong trunk by mistake. Mine must be with Lady Alexandra.' As if noticing her bare toes for the first time, she twisted her feet awkwardly to hide them under the copious material of her skirt. 'I was fetching my soap.'

'I can fetch it for you—and perhaps help to scrub your back?'

His outrageous flirting had the most wonderful effect. Her green eyes sparkled like emeralds and she threw back her shoulders like an offended queen. Something which did wonders for her full bosom beneath the thin shawl. 'No, thank you.'

'If you change your mind...'

'I won't!' She spun on her bare heel and marched back to her bedchamber, slamming the door loudly, and he found himself frowning as he heard her turn the key decisively in the lock.

A woman determined to seduce a man would have flirted back, not shut him out. She would have parried and simpered and used all her feminine wiles to lure him into her trap. Mrs Fairclough had been offended and angry. Much too keen to get out of his way. Exactly like a woman who was as surprised and horrified to see him as he was her.

Pietro winced at his own crassness.

What was the matter with him to be so unforgivably rude? He was prone to cynicism and who could blame him? But thanks to the restlessness which continually ate away at him, he was in danger of becoming *too* cynical and jaded. And perhaps too vain and arrogant in his appeal, if he was assuming she had purposely been patrolling the hallway in a state of partial undress simply to meet him and seduce him—when there was no possible way she could have known he would come back when he had. In fact, he had told his sister he would not be home that night as he had a longstanding meeting with an old friend in Napoli he could not possibly cancel.

The old friend had really been one of his stalwarts, the American widow Mrs Ida Wayfair, whose house was but a stone's throw from here. But like the paintings he bought and sold, he kept his affairs ruthlessly discreet. In public he was widely known as a charmer—but was careful nobody knew which of the women's beds he actually visited.

Ida had an insatiable physical appetite, a liberal attitude in the bedroom and the same strict views on any sort of serious, emotional and permanent attachment as he had. She was also very discreet—something he liked her a great deal for. Except the thought of slipping between Ida's well-used sheets again hadn't been enough to tempt him from feeling sorry for himself this evening, and he had cancelled. Then taken his frustration at his own dissatisfaction and bad mood out on Carlotta's unexpected guest because the sight of her had unnerved him.

Again.

She hadn't deserved that.

He would apologise to her later for being crass and for offending her delicate sensibilities with his outrageous and indelicate flirting. He never usually behaved so clumsily—especially if he found the lady as attractive as he did in this case. Usually, Pietro prided himself on being a charming flirt, who enjoyed the subtle art of seducing as much as the ultimate seduction itself.

He wasn't entirely sure what had just come over him, but knew he had to make amends. She was a guest in his house and of his sister's. He shouldn't be shamelessly flirting with her for exactly those two reasons. Firstly, it was a point of principal to never dally with any friends of the family, because it was much too close to home for comfort. And secondly, he never ever dallied at home because it was much too personal. He might use the house as a way to seduce them, but he would never seduce them in it. The only person who had ever slept in his bed here in the *palazzo* was him and that was the way he intended to keep things.

He could leave a strange bed at exactly the time of his choosing, which was always before the lady beside him woke up. Cosy breakfasts gave ladies ideas—even ladies like Ida—and daylight brought a truth to the proceedings which Pietro would rather not experience. He liked to keep his emotions detached from his desires and to do that required distance. For both those reasons, Mrs Fairclough and her potent kisses were strictly out of bounds henceforth. He had no place flirting with her because she was already much too close for comfort.

Although Mrs Fairclough had looked like a woman who needed a bit of flirting in her life. That was probably what had drawn him to her last winter. That and her lovely green eyes which had called to him. She had seemed burdened then, worried, and he had taken it upon himself to make her feel better. He still had no idea why he had needed to do that. He wasn't completely heartless, it was true, but he was no Good Samaritan either. Yet her quiet sadness had lured him to her and once he was with her, he had fallen completely under her spell. Then fate had placed them in the same carriage unchaperoned and he had kissed her because…well…he still wasn't entirely sure how to explain that. Other than it had felt entirely right at the time. She had responded with more passion than her prim, no-nonsense attire had suggested she would. More passion than either of them had expected. Certainly enough to keep her fresh in his mind these past four months. The little oasis of excitement in the barren desert of dissatisfaction he seemed doomed to wallow in.

Chapter Three

Lilian had to give herself a stiff talking to before plucking up the courage to go down to dinner, and that was after the stiff talking to she gave Alexandra. Typically, her cousin brushed it aside as an oversight, claiming she hadn't remembered introducing the Duca to Lilian at Lady Fentree's party. Without confessing to her they had shared a heated kiss in a carriage all alone, and that kiss now rendered her situation very awkward, to say the least, it was difficult for Lilian to convey exactly how miffed she was about being kept in the dark about the situation.

She was even more miffed at his behaviour earlier, because his shallow, unsubtle flirting had soured a memory which she had stupidly treasured since. In that carriage, she had felt special, interesting and appealing in a way she hadn't in years. Or so she had thought after three large glasses of wine and some of the worst weeks of her life. His clumsy attempt at seduction on the landing this evening had made her realise he hadn't thought her particularly special or interesting at all. Merely convenient, needy and pathetically malleable and that galled. Because she had been all of those things that fateful night in that carriage.

But as a guest in his house, she would have to remain polite even if she was annoyed at him for making her feel cheap and convenient. Besides, she would not allow the despicable actions of one overly charming Lothario to spoil her great Italian adventure. Better to face it head on, learn from it and consign it to the past like the foolish mistake it was. At some point this evening, she would talk to him and politely explain it had not been his charm which had led to her kissing him back, but the alcohol and that she had realised it had been a huge mistake from the outset. One she had absolutely no intention of repeating. Then, the air cleared, she would keep herself occupied with Rome and all the delights it offered and avoid her now-distasteful host wherever possible.

Lilian took a deep breath, then sailed into the drawing room, or *salotto* as Alexandra had called it when they had arrived, with what she hoped resembled more confidence than she was feeling. Carlotta rushed towards her smiling, so she was able to ignore the arrogant Duke leaning against the fireplace directly across from the door. Or at least her eyes could. Her body apparently had a mind of its own. Her skin felt decidedly odd, her nerves a bit bouncy and her stupid pulse a tad too fast.

'Lilian…you look beautiful. Those colours really suit you.' She had argued against a dress as bold and as fashionable as this one, assuming the vibrant printed coral stripes on the cream brocade, complete with the sweeping ruffled neckline and short sleeves, was too young for her. It had been Lottie who had convinced her to get it, pointing out that older women than she had worn gowns far bolder at Millie and Cassius's society wedding celebration—and looked lovely in them. Lilian had relented, but never actually intended wearing it, but for some reason tonight she had needed to feel bold and lovely, so had donned it on a whim. It was too late to regret it now, despite the rakish Duca's obvious expression of appreciation as he sauntered towards her and her recklessly bouncing nerve endings.

'Indeed she does.' He bowed politely and

kissed her hand. She withdrew it quickly in case he had a mind to linger again, but felt her pulse quicken anyway. The accent, combined with his undeniably rugged, handsome features, sublime spicy smell and impressive height called to the passionate female within her despite all her common sense. 'Welcome to my home, Mrs Fairclough. My sister tells me you have had no time at all today to explore the *palazzo*. I should be delighted to take you on a little tour of the ground floor now.'

Seeing her hesitation, Carlotta got the wrong end of the stick. 'You might as well. Dinner is not for another thirty minutes at least and I am still awaiting Alexandra. Be sure to show her the fresco in the *gran salone*, Pietro. Lilian is a huge lover of art. Something you both have in common, no?' Or perhaps she had completely the right end of the stick and was matchmaking as Pietro had suspected. Yet either way, she had been pushed into a corner. Refusing would be impolite and would cast an atmosphere over the entire holiday.

He offered his arm and she took it, pasting what she hoped was a polite and indifferent smile on her face. At least this unwelcome time alone with him would give her the opportunity to clarify his misapprehensions about their kiss and her presence in his house. She might well be at a metaphorical crossroads, but not one of the paths ahead of her included a man!

He led her out of the cosy family room and along a long hallway filled with gilt panelling and a marble floor. As soon as they turned a corner he stopped dead and sighed.

'I cannot move another step until I have apologised for my disgraceful behaviour earlier. I have no defence of it, other than you caught me off guard after a taxing day and I wrongly assumed that you were complicit in my sister's incessant matchmaking. I realise that is no excuse for my ungentlemanly behaviour and I apologise unreservedly for insulting you. It was not my finest hour and I was certainly not behaving as myself. I beg of you to forgive me.'

Entirely disarmed, because he had completely taken the outraged wind out of her sails, all Lilian could do was accept his pretty apology in the manner it was given. 'You are forgiven. Because I also suspect Alexandra had a hand in it. She likes to meddle, too, and seems to have made me a bit of a project, as you can see.' She gestured to the bold gown and then regretted it when his eyes swept her body again at the invitation. There was something about the way he did it which played havoc with her insides. 'I really had no clue there was any connection between you and the Contessa until tonight.'

'I realised that the moment you rightly slammed your door in my face at my gross impertinence.' His voice was like melted chocolate and his accent made normally curt English words like 'impertinence' sound positively sinful. Or at least the goose pimples on the back of her neck found it sinful. And the least said about his intense dark eyes the better. The way they looked at her, boldly locked with hers... Gracious, he was lovely! And she had plainly taken leave of her senses to be thinking such nonsense after just one pretty apology and a foolhardy kiss in a carriage.

'It would appear we are equally reluctant to be toyed with, both the innocent victims of two scheming women. I am only relieved we discovered their machinations in time before it created any irreversible awkwardness between us. I would hate to be the reason you did not enjoy your visit to Rome.'

'Forewarned is forearmed, as we say in my country. I am glad we cleared the air.' However, there was no point in shying away from the difficult bit of the conversation. The bit which would thoroughly clear the air. 'I feel I also owe you an apology for what occurred at Christmas.' She hoped ignoring the blush which threatened to bloom might make it subside, but the ugly heat crept up her neck regardless. 'December was a particularly trying time for me and, fortified with more wine than I am used to, I might have given you the wrong impression. What I mean is…er…the…er…kiss… was a mistake.'

'And there I was, thinking it was my charm, the moonlight and the magic of the moment.' He was smiling at her, his dark eyes dancing, as he clutched at his heart as if she had wounded him. 'Have you no sympathy for my delicate male pride?' Then his eyes seemed to darken further and his deep voice became positively naughty as it dropped an octave. 'But mistake or no, it was a spectacular kiss, was it not? At least credit me with that, *signora.*'

She couldn't help smiling in response. The combination of his mischievous dark eyes, seductive voice and his knowing expression conspired to bring out the worst in her. 'It was pleasant enough, I suppose.' Good grief! Was she flirting? After twenty-five years she'd assumed she had forgotten how.

'Only pleasant? Oh, *signora,* that will not do

and it is not wise to confide it. Such a lacklustre compliment might only spur me to do better, as a matter of honour. For both the noble house of Venturi and my wounded male pride... Unless that is what you want?' He was most definitely flirting again, but more the way he had at Christmas. Witty, playful, thoroughly charming and disarming. Exactly as she so fondly remembered him. 'In which case, I shall be forced to accept the gauntlet you have thrown down. We Venturis never shy away from a challenge.'

Inside her chest, her sighing heart was doing somersaults. 'All right, then...it was quite lovely.'

'Better—but still not *spectacular*...'

'If I tell you it was spectacular, but still very much a mistake I have no intention of repeating, will you take me to see the fresco, Your Grace...is it correct to say Your Grace? My knowledge of your language is limited.' To around ten words, give or take a *cappuccino*.

'As, by your own admission, we have shared a *spectacular* if reckless and unwise kiss, and as you are my guest, you should call me Pietro. And, yes, I shall take you to see my fresco.' He offered his arm again and she took it, trying not to feel the obvious muscle in his bicep or the gentle heat coming through his sleeve and warming her suddenly inquisitive palm. 'Might I be so bold as to call you Lilian, now that we are doomed to be nothing beyond merely platonic friends?'

'You may.' Aside from the peculiar and girlish palpitations, bouncing nerves and wholly inappropriate goose pimples, this had all gone so much better than she had expected. 'Thank you for arranging to have the correct trunk brought to my bedchamber.'

'You needed your soap and it was the least I could do after my shameful behaviour when we collided. Are your accommodations to your satisfaction?'

'They have exceeded them, your Gra—I mean, *Pietro*.' How lovely that name felt on her tongue. 'You have a wonderful house.'

'It pleases me to hear that. When I inherited the *palazzo*, it was showing its age. I have made it my mission to bring it back to its former glory. I only recently had the east wing—the wing where your rooms are situated—renovated. Thankfully now, after twenty years of work, it is finally back to its former glory.'

'Your noble ancestors would be proud of the job you have done.' They reached a pair of ornate double doors and he paused before them, clearly in no hurry to move.

'The fresco is my pride and joy, Lilian. My favourite part of this old house. However, before you see it, you must first allow me to bore you with some history to give it some context. My great-great-great-great-grandfather, Amedeo Venturi, inspired by the great Palazzo Barberini, right here in Rome, commissioned several artists to paint the ceiling of his new house. Except, he was too poor or too miserly to pay one of the established masters of the time and instead paid legions of struggling apprentices to do it instead. However, and I must confess we have no actual proof of this beyond the family legend, the finished ceiling apparently bears the brushwork of both the young Raphael *and* Michelangelo.'

'Good gracious!'

'Although which piece of the fresco is theirs, nobody can hazard a guess. Not even I, who considers himself a great expert on art, can say with any certainty. But it is a good story, no?'

'A very good story.'

'And I am prolonging the agony to shamelessly build your anticipation. It is a habit of mine. I like a little theatre.'

'That is perfectly all right—I adore a bit of history.'

He grinned and threw the doors open with a flourish and her breath caught in her throat.

The vaulted ceiling was a patchwork of gilt panels surrounding one huge central fresco. She recognised the theme immediately from the enormous white wings of the unabashedly naked lovers of the tale—Cupid and Psyche. The largest painting showed their first meeting in a forest of blossom, framing the scene as if the viewer were peeking in. The heroine startled, her golden hair woven with flowers as she wanders into the clearing to find a lovestruck Cupid staring at her, a small bleeding scratch on his chiselled abdomen from where he had accidentally pierced himself with his own dart. The smaller pictures ringed it, telling the rest of the tale, of their marriage, their separations, Psyche's series of impossible trials set by the gods to win back her immortal husband and then, finally, Cupid's rescue of his sleeping lover by transforming her into an immortal, too, so they could live properly together as man and wife in his world above the clouds for all eternity.

'Look at her wedding finger...' His breath whispered over her shoulder as he pointed.

'Look at the design of the ring he has placed on her finger.' It took her a while to focus on the thin, painted gold band, but as she stared at it she could see it was actually two hands intertwined. 'If you love a bit of history, then you will adore the symbolism. Although the story is an Ancient Greek myth, that ring is Roman. It was the custom to give a betrothal ring…a *fede* ring…two hands clasped in love and agreement. A promise.'

'I would never have noticed it unless you had pointed it out.'

He shrugged. 'I have an eye for detail and a mind which likes to store them.'

'The devil is always in the detail.'

He smiled. 'I love all those quaint English phrases.'

'I love your fresco. It is stunning.'

'It is. Old Amedeo might have been a skin-flint, but he was a romantic soul at heart. This was his childhood sweetheart's favourite story and, because he loved her to distraction but she would have none of him, he had this ceiling painted in her honour…as a token and permanent declaration of his love.'

Lilian spun a slow circle, taking it all in, more than a little overwhelmed by its sheer perfection. 'Did it work?'

'They married, had twelve children and lived to be very old together. So, yes. I believe it worked perfectly.'

'Another good story.' She found herself beaming at him. 'In fact, a better one.' One which spoke entirely to her romantic soul.

Chapter Four

For the fifth time in as many minutes, he glanced at the door, literally counting the seconds till she came through it. Just as he had last night and the night before. In fact, Pietro could not seem to stop thinking about her despite completely immersing himself in work and having as little to do with her as possible this past week.

That wasn't completely true.

He had recklessly offered to be her guide at the Sistine Chapel because he wanted to see her face when she finally saw Michelangelo's greatest masterpiece after her touching and poignant reaction to his fresco, selfishly delaying her planned visit there to fit around his business commitments. And while he had avoided her as much as he could throughout the days, he couldn't resist seeking out her company at dinner, then talking and harmlessly flirting with her till bedtime. Like clockwork, his feet took him home with plenty of time to change and be seated in the *salotto* in time to watch her arrival. Something which was rapidly becoming the highlight of his day.

The Lilian who came to dinner was a very different woman from the one he had met in England at Christmas. Gone were the plain, sensible clothes, burdened demeanour and troubled eyes, replaced by a vivacious, glamourous and constantly smiling creature who laughed a great deal and whose emerald eyes sparkled with joy and intelligence. She was loving her visit to Rome and her enjoyment of it was infectious.

Each evening, he made a point of asking about her day and then listened intently as she recounted it with such exuberance and wonder, he felt as if he was seeing the place of his birth and his home for all his forty-eight years on the earth for the first time. For Lilian, everything was an adventure, from the spectacle of the Colosseum and the ghostly ruins of ancient Rome, to the everyday sights, sounds and smells of the street markets. In all cases, it was her reaction which he adored and he blamed the fresco entirely for his new obsession with her.

Pietro had lost count of the number of people he had shown it to. Its rumoured beauty was one of Rome's most well-known secrets and, aside from all the business connections he regularly brought home to see it to help aid his negotiations with them, there were also curious dinner guests who always asked to see it.

But Lilian's reaction had been special and different. When nearly everyone encouraged him to have experts study the brushwork to ascertain which parts were by the Great Masters the legend claimed, or commented on how much money that ceiling alone would bring for his house if he ever decided to sell it, she had been more interested in the story of his besotted great-great-great-great-grandparents. She saw the fresco as a declaration of deep and abiding love and was caught up in the romance of his ancestors rather than the value of the painting.

In fact, Lilian had a talent for seeing the intensely personal in everything. The gladiator's feelings as he walked into the arena of the Colosseum rather than the architecture of the amphitheatre. Bracci's human inspiration for Oceanus on the Fontana di Trevi. Even the men who carved the stones which built St Peter's. How they must have felt to be part of the creation of something so significant. In human-ising everything in the city he had taken for granted for most of his adult life, she brought a new dimension to it, a new appreciation which was filtering down into his own work. Something which had been sorely missing for a very long time.

Today he had sold a painting by *di Banco*, a lesser artist of the Renaissance. Pietro had never much cared for his work because the brushwork and skill lacked the sophistication and subtlety of many of his significantly better contemporaries. He had picked up the small portrait, done in oils, for next to nothing a few years back from a *conte* who had been systematically stripping his villa of valuables. Uninspired by this one, Pietro had consigned the little portrait to storage where it lay forgotten until he sensed he had found a buyer. The Conte didn't know who the ancestor was so had no emotional attachment to it.

The wealthy English merchant who had bought it only wanted the portrait to give credence to the expensive illusion he was creating—to convince others his money was old and his bloodline was noble, buying the nameless ancestors of others to hang in his new mansion built in the fashionably classical style. These sorts of transactions, although not exciting, were currently very lucrative. Anyone who wasn't anyone, but desperately wanted to be someone now they had money, knew if they came to Pietro Venturi, he would be able to fill their walls with suitably aged and convincing fake ancestors to impress their visitors while being guaranteed of his silence. In fact, at least a hundred forgotten and unwanted portraits hung in the private gallery behind his main one on the Via del Corso. He had never cared if his clients walked away with a stunning Canaletto cityscape to hang above their fireplace or the cracked portrait of a nameless, forgotten old lady by an unknown artist of yore. All he cared about was making the sale.

Yet Pietro had pondered that crude portrait all day, wondering for the first time about the young man who was staring tentatively out of the aged canvas rather than the handsome profit he would make from it. He wished he had shown it to Lilian before he had sent it off. She would have come up with at least twenty theories about the fellow—who he was, what he was thinking and why he was having his portrait painted in the first place—just as she did each evening when they strolled together around the *palazzo* and he pointed out some new treasure for her to speculate over. She wouldn't care how many *scudi* it had made. He had never met a person more unimpressed with money than Lilian and in turn that lack of interest made him re-evaluate his obsession with it. He had made himself far more money than he could ever spend—perhaps now he should take a leaf out of her book and begin to enjoy life? He envied her her freedom, even though all the restrictions in his life were of his own making.

She came through the door and he drank in the sight of her. 'You were right, Pietro!' Typically, she was beaming and brimming with the excitement of the day's adventure. 'The Piazza del Popolo was well worth the visit. And so unspoilt. I felt exactly as if I was walking in the Rome of the fifteenth century.'

'My feet feel as if I've been walking since the fifteenth century!' Alexandra flopped on to the sofa opposite him. 'If you are going to continually offer her new suggestions to drag me along to, I think you should take some of the responsibility for the walking. I was all done by two. But somebody...' she glared at her cousin '...insisted we traipse all the way down the Via Leonina because a certain somebody...' then she glared at him '...encouraged her to seek out the fresco at the Trinità dei Monti, which also involved the climbing of those ridiculous Spanish Steps. All one hundred and thirty-eight of them!'

He ignored Alexandra's complaining to focus on her companion. 'What did you think?'

Lilian's face said it all. 'It was a stunning fresco! And you are right, da Volterra is a master. One I had never heard of before. Yet, you can still can see the influence and genius of Michelangelo in the painting—exactly as you said.'

'It was he who gained da Volterra the commission in the first place. Volterra is said to have based it on Michelangelo's design and drawings.' It was so wonderful to be able to converse with another about art. One who reminded him why he had fallen in love with the subject in the first place. He had never met another person who seemed to feel it all as keenly as he did.

'That doesn't surprise me. The composition...the way he paints the figures. It leaps out at you. The expressions of grief on the faces of his followers as they reverently lower the body of Christ from the cross brought a tear to my eye. It was so visceral...so utterly tragic.'

Alexandra rolled her eyes, unenthused with their topic of conversation. 'The pain in my poor feet brings tears to my eyes, too. Not that anyone cares. I hope you know a good cobbler, Carlotta. Another couple of days at this pace and my walking shoes will need new soles.'

'Yet history has condemned him to be known for ever as *Il Braghettone*—literally the breeches maker—because he was hired by Pope Pius the Fourth to cover the genitalia on works of art in the Vatican.'

'Poor da Volterra. To have his greatness forgotten.' Her eyes locked with his and he realised they were kindred spirits. She understood his thoughts. He understood hers. He could see them in her eyes.

How bizarre...

'Why don't you take the carriage? You do not have to walk everywhere.' His sister, like Alexandra, couldn't see what all the fuss was about and this, too, was reflected in the amused exasperation in Lilian's lovely gaze.

'Because Lilian is determined to *immerse* herself fully in the experience and, apparently, she would miss things in the comfort of Pietro's fine conveyance. Like the charming smells wafting from some of the side streets, for instance. The heady combination of rotting vegetables, stagnant water and the sweaty bodies of the great unwashed are also apparently intrinsic to Rome's charm. It made me want to gag so I had to resort to burying my nose in my handkerchief, but Lilian didn't appear the least bit offended by the stench. I swear, all her years working at the Foundation have completely destroyed her sense of smell.'

'I am simply more robust of both body and character than you, Cousin.' Another thing Pietro liked about her. Lilian was no shrinking violet. The brief years of his marriage had proved he had no time for those. 'However, to be annoyingly magnanimous and to appease you and your poor *old* feet, we shall take the carriage to the Pantheon tomorrow.'

'But Sofia has invited us to take tea with her tomorrow. I accepted on your behalf, Alexandra.'

'Oh.' Pietro saw the flash of disappointment on Lilian's face at his sister's announcement. 'Who is Sofia?'

'The Marchesa di Gariello.'

Pietro tried not to curl his lip in disgust at the mention of her name. Sofia was one of his greatest mistakes. A conniving, shallow and spiteful woman who lived to elevate her own importance by putting down others. She had also been one of the main reasons he had made unbreakable rules about the sort of affairs he had. She had claimed to only want an affair, but, being an old friend of the family, had used her friendship with his sister to attempt to force an engagement, claiming heartbreak and broken promises. And then when those did not work—worse.

'A great friend from our youth. She hasn't seen Alexandra in for ever.' Carlotta's eyes flicked to his awkwardly. To this day she did not know the half of it. 'And we do not get to see her so much now either.' Because Pietro had banned the manipulative witch from his house and had been upfront about his refusal to make promises to any woman beyond a night of unbridled passion ever since to avoid any confusion. He'd had one wife and that experience had taught him he never wanted another. And if he did, which he obviously very much didn't, she would never be a woman like Sofia!

'I doubt Lilian has any burning desire to meet Sofia any more than Sofia would want to meet her.' Sofia liked titles and wealth, expensive things and shallow people, and for some reason he didn't want the pair of them meeting. 'If you do not mind accompanying me to my gallery briefly tomorrow, I would be delighted to be your escort at the Pantheon.' It was an offer which he hadn't intended to make until the words tumbled out of his mouth. Even after they had, he couldn't decide if he regretted them.

'What a splendid idea!' His sister and her cousin exchanged a knowing look, which thankfully Lilian missed. 'I doubt you would be particularly interested in the three of us gossiping about nonsense all afternoon and nobody would be a better guide than Pietro.'

'My poor old feet would thank you,' Alexandra said.

'Well…if you do not mind, Pietro? Only I have been dying to see Raphael's tomb.'

'It would be my pleasure.' Which he was surprised to realise it was—albeit a temptation he did not need. Nor did he appreciate the twin knowing expressions of the clearly matchmaking Carlotta and Alexandra. However, bizarrely, he did have an urge to show Lilian his gallery. And most specifically the four preliminary sketches he had been saving for exactly the right buyer for goodness knew how long.

She was already waiting for him by his carriage in the courtyard by the time he came downstairs. In deference to the beautiful spring morning, she wore no coat over her pretty, floral, long-sleeved dress and had chosen to carry her bonnet and crocheted shawl rather than put them on. Clearly looking out impatiently for him, she raised her hand in a cheery wave as he walked towards her and she wiggled her basket. 'I've stolen a few pastries for the journey in case you are hungry.' He had promised her breakfast in a charming café he knew, where they could sit outside on the cobbles and watch the busy streets she loved so much awaken, but had warned her the drive across the city could take nearly an hour. 'Unless you don't want any crumbs in your carriage, in which case I shall leave them behind.'

'What are a few crumbs between friends?' He took the basket, then her gloveless hand, indulging his urge to kiss it before he helped her into his carriage. 'As it is early and quiet, I thought we would take the scenic route. The Tiber is always at its most beautiful first thing in the morning.'

They set off and followed the road which meandered through the old city. He had chosen the river route on purpose, not only to watch her joy as she saw it all with him as he told her all about his homeland, but to show her something he knew she would particularly enjoy. He kept his own counsel until they were practically on top of it and she was engrossed by the ruins on the opposite side of the carriage as it came to its prearranged stop. 'Look to your left.'

'At the island? Or the church?'

'As lovely as they both are, they are not what I wanted to show you.' He tilted her head to look beyond towards the fast-flowing river water and enjoyed the satisfaction of her gasp.

'Is that a bridge?' The ruined, shrub-covered white arches sitting disconnected in the centre of the river had always been his favourite bit of Rome. The ornate imperial carvings of water serpents adorning it were still as crisp now as they would have been when they first emerged beneath the talented stonemason's chisel.

'It was, once upon a time. In fact, it was a great bridge in its day, the most important bridge of the old city called the Pons Aemilius. It is a true feat of Roman engineering, connecting one half of the city with the other over the most treacherous stretch of the river.' He pointed to the rapids buffering it, wondering, as he always did, how the old stones managed to withstand it and had done for two thousand years. 'But nowadays we modern Romans call it the Ponte Rotto—because that is exactly what it is.'

'Ponte Rotto?'

He loved how she spoke Italian words with

her rounded English vowels, sounding so prim and proper when he knew she was not. 'It means broken bridge in your language.'

'I much prefer the way you say it.' Her eyes were transfixed on the ruin, giving him the chance to study her face unhindered while he waited for the inevitable. Then he smiled when she said exactly what he knew she would say. 'Imagine all those thousands of people who crossed it…the carts, the horses. Men, women, children, all going about their day.' She closed her eyes briefly to picture it as she always did. 'What were they like, do you suppose?'

'Much like us, I assume. So wrapped up in the minutiae of their daily life that they forgot to marvel at the beauty around them. Or appreciate the sturdy bridge beneath their feet. But it was built to last, as you would expect from that great civilisation, and people walked across it for centuries until it was finally destroyed by a flood just three hundred years ago. Botticelli, Raphael, da Volterra and Michelangelo could feasibly all have walked over it at some point, too.'

'Gracious.' Another quaint English word he enjoyed the sound of coming from her mouth. 'If only that bridge could talk…'

'As a boy I used to come here and think

much the same thing.' He had forgotten that memory. Forgotten that he had once seen the world exactly like Lilian. 'Yet I haven't been here in years. Until you inspired me to remember it. Nor have I seen the Pantheon in for ever either. Clearly too caught up in the minutiae of my own life...' He tapped the roof of the carriage and they slowly pulled away. 'I wonder when I became so jaded by life I forgot to stop and look at the beauty?'

'Life is like that. It drags you along with it and consumes you, until you forget everything except your daily struggles and the burdens they place upon you.'

'When I met you last winter, you seemed burdened—and now you don't. What is your secret?'

'No secret—merely circumstances. Before Christmas my world seemed about to fall apart.' Her eyes clouded at the memory. 'I was worried about my son, who had disappeared from the face of the earth. I was worried about my husband's Foundation and my home because we were running out of money, and I was worried that my eldest daughter was about to marry a man she patently did not love simply to give us all some financial security. It was a trying time.'

'And now?'

She shrugged and shook her head. 'And now, everything is miraculously fixed and forgotten. Time apparently does heal all. Things are miraculously so good, my children and the Foundation no longer need me, so I am here, having my first adventure in over twenty years and remembering what it felt like to be young and only responsible for myself for a change, rather than everyone and everything.' Then she grinned, looking instantly younger. 'Is it terrible that I have discovered I love it?'

'Not terrible at all, *cara*.' Although Pietro was envious of her newfound happiness. 'Your children are all grown and married, it is your turn to have fun now. Everyone deserves the occasional adventure and I am so very glad you are enjoying yours. I have decided I need to do more things I enjoy.' Like spending time with a certain delightful English woman who was doing wonders for his restlessness.

'I have discovered a new zest for life simply by allowing myself to enjoy the little things here in Rome. You should take a leaf out of my book and do the same. Take pleasure in the little things without feeling guilty for it. You love the details…take the time to discover them. It does wonders for your mood. I have been in a ridiculously good mood since I first stepped ashore and realised I needed this holiday. And it is addictive. Each new day, each new little thing to enjoy makes me happier. So far, I have not found a single thing I dislike about this city.'

'Give it time, *cara*...you will. The heat in the summer, for instance, can be unbearable and brings out the worst in people. The roads outside the city are dreadful, making every journey a trial. Then there is the politics here...' He rolled his eyes dramatically and she laughed at the horrified face he pulled. 'It drains all the joy from your soul.'

'Politics everywhere is draining.'

'Indeed it is—but the Italian temperament suits it least of all, I think. So instead of sensible debate, reasoned arguments and compromise, all they do is shout over one another and gesticulate.' He waved his cupped hand in the air in demonstration. 'This becomes our main form of communication.'

'I've seen them do that on the streets...' She mimicked him, looking not the least bit Italian as she waved her hand in the air, because it was too reserved. Too English. 'What does it mean?'

'That basically the person gesticulating is angry.' He stared at his hand in disgust, then threw up the other in a shrug. 'Which only serves to make those around us angry as well.'

'At least you Italians let it out. I think I should love to wave my arms about and throw a tantrum sometimes. In my country we are taught to keep anger inside. I am not sure that is a better solution than yours as it festers and only serves to make us more angry. We silently seethe and speak in over-polite clipped tones when we are offended. Like this…' She sat straighter, still like a statue, and looked down her nose at him like a duchess. 'Really. I see. If you must.'

'No, thank you.'

She nodded enthusiastically at his attempt to mimic her accent. 'Exactly. That is *exactly* what a furious English person would say.'

'It is exactly what you said to me when I offered to scrub your back.' He nudged her playfully beside him, enjoying reminding her that their relationship had not always been platonic and seeing her overly polite but flustered expression each time he did. 'You look particularly lovely when you silently seethe, Lilian. I *enjoyed* your seething immensely.' Then he grinned wolfishly at her stunned face and the little spots of colour on her beautifully pale English cheeks which he very much wanted to touch, despite knowing, if he did, he wouldn't be able to stop. '*Gracious*, Lilian! Your advice works! Already my mood is brighter just thinking about how much I enjoyed that small pleasure—blessedly free of all the guilt at last.'

Chapter Five

Pietro shamelessly flirted with her all morning and, more shamelessly, she let him, telling herself it was harmless fun when it didn't feel harmless at all. It never did. A week after their embarrassing meeting on the landing and despite clearing the air and agreeing neither of them were interested in Alexandra and Carlotta's flagrant attempt at matchmaking, the constant flirting with the handsome Italian was playing havoc with her legendary sensibleness.

It felt naughty and dangerous. And the combination made her feel as light as air and attractive again. Around him she was no longer lost and stood at a crossroads, she was feminine, human, vivacious…exciting. It was as heady a feeling as three glasses of wine and made her feel two decades younger than she was. Just as she had when she and Henry had first been courting, she had constant butterflies in her tummy and an excited spring in her step which had disappeared since she had given birth to her twins a quarter of a century ago.

She had pondered it. Of course she had. Wondering what it was about Pietro which made her lie on her soft mattress each night, staring at the beautiful ceiling smiling wistfully and reliving that kiss over and over again before she fell asleep. The best theory she could come up with to explain her peculiar behaviour and her uncharacteristically selfish thoughts was that the day she gave birth to Silas and Millie she had stopped being a lovestruck newlywed, married to the man of her dreams, and became a mother of twins. From that point on, her children had come first, her husband second and the Foundation they had built together consumed everything else. Her life became one of duty and service to others. And because her beloved Henry was an earnest man, who loved her unconditionally in his typical earnest fashion, there had been no need to focus on anything even remotely frivolous or self-indulgent except the family and the good they were ultimately doing.

Then Henry had died and, exactly as she had said to Pietro, the burdens of life had consumed her like the fast-flowing Tiber river and Lilian—the woman—had been lost.

She'd had a revelation yesterday as she washed and dressed for dinner. Since she had arrived here, with all its colour and vibrancy, and since the moment she had encountered him in that hallway, she had wanted to be colourful and vibrant herself. She looked in the mirror more frequently, took more care with her hair and her dress, and was supremely grateful for the fashionable, new, younger wardrobe her daughters and her cousin had convinced her to acquire.

But last night, she had caught a glimpse of herself in the ornate full-length mirror in her dressing room, swaddled primly in a towel after her bath despite there being nobody else in the room with her, and she had stopped and stared. Then slowly, tentatively, she had allowed the towel to fall to properly look at her body—all of her body—for the first time in years.

And she was pleasantly surprised by it.

She had always assumed the additional flesh she had gained over the course of two pregnancies, which stalwartly refused to leave, had spoiled her figure. However, as she was healthy and strong, she had avoided scrutinising it—especially after she was widowed—

and in doing so had forgotten the passionate and sensual side of herself which Henry had adored. She had adored it, too. Being kissed and held, being touched, opening her body for him and losing herself in the pleasure such intimacy created.

Perhaps it was the profusion of naked art here in Rome, where one couldn't enter a room or walk more than a hundred yards without being subjected to the nude human form in all its majesty—but the body reflected back at her in the mirror did not look fat, old and haggard at all. There was no denying the years had changed it. Her breasts were fuller. Her hips were wider. Her stomach no longer as flat as it had been when she was a fresh-faced bride. It looked rounded, curvaceous, womanly and ripe. As an experiment, she had guiltily touched her breasts and gasped as her sensitive nipples puckered and something visceral and wholly carnal stirred between her legs just as it used to.

It was the ripeness which had shocked her, because the moment she had discovered her dormant body had fully reawakened, she realised she was sorry she did not have a man to share it with. Then she thought about Pietro and imagined his tanned hands on her skin, his lips on hers, his dark eyes staring down at her nakedness in appreciation, and her forgotten and neglected body suddenly hummed with desire. Desire so intense, she had not been able to sleep for hours and it still hovered close to the surface even now.

Much as it had all day, even as she had marvelled at the Pantheon.

And even though she knew he had a reputation as a ladies' man, famous for his flirting and easy charm, that detail didn't bother her overmuch either, because she wasn't looking for love or a husband. Certainly not one who lived across the seas from her family and her life. Why would she? Clearly Rome was turning her into a scandal if this reawakened wantonness was any gauge. Maybe spending the entire day with the new object of her fantasies hadn't been a wise decision. It had been fun, glorious and sinfully exciting—but it was not at all what the usually sensible and level-headed Lilian would have done in a million years. Was she disrespecting Henry's memory by wondering what it would be like to have another lover? A temporary one? A tall, dark and handsome foreign lover...

'You look suddenly very serious, Lilian. Do not tell me I tired you out this morning?' His deep voice so close to her ear in the carriage shocked her out of her reverie.

'Sorry—I was wool-gathering.'

'Wool-gathering?' When he was confused, his dark brows furrowed as his tanned face tilted to the side as if thinking on an angle made the thoughts somehow clearer. Why were the British so against sun-kissed skin when the sun did wonders for Pietro's?

'It is an old expression back home—it means daydreaming.'

'Wool-gathering...' He said it slowly, pronouncing the vowels in a convincingly British way. 'I like it... And what were you daydreaming about, *cara*?'

You. Me. The strange effect you have on my body. 'Oh, you know...my usual nonsense.' Or at least it was becoming worryingly usual on this trip. Probably because she was having an adventure in the most beautiful city on earth rather than pondering her crossroads and it made her feel like a twenty-year-old again. 'Tell me about your gallery, Pietro. I should like to hear some history before I see it. Why does the Duca della Torizia even have a gallery in the first place? Aristocrats do not usually work for a living and Carlotta complains you work too hard. Every day, in fact.'

'Alas, I was denied the idle life of an aristocrat by necessity. My ancestors spent beyond their means and, over time, their fortunes became so depleted that I inherited a mess. I suppose that is why I am so driven. My *papà* came from a long line of proud Venturis who preferred to bury their heads in the sand rather than tackle the problem. And he was…how do you say it? You have a quaint little word which means someone is too proud and full of his own importance to consider earning a living because work of any kind was out of the question for somebody with his illustrious noble blood…'

'A snob?'

'Yes! He was…' he smiled as he imitated her accent '…a dreadful snob. He would be spinning in his grave if he knew his son had gone into trade.'

'You are a duke—you could have married for a great deal of money and avoided having to work yourself.'

'I did marry for money. Dear Papà found me a suitably noble bride with a hefty dowry, but he spent it long before I inherited it.'

'You were married?' This was the first Lilian had heard of it.

'Briefly. A very long time ago.' His expression, usually so playful and open, suddenly seemed to close. 'She died.'

'I'm sorry. That is so sad.'

He shrugged, his dark eyes averted from hers. 'As you say, time heals all.' Although for some reason she got the distinct feeling it hadn't.

'Not all. I still mourn Henry's passing. Perhaps not as acutely as I did ten years ago, but I think of him still—especially regarding the children—and wonder what he would make of things if he were here.'

'We had no children.' For the briefest moment, she saw a flash of what looked like pain skitter across his face before it was gone. 'She died young. So long ago I barely think about her nowadays.'

A polite way of saying he really did not wish to talk about it today either. But how could she not when she had seen his pain? From the experience of her own grief, she knew it was cathartic to talk about it. Losing the love of your life changed you.

'How did she die?' More uncomfortable emotions played on his expression before he masked them.

'She had been unwell for a long time. Complications from an old riding accident which never healed properly. And your husband?' Obviously discomforted by her probing, he clearly wanted to change the focus of the conversation away from him. To try to get Pietro to open up, she answered with complete honesty.

'Typhoid. We had an outbreak at the Foundation in the winter of 1832. He tried to send us away to Alexandra's. In fact, he was most insistent. When I refused, we argued when we never usually argued. I reluctantly agreed to keep the family quarantined at home while he tended the sick at the Foundation. Almost as soon as we assumed the epidemic was over and he returned to us seemingly unscathed, Henry contracted it. Of course, Henry being Henry, he promptly took himself to the infirmary at the Foundation and tried to ban me from attending him.'

'An edict I suspect you ignored.'

Lilian nodded, too choked by the memory of that final argument to go into the heart-wrenching details. 'For a hale and hearty man in his prime, we were all surprised at how rapidly he declined. Within a day, he was delirious and consumed with the fever. The next morning, unconscious. I left his bedside briefly to talk to the physician and by the time I returned a few minutes later, it was too late. He had passed. I never got to say goodbye.' She had sat with his body alone for an hour. Stunned. Numb with pain. Staring blankly at the miserable, grey sky as the rained drizzled endlessly down the windowpane, wondering what she was supposed to do now when all she wanted to do was curl up and die beside him on that mattress.

'Another reason, perhaps, why I seemed burdened when we met. Even after the passing of a decade, I still find that time of year hard. I have come to loathe English winters. All the grey and the damp and the cold. It seems to crystallise the bad memories when I prefer to remember the good. And there was so much good.'

'You loved him.'

'With all my heart. I always will.' Unconsciously, she touched the wedding band she still wore and watched his eyes flick to it. 'He was the love of my life.'

'Do you believe that? That there is one special person out there who can never be replaced?'

An odd question from a man who had been married. 'I do. The human heart was made to love unconditionally. Did you love your wife?'

It was a bold question. An intrusive and personal one and for the longest time she thought he might not answer her. But then he sighed and shook his head, and she briefly witnessed the guilt he carried for it. 'We were virtual strangers when we married and soon learned we were very different people once we were. Completely incompatible. We both preferred to conduct our marriage with a healthy distance between us, which was perhaps one of the main reasons I dedicated so much time to my business. Dealing in art involves a lot of travel.' He turned to watch the street outside. 'What a maudlin topic we have stumbled into—when we were having such a wonderful day.'

Lilian had so many more questions she wanted to ask him about his past, but sensed he was done talking about it and she risked creating an awkward atmosphere if she persisted. 'Why does it involve so much travel?' It was an olive branch and one he cheerfully gripped.

'Because first you have to track down the paintings and buy them, which is a mission in itself. Yet that is the exciting part. Like treasure hunting. But I realised when I started that if my family's fortune had been depleted after all the wars and revolutions in Europe, then there were probably thousands of similarly desperate aristocrats on the Continent who were in the same situation. All with paintings gathering dust on their crumbling walls.'

'It is sad that they had to resort to selling their paintings.'

'Watercolours and oils do not put food on the table, Lilian. This I know from experience. Although to be frank, where I might wish they would, most of them do not spend it on food or investing in their own futures. They spend it on dowries and debts and living beyond their means. The biggest problem with the aristocracy is they cannot see they are a dying breed. Like my father, most think of only the here and now and their own importance, rather than building their life on a firm financial foundation.'

Another interesting insight in a man she might have assumed lived a life of privilege. He was much too forward thinking for an aristocrat. Disillusioned with status and not too proud to work. In that respect, a great deal like her husband had been.

'As a child, I remember certain rooms of the *palazzo* had become so uninhabitable, yet my father preferred to close them up rather than invest in the building's upkeep. As those rooms closed, he sold off the treasures within them and spent the profits as quickly as he received them. I never once got the sense he regretted parting with them because he took such things for granted and would prefer a new set of clothes to repairing his roof or paying his mounting bills or keeping a Canaletto. I consoled myself with the knowledge those precious heirlooms went to a new home where they would be appreciated. It is sad, but that is commerce. And my cold, shrivelled heart is always on the side of the painting. The painting always deserves better.'

An oddly romantic notion. 'I am starting to have less sympathy for the impoverished aristocrats who sell you their treasures.'

'What piqued your interest in art?'

'I don't know...'

'Why do I suspect you do—but you are too embarrassed to tell me?' Clearly he could see inside her mind. 'I promise I won't judge.'

'All right then... I always enjoyed art. The talent which goes into it and the beauty of the pictures. In my younger days, when I had no responsibilities, I seemed to live at the National Gallery. I became a very eager student and, as you know, it is always the human story and the history behind the object which truly calls to me. When I married and Henry and I started his Foundation, I was confronted daily by the ugliness of life. The cruelty of others, the cruelty of poverty, the base and humiliating decisions those less fortunate than me had to make simply to survive. The tragedy of it all… My appreciation of art almost became like a regular pilgrimage to remind myself that not everything in the world was as awful as the things I saw every day.'

'*His* Foundation?'

Had she said his?

'You made his dreams yours.'

Had she?

'I cared about the same things and he was so driven.' Exactly like Pietro, but for different reasons. 'He came from the aristocracy, too, and became thoroughly disillusioned with them and their mistreatment of those they perceived to be from the lower orders. He wanted to change things and I wanted to help him do that.'

'What were your dreams…before him?'

'I dreamed of being the curator of the National Gallery.' She shook her head, amused by the forgotten memory. 'Unfortunately, I was born in the wrong body to ever achieve that dream.' And for some reason the memory of it was bittersweet. It was Rome again and being immersed in all the richness and beauty of art everywhere. She had made Henry's dreams hers and left all hers by the wayside as wives were prone to do. Was it time to pursue her own dreams again? 'Tell me about your clientele. Who buys your rescued paintings?' She found this side of his business intriguing.

'All sorts of people. Wealthy aristocrats who appreciate art, wealthy businessmen who wish to give the impression they are connoisseurs of art. Royalty—what is left of it. Museums. Americans. That is a very fruitful market. But not as fruitful as the English new money. Three-quarters of my business now comes from your country—which was why I was there in that carriage with you before Christmas.'

She wished he would stop reminding her about Christmas, because the mere mention of the word immediately caused her to remember their kiss. Alongside the habit of his heated gaze which wandered to her lips each time he mentioned it. 'Who knew the English make up the majority of discerning art lovers?'

He gave her a rueful smile as he shook his head. 'They make up the majority of the social climbers who wish to appear more aristocratic than their humble bloodlines dictate, *cara*. So much so, I have a room dedicated to portraits specifically to appeal to their particular desires.'

'Suddenly I am afraid to ask what those desires are. But I shall. Because I know you wish to tell me and because you have that mischievous glint in your eye.'

'Have you been staring into my eyes, *cara*?'

'The portraits?'

He grinned, unoffended at her reluctance to flirt, and leaned closer as if imparting a tantalising morsel of gossip, his warm breath caressing her ear and throwing more fuel on to her constantly smouldering desire. 'They buy ancestors, *cara*. To hang in their newly built portrait galleries alongside their freshly painted plaster coats of arms.'

'That is…outrageous!' But she could not help laughing. 'Why pretend to be something you are not? To invent airs and graces rather than be proud of achieving success off your own labours? How positively daft!'

'Daft?' He almost sounded English this time. 'What a lovely little word.'

'It means silly. A nonsense.'

'Ah… *Sì.* Daft it is. Yet it paid for all my renovations in the east wing, so I am thankful for their pretentions.'

'You are clearly a canny businessman.'

'Listen!' He cupped his hand around his ear. 'Can you hear it?'

'Hear what?'

'The sound of my noble *papà* spinning furiously in his grave at your outrageous compliment.'

He winked, obviously pleased with himself, as the carriage turned a narrow corner and he gestured for her to look out of the window.

'We are almost there. This is the Via del Corso—the most important street in Rome since ancient times. It is a combination of your Rotten Row, in that it is a place to be seen, and Bond Street to shop. Because I am a canny businessman despite my highly sought-after blue blood, I knew this was the perfect place to open my gallery. For look at it—isn't it marvellous? It has everything I could possibly need. Both a glut of snobs and so many gloriously deep purses filled with lovely new money.'

Lilian wasn't entirely sure what she had been expecting after his revelations about the biggest source of his wealth, but she was strangely relieved to find his gallery, or the public-facing part of it at least, not only a gallery in every sense of the word, but one that showed Pietro had impeccable taste. Among the impressive masters adorning its high panelled walls were also a smattering of those lesser-known artists whose genius was yet to be fully appreciated and a few new artists who he was proudly sponsoring. He showed her his little private gallery at the back, too. The one he jokingly called The Palazzo delle Santafano Renovation Fund and they laughed about the sort of people who bought the battered faces of strangers to give their tarnished history provenance, then wondered about the real people behind those portraits and the sort of lives they led.

When she assumed she had seen it all, he surprised her, tugging her hand in his towards his office upstairs. 'Come, Lilian... I have something else to show you. Something truly special...' He sat her at his desk and she watched, curious, as he opened a hidden door in the panelling to reveal an enormous, elaborately decorated cast-iron safe. After unlocking it with a key from his pocket, he produced a tied leather folder of loose papers which he carried towards her reverently. 'These are my pride and joy. I've had them for a decade and still cannot bring myself to sell them.'

He undid the cord and placed it in front of her, then came to stand behind her as she opened it. No theatre this time, which somehow made them all the more intriguing.

Lilian studied the first sheet. It was an artist's preliminary sketch, showing the rough outline of what appeared to be an epic picture in the making with at least fifty separate figures drawn in the rough. Beneath that, the second drawing showed a naked figure in a dramatic pose, his arms flung back as if he were carrying something on his shoulders. Alongside him, snippets of his anatomy had been enlarged and drawn in intricate detail…a face…an arm…a hand. The next a cluster of cowering figures on a boat, the face of the naked demon they were cowering from also enlarged to show the fine details of his otherworldly features. The final drawing was another naked man in utter despair, his hand partially covering his horrified face and just one terrified, wide eye visible. It was as disturbing as it was brilliant. So brilliant it filled her with awe.

'These are wonderful. Who is the artist?'

'You tell me…but I shall give you a clue. You may have seen his rumoured early work recently. On my fresco…'

'Michelangelo?' Instinctively she lifted her fingers from the drawing and stared at it, then turned her head to Pietro's smiling face behind her above her shoulder.

'I believe so, *cara*. In fact, I am certain these are a few of his practice drawings for *The Last Judgement*. Probably just four of the hundreds he must have made. It is so difficult to prove it as he never signed anything and so many artists have imitated his work—but each time I visit the Sistine Chapel, I see these figures. The demon and the boat, that frightened man. This one...' his finger tapped the picture of the man in the dramatic pose '...is almost identical to the central figure of Christ in the original. There are similar sketches in the Vatican Archives...'

'You have been in the Vatican Archives?'

'Well, there are still some advantages to being the Duca della Torizia...'

'I am impressed.'

'With these sketches, the fact I have been in the Archives, or that I am the Duca della Torizia?'

Her eyes locked with his and she felt herself smile. 'With all of it.'

Chapter Six

He hadn't intended to kiss her. He had wanted to all day, of course he had because he was only human and she intrigued him, but he hadn't because she was both a friend of the family and a guest in his house. According to his rigid rules that rendered Lilian entirely taboo. Those rules were set in stone. He always kept his affairs and his private life intentionally separate. Kept friendship entirely separate from passion and passion entirely detached from his heart. It was easier that way. Less messy. Certainly less complicated. And, he was unashamed to admit to himself alone, less personal. Since his wife, and the devastation excessive emotion had caused in their short marriage, he had avoided the personal most of all, preferring to live his life on his own terms.

But her reaction to his precious pictures, her

delightful company all day and the unintentional intimacy of their position had all conspired against him and, before he could think better of it, his lips had brushed over hers of their own accord and all his self-imposed, rigid rules suddenly flew out the window.

It didn't help that she kissed him back—and not tentatively either. She had sighed into his mouth as if she had been waiting impatiently for him to kiss her all along, then came willingly when he tugged her from her chair into his arms, wrapping hers around his neck and skimming her hands over his shoulders and back.

Lilian was no unschooled virgin or shy about taking her pleasure. She deepened the kiss, touched her tongue to his and shamelessly pressed her lush body against his, allowing him to see their attraction was mutual and she wanted him as much as he wanted her. He liked that. There were no games and no lies.

He had no compunction about running his hands greedily over her body, because her hips did not shy away from his hardness. They sought it. She moaned when he filled his palms with her breasts. It was a moan of both pleasure and impatience at the fabric barrier of her bodice. She twisted to assist him as he wrestled with the fastenings at the back of her dress, throwing her head back as he trailed hot kisses down her neck and collarbone and not flinching as he pushed the pretty gown from her shoulders and hurried to free her bosom from the confines of her corset.

Pietro felt himself staring at them unbound in wonder before he touched them. They were full and rounded, capped with saucy dark nipples which stood out in intensely erotic contrast to her pale English skin and the rumpled fabric pooled around her waist. The groan she gave when he traced a nipple with his thumb was guttural and earthy, and when she could take no more of his teasing she grabbed his hand and pushed it to caress all of her. Touch all of her as she was greedily touching him over his clothes.

Now entirely consumed with rampant need and lust, he lifted her to sit on his desk and found himself laughing as she solicitously moved the precious drawings to the other side before she allowed him to resume his exploration. Pulling him by his lapels to kiss her again before pushing his coat from his shoulders and undoing every button on his silk waistcoat, then hauling up his shirt so she could feel his skin against her bare breasts as they kissed again. Her legs parted so he could stand between them, both of them impatiently fighting with the copious material of her skirt so he could run his hands along the gloriously smooth side of her bare thighs above her thin stockings.

She was panting, those delicious breasts rising and falling in time with her fevered breathing, when he eased her backwards so his mouth could feast upon them. They were wonderfully sensitive and every nuance of her pleasure and passion showed on her face. He didn't ask permission to go further because he didn't need it. Lilian had made the question moot the second she undid his falls and wrapped her hand possessively around his hardness.

She stared at him intently, revelling in the moment, her eyes never leaving his as he slowly edged inside her body. Then they did, her neck arching backwards and her arms looped around his neck as he began to move inside her.

'Oh, Pietro…' The breathy sigh was music to his ears as he plunged deeper and harder. 'Yes…*yes*…' Her hips greedily meeting his thrust for thrust. Her body fitted his perfectly, more perfectly than any other lover ever had before, and it overwhelmed him. She overwhelmed him. Her eyes. Her sighs. Her sultry movements as she pulled him closer. The lush feel of her as he moved inside her.

'Ah, Lilian… *Così bello…*' His brain refused to function in English as he lost himself in her body, and staccato fragments from his mother tongue tumbled out of his mouth. *'Tesoro mio...'* Words of encouragement. Words of surprise. *'Potrei guardarti tutto il giorno...'* Endearments he had never uttered to another woman before. Never felt compelled to until her.

She came for him quickly, much too quickly, writhing beneath him and calling out his name. Her green eyes, darkened with passion and unmistakable ecstasy, held his as her delectable womanly body shuddered and convulsed around him, and he felt himself drown in them. Felt himself falling over the precipice. With her. Much too fast. Much too easily. Surprising and unexpected and spectacular. Feeling oddly emotional as he collapsed against her spent and she held him close. Almost as if she were his very first woman. Almost as if it were his very first time.

Almost as if it meant something.

As soon as he had the strength to withdraw from her body, Pietro sensed Lilian withdraw from him, too. She didn't recoil or seem upset by what had happened, more she seemed displaced. Confused and bemused. It was quite apparent she had shocked herself with her passion and within seconds he watched the sensual temptress, who had lost herself entirely to the moment, don layers of stiff, English primness as she clutched the undone bodice of her gown to her breasts while she tried to fight herself back into it with one hand. Wondering why she couldn't get her other arm in the sleeve when she had shoved her first one into the garment inside out.

'Here, *cara*...allow me.' He slid his hand down the silky bare skin of her shoulder, trying not to smile at her scandalised discomfort. He adored this primness. The contrast between the unbound Lilian he had just witnessed and the buttoned-up Lilian. It was such an English thing to be. 'You have got yourself in a tangle.' They both had. She went against his self-imposed rules and he liked spending time with her. Another reason why she was perhaps an unwise choice for a lover.

She allowed him to dislodge her arm and, as he did, Pietro couldn't resist placing a soft kiss on her neck and he smiled when he heard her little sigh. Despite the fresh primness, sensual

Lilian wasn't too far from the surface. 'That was unexpected.' He nipped the sensitive shell of her ear and she arched her neck to give him better access. 'But spectacular.'

'I am not sure what came over me.' He liked that she didn't immediately apportion all the blame for what had happened on him. 'I am not normally...what I mean is I haven't been like that... It has been a long time, Pietro. I have no excuse.'

'I do not recall asking for one. And as the other half of what just transpired, the one who kissed you first, I cannot tell you how delighted I am that it did. You are a surprise, *cara*. A beautiful, unhindered and impassioned lover.' Perhaps the best he had ever had.

'I should tell you I am not in the market for another husband. My life is in London—not here. My children, the Foundation. I have no time for love...'

Thank goodness she had been the one to bring that up first. 'Nor am I. Marriage really did not suit me. Fear not, I am not about to propose.'

Arms now free of the twisted fabric, she used her spare hand to fumble with her corset. 'Then we are agreed it was a mistake... Another one. We seem to be creating a habit.'

'No, *cara*. It was not a mistake—it was perfect. Exactly what we both needed. The perfect end to the perfect day.' She was having as much success with the corset as she had had with the sleeves. 'And I for one would very much like to make it a habit for the remainder of your time here.'

'An *affair*?' Her eyes widened as if such a proposal was madness. 'I am not the sort of woman who has affairs, Pietro. I've never had one before. There has been nobody since Henry and...'

He silenced her with a kiss before boldly, simultaneously, slipping his hands inside her gaping bodice and rearranging her lush breasts to sit properly inside her corset. A task he was happy to linger over while beneath his lips she held her breath and beneath his fingers the sensitive flesh puckered against his palms. 'You like the feel of my hands on your body and I very much like your body in my hands. If neither of us wants more than passion and friendship, and as the passion between us is so very good, why not indulge the whim and enjoy each other as both friends...and lovers?'

He kissed her again and without hesitation she kissed him back. Despite her claims to the contrary, such a sensual creature as she enjoyed a man's touch too much to go without it for a decade. 'No decision needs to be made today—but it is entirely yours to make now that I have stated my intentions. All I ask is you think about it, Lilian. For now, turn around and let me lace that dress before I am tempted to peel you out of it again and let us go home.'

'And if the answer is no?'

'Then I shall abide by it...but would very much like to peel you out of that dress right now so we can say a proper goodbye. All affairs, even the briefest, deserve a *proper* goodbye.'

'Is everything all right, Lilian?'

She practically jumped out of her skin at the sound of Alexandra's voice beside her in the deserted pavement café—before guilt made her skin heat as she stared intently at the guidebook again. Hoping she didn't look exactly like a woman who had been recently ravished. Twice. Like a wanton. On her host's ornate mahogany desk. And had enjoyed every single illicit and sinful second of their couplings. So much so, she had completely forgotten about his magnificent Michelangelos. 'Yes...of course... I was just pondering Rome.'

'Pondering a certain Roman more like. I saw the heated looks you and Pietro exchanged last night over dinner. Did something finally happen between you two yesterday?'

The pink circles she had hoped merely resembled cheeks warmed by the heat of the Mediterranean spring sunshine suddenly combusted into a blush so ferocious her loosely laced corset felt tight.

'Oh, my goodness! Something *did* happen! How positively marvellous!'

'Shh… Keep your voice down.' Not that there was anyone bar them and a few pigeons on the Piazza Navona at this hour of the morning. The locals did not tend to surface till ten. Even the waiter in this café was making them wait an age, as a mark of disgruntled protest, for the strong morning *cappuccino* Lilian had developed a taste for and ordered so soon after he had unlocked the door.

'Did you kiss?'

A kiss had been the tip of the iceberg. 'It was a mistake. A *huge* mistake.'

'Was it a good kiss? I've known Pietro for ever and have always thought he would excel at kissing. He has the mouth for it.' That he did. 'And the patience.' Neither of them had been particularly patient the first time. 'He always struck me as a man who would take his time.' Although the second time he had made her wait. A little theatre to build the anticipation, he had said. And thoroughly enjoyed torturing her, by then completely naked, person immensely.

The wretch.

Lilian still couldn't quite believe she had allowed him to see her completely naked. Or to kiss her most secret places while she shamelessly moaned her encouragement from atop his desk. Places nobody had seen except Henry. At least he had been her husband and their lust sanctioned by the wedding vows and deep love which had bound them. With Pietro, there had just been the lust. Lots and lots of sinfully, exquisite lust.

'Well, was it?'

'I told you it was a mistake.'

Just as she had told Pietro on their carriage ride home afterwards, a few scant minutes after he had laced her back into her corset for the second time—as unashamedly naked as the day he was born. A splendid sight which she knew would haunt her for the rest of her life. Although he had simply shrugged when she awkwardly explained she had been seduced by the freedom of Rome and was clearly not quite herself. He let her ramble, his dark eyes clearly amused at her ridiculously English primness when he had only just buried himself to the hilt inside her.

Twice.

Just think about it, he had said. Let us not squander the precious gift fate and circumstance and the seductive freedom of Rome have given us. Especially as they clearly shared an intense mutual attraction and because the *rapporti sessuali* had been very satisfying.

Very satisfying indeed.

Her reckless body still tingled in places which had no place tingling and she couldn't seem to erase the image of the naked Pietro from her mind. His tanned broad chest, covered in a smattering of jet-black hair. Hair which narrowed like an arrow through the navel on his flat stomach, pointed to and surrounded his jutting and impressive maleness, which she had also kissed.

Gracious!

'A mistake born out of the heat of the moment!'

'Those are always the best kind.'

'Please stop matchmaking, Alexandra. I have no desire to marry again.' Unlike Pietro, she couldn't fathom engaging in the sexual act without the emotional and institutional bonds of commitment. She had never made love with a man she did not love before him. Could she truly separate her heart from her body as he was suggesting? Although for over an hour in his office she had apparently done just that. She hadn't considered her feelings beyond the obvious—that what they were doing felt good. Exceptional. Absolutely spectacular.

'Who's talking about marriage?' Her cousin finally dropped her voice to a whisper. 'Pietro is a contented bachelor and meticulously discreet and you, Lilian dear, you are a widow. An attractive woman in her prime. One with *needs.*' Oh, good gracious! Could this conversation get any more awkward? It had been her needs, or rather her neediness which had got her into this mess in the first place. '*Needs* that a fiery Italian lover as experienced as Pietro can thoroughly *satisfy.*' Apparently, he could. Although despite satisfying her twice, her greedy body still wanted more. More of what it had been denied for ten long years. Pietro had created a monster.

She had created a monster!

What had she been thinking staring at herself naked in a mirror and then revealing such impure thoughts about it? She was forty-five. Forty-five, for pity's sake! Much too old to willingly engage in seductions, or to allow a practical stranger to take her clothes off. Kiss her mouth. Her breasts. The sensitive, long-forgotten bud of nerve endings between her legs. Unconsciously, she crossed them at the memory and wished he hadn't seen it or the shocking way it made her lose her mind to nonsensical delirium. And she had showed *it* to him in broad daylight! Moaned her encouragement. Cried out in ecstasy, then lay there completely exposed for the longest time, enjoying the way his deep brown eyes devoured the sight of her undone.

'Are you suggesting I should just blithely and selfishly take a lover and to hell with the consequences?' She could hardly admit that stable door was already wide open and the horse well and truly bolted.

Twice.

'I am the mother of three! What example would I be setting my children?'

Her friend blinked, then slowly scanned the *piazza*. 'I do not see them…because they are hundreds of miles away. Separated by an entire sea and the solid and comforting land mass that is France. I wasn't suggesting you have orgies at the Foundation, dearest, merely that

you fully enjoy your holiday and all the forbidden *delights* of Rome while you are gloriously free to do so.' She raised her eyebrows
suggestively. 'I dare say the gentleman is more
than willing.'

Which was part of the problem. Pietro had
been quite explicit in his willingness. Almost
as explicit as she had been in her wantonness
when sprawled across his desk.

'I loved my husband. I still love my husband.'

'I do know how much you loved my cousin,
Lilian, and how much he loved you—but he
is gone and Henry wouldn't have wanted you
to squander the rest of your life mourning his
memory. He would want you to enjoy it.'

They both knew her beloved husband had
said as much and more on his deathbed, when
he knew he was dying. Alongside declaring his
love and trying to demand she abandon him to
save herself, Henry had begged her to move on
and marry again because she had so much love
in her heart she deserved it. She had more life
to live and he wanted her to live it. *'Live your
life, Lilian...'* Words her children had used to
cajole her into taking this trip.

'You are too selfless and sacrificing for your
own good, Lilian. Look around...nobody here

needs you.' Neither did anyone at home any more, or so it seemed. 'Not even me, as I have Carlotta and a whole host of old acquaintances to gossip with. You have several weeks of glorious Italian freedom before you have to travel home to be a mother and a paragon of self-sacrifice again. Didn't you faithfully promise your children you would enjoy every second of this gift they have given you? Why not be a little more selfish and steal a few moments with a ridiculously handsome, charming and *discreet* gentleman who doesn't see the mother or the paragon at all. One who sees only the woman. And diligently and selflessly tends to her *needs* for once?'

The sedentary approach of the ancient waiter with their coffees prevented Lilian from arguing against the preposterousness straight away. She remained closed-mouthed and quietly confused until the cups were in front of them and waited until he was gone before she eventually spoke. 'You make it all sound so simple—and normal.' And, bizarrely, she realised she was sorely tempted to heed Alexandra's advice and take Pietro up on his scandalous offer to be her lover for the duration. She did have needs. And thanks to him, and after years of ignorant dormancy, they were refusing to go away.

'What is more normal than a man and a woman doing what they were designed to do? Especially when everyone who visits this city knows—what happens in Rome, stays in Rome.'

Chapter Seven

It was a little past midnight when Pietro finally got home. It couldn't be helped. A very wealthy and enthusiastic buyer had spent all afternoon in the gallery, purchased both the Zuccarelli and Canaletto landscapes of Venice and then insisted on taking him home for dinner. Normally, he wouldn't have minded the prolonged meeting, knowing that the best business relationships needed to be nurtured—especially if the client was as ardent a collector of Italian art as this one was. However, tonight the meal had seemed interminable because he was in a hurry to leave, but couldn't. And now Lilian was probably sound asleep and any chance of repeating their delightful interlude from the day before yesterday all but a forlorn hope.

For some reason, it did not seem to matter that

she was a family friend and his houseguest. He had broken his own rigid rules and couldn't seem to muster the enthusiasm to care. She had been worth it. Passionate, unselfconscious and different from any of the women he usually dallied with. She was also clever and shared his love of art. They seemed to think alike, too, so that he enjoyed spending time with her conversing— quite aside from the physical. Which had been exceptional.

So exceptional he hoped very much to be able to enjoy it again and had intended to discuss it with her earlier, before the day ran away with him. To tell her not to be embarrassed about what they had shared, as she clearly had been the previous night over dinner when she could barely look at him without blushing, but to enjoy it for what it was. Something magical and unexpected which would make the next few weeks wonderful and keep his restlessness well and truly at bay. He never suffered from it around Lilian. Even before they had succumbed to passion. Because she made the day brighter and time pass quicker.

A lover he enjoyed talking to...whatever next?

He took another sip of his cognac and stared out of his open window at the stars, wondering if she was still awake and thinking about him as he was her. Then seemed to sense her before she tapped on his bedchamber door.

'Pietro...can we talk?'

'I would like very much if we did, *cara*.'

She came in, looking lovely. Nervous, delightfully awkward and already blushing. 'I wanted to talk about the day before yesterday... in your office when we...you know...'

'Made mad, passionate love on my desk?' He enjoyed the way she worried her bottom lip with her teeth as she nodded, struggling to meet his gaze.

'I was thinking about your offer...in the gallery...you know...'

'I know.' As much as he enjoyed teasing the prudish part of her nature, he also respected the courage it must have taken her to come here. The English were more reserved than his people and he adored that side of Lilian, too. One minute, she had been entirely in the thrall of her pleasure, the next, shy and obviously taken aback by what had transpired so quickly and explosively between them. Almost as soon as she had wriggled back into her clothes, she had become so quaintly English again.

Perhaps proposing they pursue an affair so soon after their passion had been hasty? She had certainly seemed stunned he would ask and oddly lost for words around him for the rest of the ride home.

But she hadn't said no either.

Because she now stood in front of him, practically bouncing from foot to foot, and seemed to have no idea what to do with her hands, he wandered to the decanter and poured her a glass, too. She grabbed it gratefully, but didn't sip. 'So what is it to be, *cara*? One blissful afternoon of passion we will both remember fondly or a longer, more mutually satisfying liaison until you leave?'

'I have never…um…had an affair before,' she repeated. A promising start.

'You are considering it, then?'

'Unbelievably I am.' She did take a sip then. A healthy one. 'Which has come as a great surprise to me…but as we have already…um… you know…it was probably a bit late to be all missish about it.'

'Probably.'

She laughed nervously, then started to pace. 'You see…the thing is I feel compelled to set some boundaries before I commit to it. Some rules… That is probably not at all the done thing, is it? But I am entirely ignorant of the protocols and I have a reputation and children to consider… My work at the Foundation… I would hate for word to…'

He took her hand and tugged her to sit next to him on the mattress. 'First of all, there is no protocol. We are two consenting adults. Both no longer married and free to make our own choices. And, secondly, I think it is sensible to set some boundaries and make some rules. However, before we do any of that, I must ask you one question. Did you enjoy what we did?'

The blush on her cheeks spread instantly to her neck. 'Yes. Very much.'

'And would you like to do it again?'

'I thought you had only one question?'

'Would you like to make love with me again, Lilian?'

'Yes.' She stared down into her cognac momentarily, then glanced up at him shyly through her lashes. 'Very much.'

'Then let us discuss your boundaries and mine so we both get from our affair what we want from it.'

'I would rather keep our relationship between us…private. I do not want even Alexandra or Carlotta to know about it.'

'Agreed. Both can be meddlesome and both will undoubtedly get the wrong idea. You can rely on my complete discretion at all times. What else?'

'I should like you to always be honest with me—about where you are and who you are with. I don't want to expect to…spend time with you and…'

'I will not play games, Lilian, nor will I dishonour you by seeking entertainment elsewhere for the duration of our liaison. If I cannot keep an…*appointment*…' she smiled at that, quickly looking away '…I will ensure you are aware in advance and can assure you it will only happen if business or a dire emergency pulls me elsewhere. In return, I ask for no games from you either. I insist we always lay all our cards flat on the table with one another.' She nodded, clearly relieved.

'I am too old for games.'

'Me, too. What else?'

'Just one final thing. I know your business brings you to England frequently and that your connection with my cousin will undoubtedly continue in the years to come, but I want you to promise that, when I return home, you will never attempt to seek me out to continue our affair. I want a clean break. I have five weeks left here, Pietro. No longer. Goodbye *must* mean goodbye.'

Although he should be cheering at her adamant stipulation and tried to tell himself he was relieved to hear it, something about the anticipated ending felt almost tragic before it had started. To have no hope was... What in God's name was he thinking? It had clearly been a long day. One in which he had continually yearned to taste her again. His odd reaction to the decisive time limit had nothing to do with hope and tragedy and everything to do with lust. 'Of course.' Five weeks was plenty long enough for a monogamous affair—even with a woman as tempting as Lilian. Inevitably he would become restless long before then and tire of her company. After five weeks he would be yearning for pastures new. 'Let us not cloud what we have with messy emotion and complication. You have your life and I have mine and neither of us wants any more than we have already. Not to mention the impossible logistics involved. There are too many miles between London and Rome, *cara*.'

'And what are your rules?'

He didn't want to tell her his bedchamber was out of bounds. That little detail was easily sorted without discussion. Especially as the discussion would have to be too personal and he never discussed his feelings—or his reasons for his rigidly self-imposed rules—with anyone.

'There are only two I should like to add to your very sensible and agreeable list. The first is we must remain friends also for the duration no matter what happens. There are things I want to show you, things I would like to discuss with you, while you are here in Rome.' More unprecedented boundaries he was prepared to cross with her. Friendship and pleasure. Companionship and lust. Boundaries he had never before mixed. Yet their mutual love of art and similar ideas was too alluring to discount and he wanted to share so many things with her. Artists. History. Human details. 'Michelangelo's sculpture of Moses in the Basilica di San Pietro, for instance, like the Sistine Chapel, is a place I could not bear for you to see with anyone other than me. You are the first person I have met in ages who sees art like me and that is too precious for me to deprive myself of.'

She beamed at him. 'I should like that. I enjoy spending time with you.'

'The second is more scandalous, but involves the bedroom...' He heard her softly inhale beside him. 'Never be coy or shy with me, *cara*. If you want something—demand it. Tell me what you like and what you don't. I adored the Lilian who gave herself to me on my desk. The one who forced my hands to her breasts and greedily tore off my clothes. Take your pleasure freely and let me see it always on your face. And do so without your misplaced English guilt or with any concerns about what anyone else will think if they were to find out. Because you have my solemn pledge, they will never find out from me.'

'What happens in Rome stays in Rome.'

'It does, but I didn't hear your promise.'

'I promise.'

'Excellent.' He took a fortifying sip of his own cognac and decided a good place to start was to test the resilience of her promise. 'And what do you want from me tonight, Lilian? Command it and, if it is in my power to grant it, whatever it is, it shall be yours.' Once he had manoeuvred her out of his space and back into the more impersonal confines of hers. One rule he wouldn't break. Ever.

She stared into her glass for the longest time, until he thought she had lost all the nerve it had taken her to come in here. Then she placed the glass on his nightstand and slowly, boldly, flicked her heated gaze to his. 'I want you, Pietro... Now.'

Chapter Eight

'How much further is it?'

Pietro's much longer legs meant she had to quicken her pace to keep up with him and all she was carrying was a blanket, while he was laden down with a huge basket and did not seem the least bit out of breath by the climb.

'What is the matter? Are your poor *old* bones struggling with this tiny hill?' She could hear his amusement even if she couldn't see his expression, as his face had been filled with excitement the moment he had arrived home and declared the weather this evening would be ideal to watch the sunset over Rome properly.

'Don't concern yourself with my legs, *old* man, I can keep up with you.' His bark of laughter was its own reward, but the wretch didn't slow his pace. By the time they approached his apparent destination, a wide clear-

ing on the wooded hilltop, she was more than
a little breathless.

He ordered her to stop and wait while he
deposited the basket on a suitable spot further
away and laid out the blanket on the ground.
Already, after just ten days into their affair, she
knew him well enough to know he loved the
theatre and the anticipation caused by a big reveal almost as much as the reveal itself. Only
when he was satisfied he had set the stage perfectly did he come to fetch her, arranging his
big body behind her so that he could cover her
eyes with his hands and navigate her to stand
on the blanket.

He uncovered her eyes and revelled in her
sharp intake of breath at the sight of all of
Rome laid out before her below. Every dome
and church spire and bridge nestled in a sprawl-
ing mass with the setting sun behind it, casting
it in warm, orange light.

'Oh, my goodness!'

'I know.' His arms had snaked around her
middle as he tugged her backwards to fit snug-
gly under his chin while they gazed at the scen-
ery together. 'This is the very best view of the
city, in my opinion. Made all the better by the
fact we have it all to ourselves.'

That was also true. The clearing was blanketed by trees behind them and the sheer drop beneath made it feel as if they were floating on a cloud above the city, suspended on their own private terrace. Early evening birdsong was the only sound that filled the air. None of the hustle and bustle from the city beyond made its way this far up.

'It is beautiful.'

He kissed her neck and his whisper tickled her ear. 'You're beautiful.'

And she felt beautiful. Apparently, having an illicit, secret and intensely passionate affair had been exactly what she had needed. After that first night, when she had awoken in her bed by herself, she had awoken alone every morning since because he crept out at dawn and had left for his gallery long before Lilian made it down to breakfast. She found that arrangement suited her perfectly. For the sake of the discretion she insisted upon, it would have been impossible to sit across from him with the others so soon after he had had his wicked way with her the night before—or she him. Pietro's insistence at a lack of boundaries between them in the bedroom had been both enlightening and thrilling, and as they meticulously explored one another, she learned new things about her body and the needs she had suppressed for too long, revelling in each new sensation and each new thing he taught her.

But in that, she also learned a great deal about him—the man—and their physical intimacy had also created an emotional one a great deal faster than she ever could have imagined possible. A deep friendship, kinship and affection which spoke to her soul. She was entirely comfortable with him. Almost as if she had known him for ever. They had so much in common. The same sense of humour, ideals, thirst for knowledge as well as their mutual love of art.

Twice in the past week, he had taken a few hours out of work to show her things. The first was a brief visit to see Michelangelo's sculpture of Moses in the Basilica di San Pietro, as he had promised, followed by another visit to his gallery to see the Titian portrait he had excitedly just taken delivery of. Yesterday afternoon, he had driven her around himself in an open carriage, to see each of the seven hills of Rome, telling her about the stories and legends as they travelled in a much better and immersive way than any guidebook ever could.

'How long will it take for the sun to set?'

'Thirty—perhaps forty minutes. Enough time for us to enjoy our sumptuous dinner.'

The evening breeze felt cool on her back as he let go of her and she missed his comforting heat. 'And what a feast we have, *cara*.' From the basket, and with a typical Pietro flourish, he produced a bottle of champagne dewed with condensation because it was clearly perfectly chilled. Then he retrieved two crystal glasses and handed them to her while he opened the bottle.

He clinked his glass to hers and she savoured that first sip. How different this was from the life she was used to. Lilian hadn't realised how much life had ground her down until she had arrived here. In many ways, it felt like shedding chains, except she hadn't known she was carrying them till the weight of them was gone. Here, and especially with him, she was carefree and unburdened.

'A penny for your thoughts...' He was mimicking her accent again. Pietro adored quaint English phrases and was trying to learn as many as he could from her.

'I was just contemplating how quickly life can change.' She snapped her fingers and shrugged. 'When I met you last December, everything seemed as bleak and impossible as it had been when Henry died. My whole family was in crisis and now the opposite is the case.

Everything is better. They are all happy. The world seems filled with possibilities again.'

'Time heals all wounds.'

'It does. And love conquers all.'

The picnic he was unpacking as he sat beside her on the blanket seemed never-ending. 'Such a romantic notion. Do you really believe it?'

'I do. Don't you?'

'I cannot say I have any experience to confirm it. The romantic part of me wants to believe it, but the pragmatic part believes fate has a hand, too, and fate can be fickle. We cannot all have the perfect happy ending or meet the love of our life. So perhaps, for some, love doesn't conquer all.'

He had loaded her a plate which was much too big and placed it in front of her. 'I disagree. As long as you are open to it, it can. I've watched it happen before my eyes. Since Christmas, it has transformed my family.'

'Tell this old cynic the story.' He popped a strawberry into his mouth and settled back on his hands. His dark eyes locked with hers intently, as if she were the most fascinating woman he had ever encountered. 'Perhaps you can change my jaded old mind?'

'Well, I suppose it started some months before Christmas, when my son's regular letters stopped arriving from America. He used to send money home, too, money I am ashamed to say I perhaps relied upon too much to keep a roof over our heads while I poured my heart and soul into the Foundation. I was worried sick as to where he was, assuming the worst as mothers are prone to do, but also worried for my girls because there was practically nothing left in the coffers. We were about to lose everything.'

'I know from experience that is very stressful. But also a great motivator.'

'It certainly motivated my elder daughter Millie, who very nearly accepted a wholly unsuitable marriage proposal from a very dour and humourless man called Gilbert to keep the Foundation afloat.'

'I take it she did not marry him? Because she fell in love with another…'

'Actually, through no fault of her own, she was ruined and had no choice but to marry the man everyone assumed had ruined her.'

His face clouded. 'Poor Millie. I only met her briefly at Lady Fentree's last winter and she seemed like such a lovely girl. How sad she is now trapped in a marriage of convenience.'

'That's what I thought. It kept me up at night.

Especially as it was our fault she was ruined, Pietro.'

'Ours?'

'She was waiting for me that night, not realising I had already left in the last carriage with you. She had to trudge back to Alexandra's in the snow...and, well, when the blizzard started had to seek shelter in Cassius's home. They were unchaperoned.'

'While I was kissing you in the carriage?' He made a face. 'That makes me feel very guilty.'

'Don't. It turned out they were meant to be. They fell head over heels in love and are now blissfully happy.'

'One swallow doesn't make a summer...'

He sounded almost English that time, making her laugh. 'Do you go around collecting our old sayings like paintings?'

He shrugged, suddenly looking very Italian and much too handsome for his own good against the sunset. 'I travel to your country at least twice a year and have done so for the last fifteen years. I find your language fascinating.'

'That explains why you speak it so well.'

'Necessity is the mother of invention...and it is impossible to do business with poor English and, as you know, my beloved English clients are very lucrative.'

'I love your Italian language. Especially when you speak it. I wish I understood more of it. Although I believe I am now quite fluent in the hand gestures.' She did one, making the impassioned face she so often saw the locals do when something got their dander up and he threw his head back and laughed.

'Then you are already halfway there. But we were talking about your experiences with love conquering all...' He clutched his heart and collapsed on the blanket. 'And I am afraid I will need more evidence than one paltry example if I am to be convinced by your argument.'

So she told him about Silas and Mary. About how her son, too, married more because it was the right thing to do rather than for love—yet found love regardless and was now expecting his first child. Her first grandchild. Then she told him about Lottie's desperate quest to find a better husband for Millie than the staid Gilbert and had ended up falling for the candidate she had selected herself. And finally, she went back to the beginning of her story, and Henry, and how, with little more than the love they had for each other and the shared beliefs they both held so dear, they had built the Foundation from the ground up.

'And in the last twenty years I have watched

many lost causes come through our doors, turn their lives around and go on to find happiness. So you see, love truly does conquer all. Just as long as you believe in it.' He smiled at that. 'Have you really never been in love, Pietro?' Because it seemed entirely implausible. He was a passionate man in both his outlook and his behaviours. Good-hearted. Generous. Unbelievably thoughtful thanks to his great love of the details.

He was silent for a long time, then shook his head. 'Not like that. Which is probably what makes me such a dreadful cynic about it all.' He topped up her glass and pointed to the horizon. 'Look, *cara*…it is almost time.'

While she suspected he had wanted to change the subject, he had a point. The sun was disappearing behind the city, changing the sky into a blend of hues which even Canaletto or Turner would struggle to do justice. Blues, purples, reds. The thin but persistent band of orange, then yellow which hugged the rooftops below them and bounced off the river in starbursts.

Caught in its spell, she watched it transfixed. It was the most stunning sunset she had ever seen. As the last vestiges of day turned into night, he kissed her. It was a gentle exploration. Tender and utterly perfect.

'I want to make love to you, Lilian.' His teeth nipped at the sensitive shell of her ear. 'Here.'

'Outside?' A thoroughly scandalous suggestion which oddly thrilled her. 'But someone might see.'

'There is nobody here but you and I. Do not tell me you have never been naked outside before?'

'Of course I haven't.'

'I adore your English primness…but I know you are not so prim when it comes to pleasure.' She wasn't. She never had been. 'Let me love you beneath the stars, Lilian.' His fingers had already started to remove the pins from her hair. 'Let me be your first.'

As Italy was meant to be an adventure, and because her needy body was already convinced, she did not try to argue. Instead she kissed him back and allowed him to undress her completely and lay her down on the blanket. A growing darkness cloaked them, leaving only the rising crescent moon to light their bodies. For some reason, that only heightened the pleasure and her senses. Touch and taste replaced sight as they explored one another.

Pietro loved her slowly, whispering his own delight in what they were doing in beautiful

Italian, and she drowned in it. Drowned in him. Fully savoured every goose pimple. Every shudder. Every sinfully delicious, wickedly drawn out sensation as the sky turned from lilac to purple, then from purple to black while the night air whispered over her naked body and her heart sang in her chest. As the stars began to twinkle above them, more formed behind her eyes as he took her to the edge and held her there until she thought she might die from the exquisite torture. Then finally, calling out each other's names in wonder, arms, legs and souls entwined, they toppled over the hilltop terrace together.

Perfect.

Oddly emotional. A memory she already knew she would treasure even as it was happening long before it had been fully formed.

Chapter Nine

~~~~~~~~~~~~~~~~~~~~~~

'We should probably go.' It was a lacklustre assertion. One he had muttered at least twice before, yet failed to act upon as he was perfectly content to remain lying beside her on the blanket, staring up at the stars.

'We probably should.' Her head was resting on his shoulder. Other than that they weren't touching, although he had never felt so intimate with another in his life.

'Although God only knows how I am going to navigate the horses down the hill in the dark.'

What had possessed him to linger so long when he was normally eager to be on his way once the deed was done? Affairs were about the physical, not the temporal or spiritual. Except with her, those boundaries had been crossed and he couldn't fathom why that was so. Other than this one transcended the purely physical because he wanted to spend time with her both before and after, too.

Something which had dawned on him on his way home this evening, when he found himself hurrying just to see her and talk to her. There had been no thoughts of sex at all. Until he had pondered it and decided he was on dangerous ground if their relationship wasn't entirely based on the sex. With a physical affair he knew where he stood. Knew how the game was played and knew how to play it well. Contemplating any other sort of affair made him feel worryingly off kilter and it had been that realisation which had made him shift the parameters of his keenness. Changing his haste to simply get to her, to be in a hurry to be inside her, to make it all purely physical again where he felt safe. Hence the impromptu picnic.

But he had misjudged it by timing it for sunset, because the sunset had seduced him almost as fully as she had. Now it was over, the parameters seemed to have shifted again of their own accord and he was back to simply being glad to be with her and content to remain so.

All very odd.

'Then maybe we shouldn't… Maybe it makes

more sense to sleep here, seeing as we are both perfectly comfortable, and drive home as the sun comes up.'

'You want to sleep on the ground? Under the stars?' Something which held a great deal of appeal at this precise moment. 'I suppose we could...' Because it wasn't his bedchamber, so did not really break any of his hard-and-fast rules. 'I suppose I am very tired.' He kissed the top of her head, already warming to the idea of just him, her and the universe.

'Are your poor *old* bones struggling after your exertions?' She turned and snuggled against him, wrapping her arm around him, clearly making the decision for him.

'They are. Your fault. You have worn me out, woman.'

He felt her smile against his skin. 'It was worth it though, wasn't it? Tonight truly was spectacular.' That it had been. All of it. What was it about her that intimacies were so much more satisfying than normal? Pietro had made love to many women in his life, yet all paled into insignificance alongside Lilian. 'I have never slept outside.'

'Neither have I.' Before tonight, it had never occurred to him to do so.

'Then tonight will be a first for both of us.'

He held her close, deciding not to wonder why it seemed imperative he do so, and continued to watch the stars till he felt himself drifting. Then he must have slept the sleep of the dead because he did not recall stirring once.

The promise of daylight kissed Pietro's eyelids and he felt her move next to him.

He cracked open one eye and saw her tangle of hair across his chest. As if Lilian sensed him looking, her face suddenly emerged from it, smiling as she propped herself up. Delightfully sleepy-eyed and sultry. 'Good morning.'

'Buongiorno.'

She kissed him softly and it occurred to him this was another first. He had never awoken with another in all of his forty-eight years. He always crept away before dawn. Usually as soon as his bed partner had fallen asleep. Which meant sleeping with her in his arms was yet another first to add to his growing list today.

'Look, Pietro...the sun is rising.' She shuffled to sit and he watched, transfixed, as she smiled at the spectacle. Her dark hair, hopelessly tousled from sleep, hung halfway down her pale back and over her shoulders. With the blanket pooled around her waist, the chill in the morning air had made her dusky nipples harden, but she appeared both nonplussed and unaware of her nudity. 'Have you ever seen anything so lovely?'

He hadn't ever, although they were both looking at entirely different things. He let her watch the sunrise for a few minutes before he tugged her backwards and rolled on top of her, her surprised giggle making him laugh. But then she licked her lips when she felt his hardness and the shape of her smile changed as her eyes darkened. 'Oh, Pietro...' Not a no, but there was a brief indecision before her lips started to curve in the sensual smile he had come to love. 'You will have to be quick...the world is waking.'

So he was.

Although the glorious, frantic, earthy haste of their coupling had nothing to do with the fear of being caught and everything to do with the wonderful way he was feeling. He felt more alive than he had in years. Decades younger and, for some reason, deliriously happy.

They clung together laughing and panting, rolling around on the blanket as they greedily took their pleasure, neither quite believing what they were doing until it was done and they collapsed, stunned.

Then it really was time to go. A quick check of his pocket watch declared it to be already six. In another hour his whole household would be awake, swiftly followed by Carlotta, who had always been an early riser, and he had solemnly promised Lilian they would always be discreet—even though he suspected they were failing miserably and everyone at the *palazzo* already knew.

'Where is my shirt?'

She tossed it at him, no longer the least bit prim about her nudity in front of him as she had been at the start of their affair, then twisted her hair into a slapdash knot which she secured with the two pins she had managed to find discarded in the grass.

As he watched her, Pietro wrestled with his hopelessly crumpled trousers. A feat made near impossible as they had been dampened by morning dew and stuck twisted to his skin mercilessly. They both laughed as they tried to get her into her corset. The damp laces proved impossible to undo and they had to concede defeat. Pietro stuffed it in the picnic basket instead while she wriggled into her dress.

'I cannot believe I am not wearing any underwear.' She flattened her hands against the peaks of her nipples poking through the silk in an attempt to calm them as he did her up. 'I shall cause a scandal if anyone sees me.'

'Yet your lack of underwear will certainly make the ride home interesting. I should warn you, I intend to drive very fast over the cobbles.' He winked at her look of outrage and tugged her into his arms for one last searing kiss before they finally gathered everything and made their way to his curricle, him thoroughly delighted by the excellent start to his day.

Then, both feeling very naughty but wholly unrepentant, they returned to the *palazzo* at speed, the horses' hooves beating in time to his rapid heartbeat, giggling like children when the house was still quiet, creeping up the stairs and back to their respective rooms before either Alexandra or Carlotta were any the wiser. Before she disappeared through the door, Lilian blew him a saucy kiss and he caught it in his fist, laughing softly as he went through his own door and feeling completely at one with the world.

What a morning!

What a woman!

He was going to miss her dreadfully when she was gone.

His feet slowed. Stopped. Alone in his bedchamber, he hadn't even stripped off his coat before he was swamped by the most peculiar feeling of emptiness. An emptiness he knew would go the instant he returned to her. Perhaps he should order breakfast in bed for the pair of them? Send his sister and her cousin out shopping for the day so they could be entirely alone? Spend the morning reading his newspaper with her next to him in his bed. Talking to him, passing the time. Then maybe later he would lure her out into the garden and make lazy love to her in the midday sunshine? He smiled at the thought, instantly feeling better.

Yes—that was exactly what he was going to do. He believed Lilian liked her eggs scrambled and her bread slathered in butter. She would also want tea—a drink he couldn't stand, but which always made her sigh with almost the same happiness as she did when he kissed her. While the kitchen was making them breakfast, he would also get a bath drawn and they could soak in it together. He would tell her to bring her precious soap and this time he would scrub her back. And her front. As the English said, cleanliness was next to godliness after all.

And while he was about it, perhaps he should suggest she simply move her things into his room for the duration of her stay... It made no sense tiptoeing backwards and forwards when they would spend every morning as well as every night now together...

Good grief, what was the matter with him?

If he did that, there would be no sensible boundaries left between them and he suspected he needed all those sensible boundaries with her if he was going to let her go at the end of their allotted time together with his sanity intact.

He did not want to give Lilian false hope or ideas about them, and suddenly felt uncomfortable about the idea of them living hand in hand like man and wife. Such close proximity for the next few weeks could be dangerous.

Could?

There was no could about it if the word wife had popped into his head and he had been seduced into the idea of spending every morning with her! The minx and the morning sunrise had obviously bewitched him! What was he thinking?

Pietro sat heavily on his mattress as his nerves and emotions swirled. Things were on the brink of getting out of hand and he needed to reel them in before they spiralled out of control.

All his rigid rules were there for a reason, to

protect his freedom. Freedom he adored. Freedom he had fiercely guarded for twenty-five whole years. Freedom he had no intention of relinquishing—even for her.

Yet look at what happened when he broke them.

He had lowered his guard and allowed one carefree night and one overly familiar morning and on the back of it had started to seriously consider nonsense like sharing every morning with her, when his bedchamber and the barriers around his heart had always been sacrosanct.

Was that what he truly wanted?

Every morning? Real commitment that extended beyond their allotted time?

He felt his pulse quicken with panic. No... He must be tired. Overwhelmed. The nature of this morning had made him view things through what the English quaintly called rose-tinted spectacles. This was merely a phase. Brought about by too much fresh air and not enough sleep and the magical properties of the stars and the sunrise.

He walked his own path. That was the way he liked it. There was no reason to change course or make concessions. As long as he kept things within the strict parameters which had worked perfectly for decades, all would be all right in the end. It was just a few weeks, for pity's sake! Nothing catastrophic could happen just as long as he kept his wits about him.

And at least he had come to his senses quickly. Clearly mornings were too personal for his sanity to cope with—and clearly mornings with her much too tempting if he was already contemplating the unthinkable. The untenable.

The wholly unpalatable.

He made a vow there and then which strangely depressed him rather than calmed him. No more mornings. She was just too damn irresistible.

Chapter Ten

Every night he came to her bedchamber when the house was asleep and left her before she awoke. She missed waking up in his arms, but appreciated his discretion regardless.

But today she would not see him at all, nor most of tomorrow, as he had gone to visit the villa of a *barone* somewhere between here and Naples, on the trail of a Botticelli, and would have to spend the night. It was, she decided, just as well, because as much as she was determined to keep emotion out of their relationship, it appeared to be creeping in regardless. She blamed their night under the stars for that. It had entirely seduced her. He had entirely seduced her. Body and soul. Heart and mind.

It made no difference that they kept their friendship completely separate from their nocturnal activities—where they seldom talked about anything beyond the nonsense passion elicited—the conversations and easy camaraderie between them when passion was impossible, had made her like him a great deal. He was so easy to talk to. So insightful and...nice.

She looked forward to those times as much as the nights. Perhaps more so. Yesterday, she'd had butterflies in her tummy for most of the day. The same sort she'd had when she and Henry had been courting. Butterflies which had nothing to do with how he would inevitably make love to her later and everything to do with being delighted just to breathe the same air as him.

It was a worrying development which she was determined to get over. This was an adventure. An interlude. An unexpected and thrilling happenstance which she wanted to remember fondly, not mourn the inevitable death of. A little distance from Pietro, who most definitely did not want anything complicated, would help her to detach from those unwelcome stirrings and put them into stark context. Just as soon as she stopped feeling miserable about it.

As if mirroring her disappointment, the heavens had decided to open and the bright blue skies which had been her constant companion since her arrival had decided to go with him, replaced by slate-grey clouds and vertical fat raindrops which showed no sign of abating.

To that end, she had agreed to accompany the other ladies to a small, intimate afternoon soirée at the home of their old friend the Marchesa di Gariello, where a renowned *modista* from Milan was coming to tout her wares. This was a cause of great excitement to both Carlotta and Alexandra, who had been wittering for most of the morning about the woman's exquisite and daring gowns. A topic which held practically no appeal for Lilian, but as she was at a loose end, needed a distraction from pondering on Pietro and they had welcomed her with open arms, she made an effort to at least appear interested in the close confines of the carriage as they pulled up outside.

'Of course her clothes cost a fortune,' said her cousin as if this alone made them more desirable. 'Signora Ferretti specialises in hand-painted silks, Lilian, and has so many commissions, it takes months for any clothes to be shipped. But when they eventually arrive— they are worth it.'

If they cost a fortune, Lilian was certainly not going to be swayed into purchasing one. She had spending money, a decent amount, too, but she appreciated the value of money too much to waste a fortune on a hand-painted silk gown. And where would she wear it? She didn't go to many fancy balls or parties. Aside from her new holiday wardrobe, her normal clothes were sensible and serviceable, although she was now prepared to concede they were a bit drab. She had grown to rather like the colourful and light gowns her daughters had introduced her to. Especially when she watched her scandalous new lover's dark eyes smoulder with appreciation when he saw her in one. The more he appreciated the gown, the slower he unwrapped her at night until she stood or lay before him quite naked. It had come as an entirely unexpected revelation that she appeared to enjoy being naked most of all nowadays.

Well... What happened in Rome and all that...even if she still did harbour a great deal of guilt about her scandalous behaviour.

Servants with umbrellas helped them out of the carriage and into the Marchesa's apartments, where Lilian quickly learned the soirée was anything but small and intimate. At least forty women were crammed on dainty chairs in the ornately gilded parlour, ringing the room like the eager spectators in a gladiatorial arena. The bold, Mediterranean colours of their fashionable dresses and excited, rapid Italian as they all fought to be heard above the cacophony of chatter made them all appear like strange exotic birds. A plethora of servants hovered, attentively and silently serving them with steaming silver coffee pots and platters of exquisite little cakes and pastries which they lifted on to little gilded plates with tiny tongs.

'I see Signora Ferretti has attracted quite the crowd.' Alexandra kissed both cheeks of a beautiful woman of indiscriminate age and jet-black hair who was, in Lilian's humble opinion, much too thin. Her olive skin was draped like translucent parchment over prominent collar-bones and all the tendons in her neck were visible as she turned to greet Carlotta.

'Darlings! So glad you could come.' Her dark eyes flicked to Lilian with barely disguised interest. 'And this must be the Mrs Fairclough I hear so much of lately.'

'It is a pleasure to finally meet you, Marchesa.' She curtsied politely and the other woman inclined her head like a queen, the brittle smile on her face not reaching her eyes.

'Enchanted. I am sure we shall talk later. But at the moment...well, as you can see, things are busy. Hurry and sit. Signora Ferretti is about to start.' She shooed them towards the few empty seats at the side and scurried off.

For some odd reason, and although Lilian prided herself on not making snap judgements about people, she had taken an instant and irrational dislike to her hostess. Something she would have to ponder because it was so unusual.

They squeezed themselves on to three chairs at the furthest end of the room and she smiled apologetically to the woman next to her as she wrestled her full skirt and petticoats into a respectable size before gratefully accepting a cup of steaming hot coffee and a plate of delicious-looking confections from the two servants who immediately came towards them.

'Thank you... I mean *grazie*.' Both servants smiled at her for acknowledging them. The rudeness some of the aristocracy displayed to their servants had always been one of her biggest vexations and, regardless of whether it was the done thing or not, she liked to make a point of being polite around them in the vain hope it might rub off.

'English?'

The woman beside her was smiling, her accent distinctly American. 'Yes, indeed. From London actually. I am Mrs Lilian Fairclough.'

The steaming coffee and the plate of cakes prevented her from offering her hand.

'Mrs Ida Wayfair—from New York originally, but I have lived here in Rome for over a decade now, so it feels more like home than home does nowadays. My husband used to be the American Ambassador to the Vatican.'

'And what does he do now?'

'Mostly pushes up the daisies.' The woman smiled at Lilian's discomforted expression, obviously amused and delighted to have shocked her. 'He died three years ago and I cannot say I was sorry to see the back of him. He was a most disagreeable man, by and large. I hope you have had better luck with Mr Fairclough.'

'He was a wonderful man—but like yours, also deceased.'

'Recently?'

'Ten years ago now. Nearly eleven.'

'Then we are both merry widows—free to live our lives as we choose. Isn't it *glorious*? What brings you to Rome?'

'A little holiday. I came with my cousin through marriage, Lady Alexandra Malverly, and am staying with the Contessa di Bagnoregio.' She gestured to her companions, who were too engaged in a discussion with another couple of ladies in the seats behind them for her to interrupt and perform the introductions.

'The Contessa and I have collided on occasion. I know her brother, Pietro, better.'

'You know Pietro?'

'I have a love of Rococo art and he has found me many a lovely painting to hang on my walls.'

'I love all art—but most specifically that from the Renaissance. It was one of the reasons I came here to Rome. It has such a rich artistic history.' And thanks to that, and Pietro, she couldn't seem to shake the feeling that perhaps it was her love of art, rather than the Foundation, which might shape her future. An idea which had blossomed in his gallery and which seemed to have taken root. A little shop, perhaps—not for great masters like his, because Lord only knew she couldn't afford them—but to show the work of new artists, selling a little beauty to women like her to cherish in their houses.

'That it does. Have you seen the Sistine Chapel yet?'

'Pietro has promised to take me soon.'

'Then you are lucky as you have the best possible guide. He is the font of all knowledge on Italian art. How long are you staying at the *palazzo*?'

'A little while yet.'

'Then you must come to my ball! I hold one every year. A tradition started by my husband to grease the wheels of diplomatic relations and commerce, and one of the few things he did I enjoyed so much I continued. Pietro has already accepted my invitation on his and the Contessa's behalf weeks ago—so now I shall extend it to include you and your cousin. It will be so nice to have two more guests who speak my language and I should like to show a fellow art lover my little collection.'

'That would be lovely.' Perhaps she did have an occasion to wear one of Signora Ferretti's confections—not that she could afford one. But the thought of wearing something stunning and daring for Pietro at a fancy ball suddenly held a great deal of appeal. He had the most expressive eyes. Eyes that positively ate her up when he liked what he saw.

As if reading her mind, Mrs Wayfair whispered in her ear as their hostess took centre stage to introduce the *modista*. 'Because we are now friends, I shall let you in on a secret, Mrs Fairclough. Although Signora Ferretti charges a fortune for commissions, if you see anything you fancy on one of the models and ask her quietly for it at the end, she will sell you her samples for an absolute steal. She absolutely loathes carting it all back to Milan. My own wardrobe is full of them—but please don't tell anyone. These people are such snobs, I would never live it down.'

Signora Ferretti's gowns were stunning and, although Lilian had never put much stock in fashion, she found herself coveting one in particular as the pretty models circled the floor wearing them. It was pale green, the full bell skirt decorated along the hem with a profusion of hand-painted flowers which wove together among twisting fronds of ivy. The rest of the dress was plain—yet elegantly so. The tight bodice nipped in tight at the waist, while the daring neckline was cut in a low V to sit off the shoulders.

When the show was done and the models mingled among the ladies so they could examine the details, Lilian gave in to the temptation to examine it more closely.

'You have the figure for it, *signora*.' The *modista* silently appeared at her shoulder. 'This gown demands a figure with a voluptuous shape to hold it up. You are one of the few ladies in the room with the décolleté necessary I think. It could have been made for you.'

'I fear it is too expensive for me to consider,

signora—but it is lovely.' Should she broach the idea of purchasing the sample?

'That is a shame.'

'Unless this *used* gown is for sale?'

The *modista* took her arm and guided her away from listening ears. 'It could be. I would take nine *scudi* for it.'

Lilian quickly did the mental arithmetic and her heart sank. Nearly three pounds! Three-quarters of her entire spending money for the entire trip and three times the price of any dress she had ever bought before. 'That is too expensive.'

'That gown is made of the finest oriental silk. I painted the flowers on the hem myself. It took many hours to complete, *signora*.'

'I am not trying to diminish the value of your excellent work, Signora Ferretti. I am merely stating a fact—for me, nine *scudi* is a fortune.'

'I could go to eight...but no lower.'

For a second, she seriously considered it, then shook her head as common sense returned. As beautiful as the gown was, it was a ridiculous extravagance. A few months ago, three pounds had meant the difference between a roof over her head and destitution. Just because her financial woes were over and the family funds buoyant once again, it did not mean she could waste good money on a selfish purchase for herself simply to watch the effect the daring gown would have on Pietro's eyes, because here in Rome she was a bolder, braver, more sophisticated and passionate version of her usual self. 'I appreciate your honesty, *signora*, but alas, I must decline. I am sure somebody else will snap it up soon enough.'

'I am certain of it. But for the next hour, I shall say it is already sold in case you change your mind.' The *modista* was clearly a canny businesswoman. 'Because for me, that gown belongs on you.' She looked her up and down. 'In fact, if my excellent eye is correct, it will not even require any alteration. You and the model wearing it are exactly the same size.'

Words not conducive to strengthening her resolve. 'Really, I...' The rest of the sentence became redundant as Lilian spoke to the woman's retreating back as she disappeared back into the clucking melee of eager buyers all vying for her attention.

Feeling a little deflated, heartily ashamed to be so waylaid by a dress, and unable to see either her companions or Mrs Wayfair in the gaggle, she decided to visit the retiring room and give herself a stiff talking to rather than attempt to converse in her pathetic, paltry attempts at Italian. Rome was clearly seducing her too much if she had considered for one second spending a king's ransom on one gown. Was it not bad enough she had taken a lover who she allowed to take sinful liberties with her person? At this rate, the sensible woman she had always been would evaporate and she would return home putting more stock in shoes or lace or other fripperies than she did her own character.

She would become a spendthrift as well as a wanton!

Pietro's fault.

He made her feel special and beautiful and more alive than she had felt in for ever and she so wanted to look beautiful for him. She loitered behind the privacy of the plush velvet curtain, hoping that in avoiding the coveted gown, some other lady would covet it more and offer the *modista* a price she simply couldn't refuse. Until she heard the unmistakable sounds of another woman entering the chamber and knew her time for avoidance was done. Lilian pulled back the curtain to stare straight into the face of her hostess. Caught off guard by the one lady she was happy not to collide with ever again, she pasted a smile on her face.

'This is a lovely gathering, my lady. Signora Ferretti's gowns are stunning.'

'They are indeed. Which did you purchase?'

'None. As lovely as they are, I have nowhere to wear one.'

'Such a shame...but I am not surprised. They are a little too bold for you, I think.' That galled. 'Although I must say—you are not at all what I expected, Mrs Fairclough.'

'How so?'

'From the accounts I had heard of you, I was expecting someone much more glamorous.' As insults went, in this gilded gaggle of exotic birds in expensively fashionable dresses, it was a cutting barb and one which took Lilian aback.

'Then I am sorry to disappoint, my lady.'

'Oh, I am not disappointed, Mrs Fairclough, and I meant no offence in stating my impressions.'

Lilian was in no doubt that she had, although couldn't for the life of her think why this strange woman had cause to dislike her or grievously insult her so.

'Merely that one hears rumours in a city such as this...' The tinkling laugh was as fake as the streak-free black hair on the Marchessa's head. 'And when the rumours concerning you go hand in hand with a certain handsome *duca* who has been dragging you all over the city, one assumes he has been captivated by a siren rather than a…matron. It is…refreshing. That is all. If a little strange.'

Lilian was more bothered by the rumours than being called a matron. Rumours, in her experience, tended to spread and she had been so certain they had been discreet. *'Captivated?'* She hoped her tinkling laugh sounded more genuine than her hostess's. 'I hardly think so. But if you are alluding to the few excursions the Duca della Torizia and I have enjoyed together, then alas, they come from a mutual love of the great art of the Renaissance rather than anything else.' Years of experience with rampant gossip among the women at the Foundation had taught her the best way to deal with an unsavoury rumour, or an unsavoury character, was to tackle them head on.

'I suspected the rumours were exaggerated, my dear Mrs Fairclough, because…' she paused to look her up and down '…now that I see you, it is quite apparent you are not Pietro's type. He likes his women less…homely and plain. Silly me.' She fluttered her hand, something which made the gnarly tendons in the woman's skinny arm bulge in sharp relief. 'As we are not at all alike.'

'Are you telling me you are more his type?' Lilian hated herself for asking the question the Marchessa had clearly intended for her to ask if the brief flash of triumph skittering across her features was any gauge, but the rush of jealousy had been too acute to ignore.

'He *did* ask me to marry him.' The woman had turned her back on Lilian to stare at herself in the mirror while she adjusted a hairpin. 'And was heartbroken when I turned him down. Poor Pietro. I still feel bad for hurting him—but I promised myself that if I ever married again it would be for love. I tried to feel that for Pietro. Really, I did. And he did everything he could to encourage my affections... but despite being lovers for a while there was no *passione*. At least not from my perspective.' She shrugged and turned back to face Lilian. 'But he still tries—bless him. Even after all these years. I am dreading the Wayfair ball. He knows I always attend for Ida and every year he reiterates that his feelings have not changed.' Then her cold, calculating eyes swept Lilian's entire body again slowly. 'You should give me the name of your *modista*, Mrs Fairclough. Perhaps if I dress a little more like you Pietro will finally lose interest?'

And with that she sailed out of the room.

For the longest time Lilian simply stood there, allowing the hurt, the shock, the intense and irrational jealousy and the outrage to settle. Except it didn't. How dared she? *How dared she?* Then, as outrage turned to fury, Lilian did something completely un-Lilian-like.

She stormed out of the retiring room and straight towards Signora Ferretti, who stood all alone near the door.

'Six *scudi* and not a penny more!'

Chapter Eleven

Her index finger was tracing lazy circles on his chest, a state of affairs Pietro was perfectly content to let continue till she fell back asleep and he had to leave her. They hadn't made love either, something he had neither minded nor expected when he had arrived home well after midnight as she had been fast asleep when he had slid in the bed beside her and cuddled her close. He had craved her constantly in the two days he had been gone, missing her conversation and company as much as he missed her passion. Hence he was here, simply to be with her because he couldn't wait till morning to see her again. He hadn't even expected conversation, yet she had sleepily asked the odd question as he had rambled about his trip. He liked that she was as happy to see him as he was her.

Not for the first time today, he considered

how relieved he was their time together was finite because she was getting under his skin. He had tried to conduct their affair exactly as he had all the others—yet even when he tried, with her it was different. Special. He couldn't remember the last time he had not quite been as occupied with business as he should be because a part of his mind was always with her. It wasn't the usual restlessness this time either. He knew all the symptoms of that intimately. It was an eagerness. A keenness. A sense the world was not quite right because she was not there with him.

Something which should probably worry him more than it did at this precise moment.

But because their time together was ticking away and because she was rigidly abiding by her own rules, he decided not to allow their unique connection and growing friendship to spoil the wonderful sanctuary from life their affair was creating. He had a little more time to enjoy her to the fullest and then Lilian, her delectable, responsive, comforting body and her keen mind would be gone.

All was as it should be.

'When will the Botticelli arrive? I hope I get to see it.' She was so soft and warm, he wrapped his arms tighter around her, enjoying the subtle rose scent of the fancy soap she liked to bathe with.

'Next week—I hope.' The impressive circular *tondo* of the Madonna was undoubtedly a coup. One which would bring him an extortionate price. An insignificant detail she would not care about. 'It is in superb condition, *cara*. The colours still as vibrant as the day he painted her. Even the frame is original. Exceptionally carved. You will love it.' He had known that the second he had laid eyes on it and his first thoughts had been to imagine Lilian's reaction. She would love to touch a real Botticelli rather than have to gaze at one from a safe distance. He could imagine her delicate hands tracing the brushstrokes and the carvings on the frame as she pictured the person who had made them and wondered about their life. It was why he had bought it with his heart rather than his head and only offering token resistance when the owner had haggled for more money despite knowing it was an inferior example of the artist's. Something he hadn't done in years.

'Then you must take me to see it the second it arrives.' She snuggled against him. 'I am glad you are home.'

'Did you miss me?' Why was he asking that? Why did he care?

'I did. But do not let it go to your head. When you left, you literally took the sunshine with you, it has rained nonstop and I have been stuck indoors. Worse, I got dragged to an interminable tea party.'

'Oh, dear. Was it bad?'

'A room full of snobs and empty heads.' She propped herself up on one elbow to stare at his face in the moonlight. 'I met the Marchesa di Gariello...' His frown was instinctual and unguarded. 'She seemed to take an instant dislike to me.'

'I wouldn't take it personally.' Sofia was hideous. Mean. Judgemental. Conniving. 'She takes a dislike to most people she meets. Wear it like a badge of honour. I do.'

'I got the impression it was because of you.' Of course it was because of him. 'She mentioned you were betrothed once.'

He felt his eyebrows disappear into his hair with shock. 'We most certainly were not!' What was the witch up to now? 'I would rather spend eternity in purgatory than a day married to her. Although that was not for a great want of trying on her part. I would have thought after all these years she would have got over it...'

'That is exactly what she said about you.' Her expression was a little too casually dismissive. 'In fact—she said you continue to pursue her. Even now.'

'Did she?' He shook his head, wondering if he should be furious with the woman who was plainly causing mischief or pleased the one in his bed was clearly put out by the connection. 'Bizarrely, I am not surprised at her lies. Nor that she sought you out specifically to tell them to you. Carlotta or Alexandra must have mentioned our friendship to her. She always was a manipulative and nasty piece of work. It is why she is banned from the *palazzo*.'

'You banned her?'

'Fifteen years ago. I cannot abide the sight of her. She knows that.' Because in an entirely unregretted lapse in gentlemanly manners, he had told her to her face. Vociferously.

'Were you really lovers?' Lilian and Sofia had clearly had quite a frank conversation.

'Are you jealous, *cara*?' He liked it that she was.

'Were you?'

'Once. Just once. The biggest mistake of my life.' He still remembered that dreadful morning as if it were yesterday. Her appearing in his bedchamber, refusing to leave until he agreed to marry her. Threatening to tell the world he had raped her when he refused, ruining his reputation unless he capitulated to her demands. Him calling her bluff, telling her to do her worst and then throwing her out. The anxious wait in the coming months to see if she would come good on her threats and hideous lies. Feeling sick with worry every day and not knowing what the hell he could do to stop it except avoid her. Something he had done for many years.

Another self-centred, conniving, manipulative woman exactly like his wife. But at least Isabetta had been his father's mistake—not his. His bride had not been of his choosing—not that he would have chosen Isabetta in a million years. She had been spoiled and selfish, prone to tantrums and weak of character. He had disliked her from the outset and hated her by the end. He'd hated Sofia from that first morning. 'I've never felt the compunction to repeat it.'

'I see.' His temper flared at her blatant disappointment and disapproval as she shuffled away from him and sat up in the bed.

'This is ridiculous! It was a long time ago.'

'But it was with her! That horrible woman!'

As much as he regretted that unfortunate liaison with Sofia, it galled him that Lilian should make him feel ashamed for it. 'Did you think I didn't have a past? That I had remained celibate since Isabetta died twenty years ago?'

'I knew you had a certain reputation.'

'One I have no intention of apologising for. Like you, I have no spouse to answer to. I've broken no rules. Yet you expect me to still apologise for an error of judgement from years ago? One which happened long before I even knew you existed.' His good mood now royally spoiled, he got up from the bed to pace, raking his hand through his hair as he tried to calm down. 'Have you never made a mistake about a person? Put your trust in someone and then have them betray that trust?' He could tell by her face she had. 'This is no different. It happened. I wish it hadn't. But I cannot turn back time, Lilian.'

'Do you promise it is over between you?'

'I shouldn't need to!' Incensed, hurt and entirely bewildered as to why it bothered her so much, he snatched up his robe and stuffed his arms into it. 'You being jealous of Sofia is like me being jealous of Henry! We cannot erase our pasts—therefore what purpose does it serve above making us both miserable?'

With that he stalked out.

Back in his own rooms he poured himself a healthy snifter of cognac which he did not want and went to the window to stare sightlessly at the night sky. For two days he had missed her. For two days he had yearned for her company and her smile and the easy way she made him feel. Now, he was seething and filled with righteous indignation. Because her argument had been stupid and petty. Oddly reminiscent of so many stupid and fruitless arguments with Isabetta because he couldn't turn back time and there was really nothing he could do about it other than apologise for breathing—and he had done much too much of that in his awful marriage to want to engage in it now, twenty years later, with a lover who had got under his skin when he was always so careful to keep it tightly nailed down.

This was exactly what happened when he allowed emotions to cloud things. His fault, because he enjoyed her company so much and, he was prepared to admit, a little of her possessive jealousy. He had shown Lilian more of himself than he was comfortable sharing because they had so much in common. She was different.

Or perhaps she wasn't if that nonsense was anything to go by.

'Pietro...' He rolled his eyes as he heard his bedchamber door creak open, not quite ready for the next round of nonsense in a fight nobody could win. This was exactly what he hated about the relationships between men and women. The nonsense. The histrionics. Endless fighting about nothing. 'I'm sorry.'

He stiffened at the apology, the ghosts of too many past apologies too fresh in his mind. Apologies which meant nothing. Which merely served as a way for the woman making it to begin her unreasonable attack again, hammering a wedge between them so deep, there was no coming back from it.

'I was entirely unreasonable just now. I am heartily ashamed of myself...' He heard the bed creak as she sat down on his mattress. 'I allowed her to get inside my head and chip away at all my insecurities, despite knowing she had, as you rightly just said, sought me out on purpose with the sole intention of insulting me and spoiling my day.' He still refused to turn around, although to give her some credit, Lilian's apology did sound a little bit genuine. 'I am angry with myself for giving her the last word and angrier still that I have allowed her cruel words to wound me. It is ridiculous. I am a mature and normally level-headed woman, not some silly girl who believes every outrage or insult that she hears without question. Nor should I allow a shallow and mean creature like the Marchesa the power to destroy my confidence, when I had worked out her character from the outset. Please forgive me, Pietro. I was half-asleep and snippy and not very rational. None of this is your fault.' He heard the contrition in her sad sigh. 'I do not want to go to bed on a fight.'

As apologies went, it was one of the most selfless he had ever heard—yet he still wasn't entirely ready to accept it. Not until he understood it was genuine. 'How did she try to destroy your confidence?'

'It is silly... I know it is silly. And I also know I should allow it to wash over me, but I was out of my depth in that room full of aristocratic women, all dressed in their finery and all looking much more like they belonged there than I did. Then there were all the gowns they were clamouring over. Signora Ferretti's ridiculously expensive fripperies well out of my price range... I was feeling like a fish out of water and went to hide in the retiring room to give myself a stiff talking to...and she was there waiting as soon as I came out.'

'She must have said something atrocious to have upset you so.'

'She declared me more a matron than a siren...which of course I am...and said she was surprised such a homely, plain and unglamorous woman could captivate you. Then she told me about your betrothal and…well, I have no defence. I did feel irrationally jealous and I did feel like a common English sparrow in a room full of exotic birds. I did feel homely and plain—before she said I was.'

'If I were to liken Sofia to a bird, *cara*, it would be to a vulture. Aside from the fact it suits her personality, which feeds on decay and destruction, there are some unfortunate similarities in their wrinkly bald heads.' He found himself smiling. 'The years have not been kind to Sofia. Not helped by her obsession with emaciation.'

'I did think she needed a good meal.'

'She resembles a skeleton draped in skin. Even Signora Ferretti's outrageously expensive gowns cannot disguise how gaunt and painfully thin she is. Nor can they minimise the imprint her mean-spirited character has ground into her face. As flattered as my shallow male ego is, you have no reason to be jealous of her, my darling. I like my women to look like those Botticelli painted. I love curves and flesh and women who enjoy their food rather than pick at it. And much as it shames this proud Italian to admit it, I have discovered I much prefer your

English rose complexion to that of my country-women. And as to your being a matron…well, I suppose I could flatter my ego with a younger woman, but what would we talk about? And you are a siren to me. I cannot resist you.'

'You are being awfully nice about my little tantrum.'

'That is because I want my wicked way with you.'

'Even though I am homely and plain.' Finally, she was smiling and despite the fact she sat on his bed—in his personal sanctuary—he found his feet walking towards her, tugging her to stand before him and loosening the knot in her silk robe.

'I can see it may take me many hours to re-build your tattered confidence, *cara*.' He slid the silk from her shoulders, his eyes heating at the sight of her nakedness beneath. 'Thank goodness we still have all night…'

Chapter Twelve

Lilian woke wrapped in his arms for only the second time in their relationship and decided it was exactly where she wanted to be. The first rays of the sun were streaming through the shutters, bathing his bronzed skin in light. Beneath her palm, she could feel the rhythmic rise and fall of his chest as he slept and was in no hurry to wake him as she knew that would only hasten his departure to the gallery which took up so much of his time and spoil this cosy intimacy which she was enjoying. They had never awoken together in a bed before. Pietro always crept out before she woke and it was usually hours before she got to see him again. Because the man worked too hard. Selfishly, she wanted more of him now. More than just the nights and a few snatched hours on the odd day he could spare them.

There was no denying she was developing feelings for him. Not after her uncharacteristic flash of jealousy last night, followed by her body's honesty as they had made love afterwards. For her, it had been more than the sexual act, more than pleasure and more than an affair. She felt a connection to him, a sense of kinship and rightness she had not known with anyone other than Henry. It wasn't love yet, because there was still so much she needed to know about him and she wasn't entirely sure her feelings were strong enough to eschew her old life to embrace his new one. But she was certainly on the way towards it. She felt a deep affection towards Pietro and was starting to believe he reciprocated those feelings.

Which was a complication, to be sure—but not an insurmountable one. If it was meant to be, they would find a way to make it work and, as they still had just over two weeks left before she had to leave and the relationship between them was still in its infancy, there also seemed little point in discussing things now. Or perhaps at all.

She felt him stir and snuggled against him, pressing her lips softly to his before propping her head on her elbow to smile down at his sleepy face. 'Good morning.'

His hooded eyes stared back, a little surprised to see her. '*Buongiorno, cara*... What time is it?'

'I have no idea.' She kissed his chest. 'Does it matter?'

'I do not want the servants to find you here and start to gossip. And I have to get to the gallery early.' He shuffled out from beneath her and sat up, putting a distance between them she did not want. 'I have a mountain of things to do today.' He seemed uncharacteristically awkward, although why she couldn't fathom.

'You work too hard.' Much too hard. As robust as he was, it wasn't healthy for him to keep the hours he did.

But he was already up, not listening and striding to his dressing room. 'I need to arrange payment for the Botticelli and send my man to fetch it.' Behind the half-open door she heard him rifling through his wardrobe. Heard him splash water into a bowl. Readying himself to leave. Or bolt, more like.

'You could do both of those things from here using a messenger.'

'I could—but I like to do them myself.'

'Why?' He seemed stunned to see her suddenly standing, swathed in a sheet in the doorframe.

'Because... My business doesn't run itself.'

'I see. Are your staff lazy and incompetent?'

'I have no complaints about my staff. They are all diligent and able...' He was looking at her as if she had gone mad. 'You have met them. You know they are excellent.'

'You believe you are indispensable, then?' As she had for years. Before the shoots of a new idea, a new venture, one which was entirely her dream rather than her husband's, had begun to change her way of thinking. 'In which case, why do you bother to pay so many people to work for you?'

'I have responsibilities. Things that must be done.'

'I have been here for nearly four weeks, Pietro.'

'And?'

'In almost a month I have not seen you take a full day off. Not one. According to your sister, you take one once in a blue moon.'

'I never promised to be your constant companion, Lilian!' He was getting snippy now. Misinterpreting her concern for him as selfishness on her part.

'I do not recall ever asking you to be. I enjoy your company, Pietro—but I do not waste my days pining for you when you are not around.' He blinked at that and frowned. 'This has nothing to do with me. Other than the fact that I am worried about you. It is not healthy to simply work, work, work.'

'I don't just work.'

'True—you snatch a few stolen hours here and there, taking it upon yourself to escort me to places I am perfectly capable of taking myself. Staying up late. Last night, for instance, you didn't come home till after midnight, then it was gone two before you finally went to sleep…'

'I did not hear you complaining last night. Quite the opposite happened, in fact.'

'Yes, I know. Which is part of the problem. I feel very guilty for taking up so much of your valuable rest time when I know you get up at the crack of dawn to start your day.' Even though his wary and confrontational stance was doing everything in its power to repel her, Lilian walked towards him and cupped his cheek. 'You look tired, Pietro. Exhausted. Come back to bed.'

'I can't. I have things to do.'

'Can't…or won't? You are two years shy of fifty, Pietro…'

'With the energy and fitness of a man half my age!'

'Something I cannot deny—but you are

missing my point. You are going to make yourself ill with your punishing schedule.'

'I am never ill.'

'One day you will be. And if you are not careful it will knock you sideways.'

'It is lovely that you are worried about me, *cara...*' He was stubbornly determined to work up a lather from his shaving soap. 'But I have the Venturi constitution. Aside from the chickenpox as a child, I have never spent a day in the sick bed in my life. And even then I had it so mildly I was running around again in no time.'

She clearly needed to try a different tack. 'All right, then... You have built up a successful business, replenished the family fortunes and renovated this beautiful *palazzo*. When, exactly, are you going to take a day out to enjoy it?' Before he could argue, she took his hand and he stared at it. 'Do you remember what you said that day at the bridge? Because I do. You said you needed to take more time to enjoy the simple pleasures in life. How can you do that, if you work all the time? Even when you plainly do not need to.'

'I suppose working every day has become a habit.'

'But it cannot be your entire world, Pietro. I made the Foundation and my children my entire world and, while I do not regret it, I am grateful I no longer have to dedicate all my time to it. I had to be convinced to take this holiday. I felt lost and redundant. I felt guilty for leaving and at a loose end without my responsibilities. But I am so glad I did. It has been wonderful to take some time to smell the roses. It is Sunday. Why not take some time to enjoy all the blessings your hard work has created?'

'I suppose I could spare you a day.'

'Not me—*you*, silly.'

'I don't understand.'

'I want you to make today about you. I want you to get back in that bed and sleep for a few more hours. Then I want you to enjoy a leisurely breakfast. Perhaps an hour lying in a nice hot bath. I want you to walk around the gardens or the rooms of this beautiful house you have created. Read a book. Stare at the walls. Amedeo's stunning fresco. Just breathe.'

'Breathe…'

'You are a stubborn, driven, lovely man, Pietro. A diligent host, generous lover and fascinating companion. And today, I am going to look after you.'

'But I need to…'

'I will send a messenger to your gallery manager, informing him to arrange collection of your precious Botticelli on the morrow and I shall set Carlotta to paying for it. What else do you need to do?'

'Er...'

'Nothing, then? Nothing else is pressing.' She could see he was wavering, so she tugged him to follow her, gently pushing him down on the mattress and then tucking him into bed. 'You are taking the whole day off. And you are doing absolutely nothing. That is an order.'

He made her wait outside the huge wooden double doors at the entrance to the Sistine Chapel to tell her some of the history, knowing full well she knew it already but to build her anticipation. Pietro's theatre again. She allowed him to have his fun because she had won. Not only had he taken all day Sunday off, he had suggested himself he take today, too, and because it was still pouring with rain outside it had been he who suggested they bring their planned trip to the Vatican forward.

So far they had wandered the museum and marvelled at its treasures, but he purposely saved the chapel till last, explaining that seeing it first would only overshadow and spoil her enjoyment of everything else.

She rolled her eyes when he tried to go into great detail about the sixteenth-century *opus alexandrinum* pavement. 'I do not care about the floor, Pietro darling. I want to see the ceiling. A ceiling I have been denied long enough thanks to you. I've waited too long already, you wretch. Please stop prolonging my agony for your own cruel amusement.'

He grinned. 'Patience is a virtue.'

'And mine is worn thin.'

'Ah, very well…' He walked towards the giant doors and waited for her to go inside.

Lilian had expected to be impressed, even taken aback by the sight of the frescos, but she hadn't expected the visceral, emotional reaction or the sudden tears which pricked her eyes. Despite knowing the walls held panels painted by masters like Perugino, Rosselli and Botticelli, it was Michelangelo's epic depiction of the Book of Genesis on the ceiling which rendered everything else insignificant.

Slowly she walked along the length of the chapel, her eyes cast heavenwards as she tried to take it all in. 'Oh, my…' It was overwhelming and so much more than she had ever hoped. The colours… The sublime details of each separate panel. The huge, aquamarine expanse of *The Last Judgement* on the far wall behind the altar and crucifix. 'It is so beautiful.' Pietro seemed content to simply stare at her as she spun in a slow circle. 'Now I see why it took him years to paint it.'

'He did not want to do it. He had to be bullied into it. Did you know that, *cara*?'

'I didn't. Why would he not want to paint this?'

'Because in his head, he was a sculptor first and he did not think he was capable of doing this great chapel justice. He doubted his capabilities. Can you imagine that?'

She had seen many of his sculptures, all stunning, but none compared to this. 'I like that story. It makes him seem more...'

'Human?'

'Yes.'

'I knew you would say that.' He pointed out the most famous aspects of the ceiling, as they continued further down the long room, before pausing beneath the story of the creation directly above the altar. 'This is my favourite part.' The figure of God dressed in red was separating the light from the darkness, symbolised by two contrasting clouds. It was well painted, but to Lilian's eye nowhere near as dramatic or as detailed or as breathtaking as some of the other panels.

'This? Over *The Creation of Adam* or *The Great Flood*?'

'Yes, this. For two reasons. Firstly, Michelangelo painted this final panel in just one day.' Which probably explained why it lacked the detail of some of the others. 'And because it is rumoured he painted himself within it.'

'As God?'

'Perhaps…although I do not think he believed he was a god by any means. But I think by the time he finally came to paint this last panel and because he never signed his painting, he wanted to leave his mark on it. I think he chose this subject—creation—as it was a struggle. He had to create something magnificent, something worthy, out of nothing but the vision in his heart. That panel shows his struggle. For me, this makes him seem more human, too. He doubted himself, but then he surprised himself as humans so often do. And he was proud of what he had created.'

She stared up at the image again, taking in the man's features, his intense concentration on the task, his hands outstretched as he reached up to touch the sky, struggling to separate the clouds with his bare hands aloft—just as the artist must have done to paint this ceiling. Then she remembered something else Pietro had told her outside. Another of the fascinating little details he had stored in his head. That Michelangelo had painted it all standing up, not lying flat on the scaffold as everyone always assumed. Neck cricked, arms outstretched above him, aching, every brushstroke a struggle and a labour of love. 'I like your theory.'

'He often painted himself into his pictures—that is his signature. But subtly and often ironically.' He turned her head to face the end wall, rather than the ceiling, and her breath caught again at her first close sight of *The Last Judgement*. 'See if you can find him.'

The sheer size and scope of this painting was awe inspiring. Hundreds of figures, angels and souls, finding their final place in eternity after being judged by Christ. 'Ironically...is that a clue?'

He pointed back towards the entrance of the chapel behind them. 'Do you see that panel in the corner—the depiction of Judith carrying the head of Holofernes on a platter? The head is his. Michelangelo put his head on the platter.'

'Why?'

'Who knows? I suspect it had something to do with his faith and his own fears for the future of his soul. Despite his very human faults and carnal desires, he was also a very devout and pious man, hopeful his depictions of himself acknowledging his many sins might one day, when the Almighty judged him, save his own skin. And that, in case you were wondering is another very big clue, *cara*.'

There were several similar older, bearded men in the picture, especially towards the centre, any one of which could potentially be the painter. Save his own skin? She stared at the section intently, at the faces of the saints surrounding the son of God and all the faces poking out from behind them before finally focusing on the peculiar human-shaped flayed skin in one of the figures' clutched fist. As she looked closer, the artist's features could be clearly defined in the sadly sagging face.

'Ew...gruesome.'

'But intriguing, no? What was your phrase...? The devil is in the detail? Fitting in this case, I think. By then, they called him *il divino*...the divine one...and he despised that name because he felt it was hubris. And that conflicted with his faith. For him, he was just a man—plain and simple. I think that is why he reduced himself to flesh in this painting. To prove he was as human and as flawed as the next man before God and not the least bit divine. I love that about him.' He turned to her, his expression still a little awed. 'And I love this altarpiece more than any of his other works. Both the chaos of it—and the simplicity.'

'There is nothing simple about this painting.'

'Ah, but there is, *cara*. The subject is simple. It is about death—the end of the world—and what becomes of each human soul on this final Judgement Day when they answer for their sins. Do they go to Heaven or Hell? This complicated picture has but one message. Either yes, or no. There is no indecision. No mercy for the sinners. No more chances to make amends because time has run out. As it does for all of us mere mortals.'

She stared at the painting again, slowly taking in every face among the hundreds, and realised Pietro was right. The expressions on the faces depended on the judgement. Relief for those accepted. Dread for those banished and trepidation on those still awaiting their fate. But she gasped as she saw the demon at the bottom.

'From your sketch!' She pointed to the grotesque figure on the boat, an exact, giant-coloured replica. Excited, her gaze hunted for more evidence and was rewarded with the sight of the man cowering, his hand covering his face as more demons dragged him to the underworld. Then, unbelievably, the central figure

of Christ was the image of the lone man, his
arm thrown back in a dramatic fashion. Pietro
watched her features as realisation dawned,
making no attempt to hide his enjoyment as the
penny finally dropped 'Pietro—it is the same.
All of it is the same! Your sketches must be by
the hand of Michelangelo!'

'Which is probably why after all these years
I still cannot bear to part with them. Which
also means my canny investment wasn't clever
at all. I paid a fortune for them, *cara*, at a time
when I had no fortune to spare.'

'I'll bet you don't regret spending it, though.
You adore the history as much as I do.'

'You are correct. Even when I had barely any
money and a mountain of my father's debts still
to pay, it never occurred to me to sell them, yet
I still fool myself into thinking I am a businessman first and keep them at my gallery in case
the right buyer turns up.'

'He will never turn up. Perhaps it is time you
took them home, Pietro, and stopped feeling so
guilty for loving them?'

'Guilt is the Catholic's curse, *cara*. We must
carry it with us always. I am certain that is
written in stone somewhere.' He turned back
to the painting before them, folding his arms
as he studied it, the smile on his face inform-

ing her he was about to tell her something he knew she would find fascinating. 'There is one distinct difference between my drawings and the finished fresco—have you noticed? In my sketches all the figures are nude and in this one their modesty is draped in loincloths. Loincloths which were added after Michelangelo died—by his friend and student Daniele da Volterra.'

'Il Braghettone...'

'Indeed—the underappreciated breeches-maker. The only man talented enough to be able to overpaint a Michelangelo and make it look as if those modest, pious loincloths had been there all along. I wish you could see all the other preliminary sketches in the Archives, *cara*. To see what it all would have looked like before it had been censored. But...' He shrugged, turning to her apologetic. 'They are very particular about who they let in.'

'At least you have seen it and can tell me about it.' There was no point mourning the loss of something she would never see. She wasn't a Catholic, an Italian aristocrat or even a man. 'And as much as I would love to see those other drawings with you, I have never expected or even dreamed to be privy to the Archives.' She slipped her arm through his, touched that he was pained on her behalf. 'Does it tell you how expensive it was? All that blue…' Bright blue paint was always used sparingly in those days because of its cost.

'Expensive does not begin to describe it, but Michelangelo knew what he wanted. He was older this time. Well into his sixtieth year and much more confident and assured in both his talent and his vision than the more cautious younger artist who painted the ceiling thirty years before.'

'With age comes wisdom, or so they say, and the self-assurance to know one's own limitations and one's strengths.'

'And it shows in every brushstroke—and indeed, in his particular and specific choice of colour. This blue is no normal blue, *cara*…' He was so animated when he talked about art, his dark eyes dancing with excitement, his beautiful accent thicker as the words came out in a hurry. No wonder people bought from him. She hoped she would be as inspiring when she opened her little shop.

'This is *ultramarine*. Very rare and made out of crushed lapis lazuli all the way from Afghanistan. It was more expensive than gold in its day, but he wanted this picture to be special… It was his *opus magnus*. He rarely painted again after he completed this, preferring architecture or to stick with the safety of sculpture. I think that is because he knew he could never match it. Just look at the complexity. Well over three hundred individual figures, all intertwined and fighting for space. Yet despite there being plenty of opportunities within the composition to cut corners, he challenged himself. He never took the easy path. I admire that about him. Look at all the hands, *cara*... equally as expressive as the faces and so much harder to paint. Even the subject matter shows a man fully confident in his talents. An educated and brave man unafraid to break with tradition. There are many artists who have tackled this Biblical prophecy over the years, yet all are so simplistic when compared to this. There is a heaven and there is a hell—but in Michelangelo's depiction of Judgement Day we can see the influence of Dante in the tiers. The Seven Deadly Sins woven into the tableau. A tragic acceptance of the poor decisions we make as people and a celebration for both faith and life...'

He caught her looking at him smiling.

'Am I being a dreadful bore?'

'Not at all.' He was charming. Lovely. Perfect. And exactly what she had not known she was looking for. Which certainly was an unforeseen complication she would need to give serious thought to. 'You are fascinating. Were you always so passionate about art?'

He paused, considering it. 'Probably not... I have always loved it and, like you, been attracted and drawn to its beauty. However, the older I get, the more I appreciate the efforts it took to create. The stories behind it.'

'The human side.' The details.

'*Sì*... When I look at this, I wonder what he was like. Both the younger man and the elder. When he stood here and painted his *Last Judgement*, did he gaze at the ceiling he had done all those years before and find fault with it? Harbour bitter regrets... Wish he had done things differently? Or did he accept it as who and what he was in that moment in time? I wonder which man I would have preferred.'

'I suppose that would depend on which Pietro was asking—wouldn't it? I suspect the younger one would have been frustrated with the older artist. Found him stubborn and set in his ways. A little pompous, perhaps. Someone to rebel against. The Pietro standing in front of me would probably see the genius and the flaws in both. With age, comes wisdom after all.' She slipped her arm through his and stared at the painting. 'I wonder which Pietro I would prefer? What were you like as a young man?'

'Impatient. Ambitious. A little rebellious, but perhaps not as confident as I am now. Probably less selfish. Back then, I allowed other people to dictate aspects of my life which I now much prefer to control.'

An interesting insight. 'Like what?'

'The path I took. I wish I had taken it sooner rather than waiting for my father to die. If I had refused to do what he wanted me to, been brave enough to follow my heart rather than his edicts, then perhaps...' He shrugged, his expression suddenly closing as if he had said much more than he was comfortable with.

'You have regrets?'

'Too many to count. Who doesn't? You must have them, too.'

'That which doesn't kill us makes us stronger...' She shook her head, suddenly wistful in the face of the truth. 'But only one real regret I would gladly change if I could. I wish I could have been there when Henry died. Held his hand. Let him know he was loved and not alone in those last moments. Those haunt me.'

He took her hand and held it tight. 'He knew he was loved, *cara*. He always knew he was loved. Be in no doubt of that. And clearly loved you deeply in return. Why else would he have tried so very hard to send you and your children away? Why he chose to die in the infirmary rather than bring the danger to those he loved above all else? He wanted to protect you. I would have done exactly the same in his shoes—or at least like to think I am brave enough to be so selfless in the face of death.' He exhaled slowly and gripped her hand tighter. 'Although I suspect I am too selfish. I have always been too selfish.'

What an odd thing to say when he was such a generous, deep-feeling man. 'Were you there when Isabetta died?'

'No. Nobody was.' She saw intense pain quickly followed by intense guilt. 'Although that was of her choosing, I think.' She could tell he regretted the words the second he spoke them because he frowned, instantly letting go of her hand to turn away as if suddenly captivated by another bit of Michelangelo's genius.

'You think?' What a strange response. One which probably said a great deal about his marriage and what he continued to feel about it.

'A miserable and depressing story, *cara*, and one not for today.' His gaze resolutely avoided her obviously curious one as he began to lead her from the room. 'Today is all about this place, you and me…and Michelangelo.'

'But, Pietro…'

'No, *cara*…not today.' He shook his head and tugged her forward. All the regret and pain she had seen briefly on his face was now gone, ruthlessly masked and replaced by that of the charming escort. Yet she knew the wound was deep and still open. Perhaps festering. How could she leave him like that?

'By not today you really mean never, don't you?' An unhealthy state of affairs.

'I prefer not to talk about it.'

'And does that work? Does it prevent you from thinking about it? Does it stop the guilt? The pain I just witnessed in your eyes?'

She saw the flash of anger at her question, then, after a battle with himself, watched him deflate in defeat. 'No. Nothing does.' He stared back up at the painting, at the sinners consigned to hell directly in front of him, and closed his eyes briefly, deep ridges of sorrow etched on his face, then, as if he had made a momentous decision turned to her, his voice a whisper. A confession. 'Because she killed herself, Lilian. Either intentionally or by mistake. And as usual, I was as many miles away from her when she did it as it was possible to be—because I couldn't stand to be in the same room as her. Couldn't stand to even breathe the same air as her.'

'Oh, my darling…' She took his hand this time and squeezed it, wanting to wrap her arms around him, but mindful of the few other tourists dotted around the gallery and the inevitable discomfort of the proud man she stood with if she tried. Her heart breaking for him and the guilt which obviously still burdened him from the admission. 'I don't know what to say.'

'Neither do I…because there is nothing that can be said to excuse it… So ask me about art, *cara*, and let us never speak of it again.'

Chapter Thirteen

Amore mio… Buon Dio!

Things had gone too far! Pietro wrestled
with the straps of his saddle in the darkness,
his heart racing and his mind whirring. Part of
that was to do with the fact she had been lying
cuddled against him again for the third night in
a row, in his private and sacrosanct bedchamber after a bout of fervent and uncharacteristically emotional lovemaking, but a bigger part
was because of what he had said during that
lovemaking.

Amore mio.

My love.

Not only had he said it—but he had also apparently meant it, because the words had come
out choked of their own volition, tumbling out
of his mouth in a rush. Out of necessity. Because in that moment he wanted to tell her what

she meant to him because he was feeling vulnerable and raw and he was just so damned relieved she was there with him. When he had gone to bed alone earlier it had been specifically so she would not be there with him.

He should have locked his door.

He had even thought about it as he had slammed into his bedchamber straight after dinner, pleading exhaustion, his hand hovering over the key momentarily before he had retracted it. He knew now he had subconsciously left it unlocked because he had hoped she would come, because he had been in a state since the second he had confessed the truth about Isabetta. A truth he had never uttered to another soul—not even Carlotta—because he meticulously stuck to the official story. The story written in black and white on her death certificate. The one in which she had accidentally taken too high a dose of her prescribed medication when she had long before stopped procuring her opium in controlled batches from the physician.

Not that Pietro had cared. He had taught himself not to care because all the worry in the world, all his pleading and all his interventions achieved nothing. He had told himself Isabetta was beyond help and that she needed to help herself. Washed his hands of her, her vitriol, her self-pity and her addictions, when a decent man, a less selfish man, would have continued to fight.

What sort of monster felt that in the wake of a tragedy? But he had then and still felt the same way now. He had never mourned her because he couldn't stand her and, the day she died, the constricting chains of marriage which had bound him disappeared and he felt he could breathe again. Restart his life. Blithely follow his own path, blessedly unencumbered by the heavy yoke which came alongside being responsible for someone else. And he had loved that life, that solitary path, never wanting to deviate from it or glance backwards. Only forwards. Except since he had met Lilian his path no longer seemed straight and now he had reached a fork he had never anticipated or wanted to encounter.

Continue on the solitary, safe path he had always wanted or allow his feet to edge along the other one? The one with her on it, too. The path which inevitably would involve more shackles and chains and the death of his hard-earned freedom.

He wasn't ready to relinquish that—even for her.

Amore mio…

Yet he had meant what he said in the moment he had said it. Two hours since his unexpected declaration and he still meant it. Something that frankly scared the hell out of him. As it wasn't just about passion or shared interests or friendship. It was about compatibility and his heart, honesty and all the tangled, complicated and uncomfortable emotions he had always promised himself he would avoid.

He wanted to blame Michelangelo for his uncharacteristic lapse into sentimentality— as her reaction to the Sistine Chapel had thoroughly charmed and disarmed him. He wanted to blame tiredness, but thanks to her insistence he take some time off, he felt refreshed and full of life and ridiculously satisfied with the state of it. He wanted to blame his innate and annoying restlessness, despite it being oddly missing this past month, replaced by an alien sense of contentedness he had never experienced before. He wanted to blame Lilian—because she was certainly the catalyst for all of this and had quietly forced herself into aspects of his life he had never allowed another person into. But knew it had been he who had let her in and seemingly without any care. He wanted to blame all those things for his foolhardy and worrying outburst tonight—but could only blame himself.

What had made him vulnerable in the first place was the niggling suspicion that with Lilian things might be different. That he could love as deeply and as selflessly as all the poets and painters suggested a man could, when he had long ago made his peace with the realisation, he was not made that way and felt suffocated by any thoughts of commitment. Suffocated and desperate to run.

He hauled himself on to his horse and set off down the moonlit drive, cursing fate for bringing her back into his life and his sister and Alexandra for purposely wafting her under his nose. With no other destination in mind, at least two hours before the dawn sun lit the poorly maintained roads out of Rome and nothing packed for a long journey, he decided to head to his gallery first. Regroup. Consider his options and plan his next course of action. He had a little under two weeks left before Lilian returned to her life. All he had to do was come up with a foolproof way to survive that. Surely he could do that without his world imploding?

What had possessed him to break all his carefully considered rigid rules with her from the very beginning? He actively sought out her company outside the bedroom, when he knew from the outset something about her called to him which went beyond the need in his loins. Allowed himself to feel too comfortable with her. To speak too freely about things that mattered. Letting friendship mix with passion. Why had he allowed her to interfere in the way he conducted his life? Allowed her to look after him, make him feel unwanted tenderness towards her. Stupidly, he had allowed himself to wake up with her and share his mornings. Hell—for two days that had been the thing he had enjoyed the most. That intimacy. That stark honesty. The closeness… All the things he avoided! And in allowing her those liberties, and drunk on that heady honesty, he had lowered his guard and allowed affection to germinate unbidden alongside their passion. Then he'd told her exactly what he felt in a moment of weakness when he should have been running for the hills rather than give another woman such power over him.

What a mess!

One which his head screamed necessitated the need to end things between them. Cut their affair short and make a clean break of it so he could lick his wounds and move on. He had never wanted a lover who meant something to him! Never wanted a soulmate or a confidant.

But was he ready to cut all ties now? Most definitely not. His feelings were too confused. His head, his heart and his body were all jumbled up and he needed to make sense of all that before he did something hasty and spoiled something which would be done shortly anyway. This current vulnerability was temporary and he could overcome it. Surely he could? All he needed was a little space and distance to get it all straight in his head. And once he did, there would be no terrifying forks in his path and the world would stop wildly tilting on its axis.

Two days later and Pietro felt himself again as he mentally steeled himself to step through his own front door. All he had needed to do, really, was reset the boundaries in his own head which had become a little skewed. And now that he had shown her the Vatican as he had promised, there really was no need to socialise with the woman beyond their physical relationship in the bedroom. This was an affair, not a great romance or the road to his future. He liked Lilian. Of course he did. But he didn't love her and he didn't want anything beyond the remaining time they had left. As long as he repeated that comforting mantra, everything would remain as it should be.

'Ah…look what the cat dragged in.' His sister flounced into the hallway to investigate the noise and, hands on hips, stared at him in disgust. 'Would you care to explain where you have been?'

He was master of this house and certainly did not need to explain anything, but he would, because he was a gentleman and he didn't want anyone—especially his sister—coming to the conclusion he had run away.

'Pomezia. On the quest for a Marieschi. It's a cityscape of Venice.'

'Because you urgently needed another painting of Venice? When your gallery is already full of them?'

'Venice sells.' He brushed past her, intent on heading directly to his rooms, ostensibly to change before dinner when he knew deep down it was to hide from Lilian for as long as he feasibly could.

'At least you are back for tonight. Hurry and get ready and I will have the carriage delayed.'

It was only then he noticed his sister was dressed in an evening gown and glittering with gemstones. 'Tonight?'

'The Wayfair ball? Do not tell me you have forgotten?'

He had and it was the last thing he needed. No more cosy social outings. No more enforced proximity or conversations unless they were entirely about sex. 'I am too tired…' His attention was distracted by the sound of footsteps on the marble stairs and his breath caught in his throat.

'Hello, Pietro. You are home. We were all beginning to wonder.'

The usually lovely Lilian had been replaced by a temptress he barely recognised. The daring gown was unlike anything he had ever seen her in before, the full soft green-silk skirt moving like liquid as she undulated down the stairs. The tight bodice hugged her curves like a second skin, the low neckline offering up her full breasts like a feast on a platter for his greedy eyes. Acres of her creamy alabaster skin was on display—her shoulders, her back, her swanlike neck. A hint of red stained her plump lips, making them look as full and as swollen as they did after they had had their way with each other. And her hair…the loose curls arranged with such abandon, all tousled and sensual—she resembled a woman freshly seduced. He felt the sharp pang in his heart a split second before the floor tilted and knew he was in trouble.

'He's not coming.' Carlotta shook her head, clearly furious at him. 'He's *tired*.'

'Oh, well, never mind.' Lilian breezed past him, enveloping him in a cloud of her sultry rose perfume, barely casting him a glace as she disappeared into the *salotto*. 'Have you seen my lace shawl? I think I left it here.'

'On the sofa.' Carlotta glared at him. 'Not a word? Not a note? We were all worried sick.'

Lilian worried? Part of him hated the thought. Another part was thrilled. 'Yet I sent for the carriage and a trunk, and you had them both delivered to the gallery within the hour so you knew full well I was going away.' He was ridiculously aware of her in the room beyond, his eyes straying to where he could see her leaning over his furniture to fetch her dratted shawl. Latching themselves to her as she took her precious time about coming back.

As Alexandra, too, began to descend the stairs, his butler appeared. 'The carriage is outside, my lady.' His eyes flicked to his master in question. 'Shall I tell it to wait?'

'No need. My brother is staying at home.'

'Is it just the three of us?' By the look on her face, Alexandra seemed thrilled at the prospect. 'Not that we won't sorely miss your charming presence, Pietro...' And as soon as she looked away from him, he was instantly forgotten. 'Oh, Lilian...what a gown! You shall be the belle of the ball. In fact, I'd even go as far as to say you will give some of those young debutantes a run for their money and doubtless steal all the young bucks away from them. You may even fill your dance card.'

'How exciting.' The temptress linked her arm through her cousin's, as if he did not exist at all. 'It has been for ever since I danced and this gown was definitely meant for dancing.'

'I'd have thought you were all a little old for dancing.' The churlish remark had popped out of his mouth before he could stop it, earning him a simultaneous affronted glare from all three women.

'Oh, really, Pietro?' His sister's eyes were shooting daggers. 'We shall see about that. As I happen to know that many a handsome young gentleman prefers a woman with experience.'

What was that supposed to mean? Jealousy at the thought of any young bucks eyeing up Lilian made his eyes narrow.

'And ladies of experience love nothing more than a young buck to share it with.' Alexandra grinned saucily at her friends. 'Come, ladies.

Let us leave this old curmudgeon to his pipe and slippers. Our carriage awaits…'

Then they left. Without as much as a backward glance or another attempt at tempting him to accompany them. All three of them chattering like parrots as *his* servants helped them into *his* carriage. Where *his* coachmen would deliver them to a ball on an invitation meant for *him*.

And where *his* woman apparently intended to dance with other men wearing a scandalous dress she had absolutely no right to be wearing. A dress which would draw every filthy male eye, giving them erotic ideas they had no place having.

Well—he would see about that!

He bolted up the stairs two at a time, impatiently clicking his fingers at a servant, ordering them to fetch his valet and have a second carriage readied as soon as was humanly possible. Then he slammed through the door to his bedchamber before coming to a shuddering halt as he realised exactly what it was he had just thought.

His woman.

Amore mio!

So much for time and blasted distance!

Chapter Fourteen

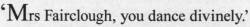

'Mrs Fairclough, you dance divinely.'

She smiled politely at the contrived compliment, narrowly avoiding rolling her eyes at his eagerness and transparent intentions. Her current dance partner was at least a decade too young for her, but irritatingly determined to seduce her regardless, oblivious to the fact she was as uninterested in him as it was possible to be. But when she sensed Pietro glaring at her from across the room, simply because she was annoyed with him, she smiled up at her flirtatious dance partner's face and ignored him.

Exasperating man! Creeping out in the middle of the night without waking her and then nothing but silence for days. If she hadn't understood some of his reasons, she'd be fuming at his disappearing act. However, she did and they softened her temper.

She had seen first hand his pain in admitting how his wife had died and his lack of feelings for her, and realised in that instant there had to have been some pretty damning and serious reasons for his dislike of her. Pietro did not possess a cruel bone in his body. He was hardworking, sociable and possessed a soft heart. She knew that, too, as she had seen it as plain as day on his face when he talked about art or history or even how much his sister drove him mad with her meddling.

She had also borne witness to his discomfort after he had let that tiny bit of his past slip. He had covered it with his usual charming bravado and to an indifferent acquaintance they would see nothing amiss at all. But Lilian wasn't an indifferent stranger. Living cheek by jowl with the man for a month, sharing his bed and his intimate company, she knew his moods. She could see when he was tired. See when he was mischievous or passionate or engrossed. And that day at the Vatican, for the very first time she saw him truly vulnerable.

His admission had churned up complicated and unpalatable emotions and they had unsettled him for the rest of the day. Which was why she wasn't in any way convinced by his vociferous plea of tiredness and a need for an early night, so when the house was quiet she had gone to him, slipped quietly between his sheets to be with him and he had turned and clung to her as if she were the only piece of driftwood in a storm.

Lilian would have held him all night, just like that, but he had needed her love almost like a reassurance. For Pietro, it was a somewhat clumsy and rushed coupling, yet despite that, she also knew he gave his whole self to her and felt, again for the first time, his heart as engaged in their lovemaking completely. So much so, she could hear the emotion and affection in his breathless Italian endearments as he collapsed on top of her and she felt the tremors in his big body as she snuggled up against him afterwards as the aftershocks of that same emotion lingered.

Then, in a panic, he had run rather than talk to her and therein lay the root cause of her annoyance. There were things to say. Important things. And by the end of tonight she would be the one to instigate the necessary conversation. Because it was now quite apparent their illicit and brief affair had grown into something else for the both of them and they had to start talking about what happened next. Uprooting two lives to find a compromise which worked for them as a couple was not a decision which could be rushed. Especially when the bulk of his life was here in Italy and the bulk of hers hundreds of miles across an entire continent.

'I told you he would come!'

Carlotta spun past her in the arms of an equally young partner and she shot a triumphant look at Lilian. Her new friend had been right. Pietro had come and was wonderfully jealous. She could thank Signora Ferretti's daring gown for that, just as she could thank the *modista* for the list of eager names on her dance card. But despite the encouragement of both his sister and Alexandra, she had not allowed her card to be filled up. She wasn't a silly young girl and she wouldn't play games. As soon as he asked her, she would dance with him, because he was the only man in the room in whose arms she wanted to be.

The dance came to an end and she curtsied to her partner, then wanted to roll her eyes when his fixed to her cleavage. Clearly all women of middle years and in possession of their own teeth were considered fair game here in Rome if her glut of eager new suitors was any gauge. They all assumed she was wearing this gown to snare a fresh crop of lovers when she was wearing it solely for Pietro. Not only her lover now, but the man she was in grave danger of falling hopelessly in love with. Or perhaps had already fallen in love with if she listened entirely to her heart and not her head. But her head had to be listened to.

In a strange sort of way, the enforced distance had given her the opportunity to consider her relationship with him properly. The original parameters had changed. She knew in her heart the thought of saying goodbye to him was too dreadful to consider. She wanted more and she was pretty sure he did, too. It was indeed a complication she had not foreseen— but then neither would she ever have imagined in her wildest dreams she would indulge in a romance while in Rome. And it was a romance now rather than an affair. As much as she had enjoyed their affair, she had also come to quickly discover she really wasn't made for affairs. She couldn't separate her heart from her body. The two came as a pair and she had given him both now, although initially unconsciously, from pretty much the first time they had made love. She might never have said the words, but she felt them. They were friends and lovers and she wanted them to continue to be both.

If they had a future together, and she hoped

with all her heart they did, then it had to be on more solid terms than their arrangement now. She didn't want to pretend they weren't a couple and she didn't want to tiptoe around like a thief in the night. She wanted him to be part of her family and part of her life—and all that that entailed. Lilian believed in commitment and promises and honesty. And while there had always been complete honesty in her relationship with him, they had made no lasting commitments and certainly no promises. Nothing apart from their shared interests, passion and growing affection bound them and now she was prepared to concede she wanted those things, too. Not immediately. She was in no rush. But she did not want there to be secrets from those she loved either when she went home.

If marriage wasn't for Pietro, then she would respect that and mourn the loss of him because what was the point of all the pain without a defined purpose? All the upheaval? All the inevitable compromises which would toss her ordered existence up in the air and make her have to revalue the new dreams which her heart was still nurturing? Trying to alter a person's path for your own selfish reasons never ended well. She had clashed horribly with her son when he had declared his intention to leave the Foundation and pursue his own desire to be an engineer. It had been borne out of worry more than anything else. She didn't want her son hundreds of miles away while he trained or on the other side of the world when he pursued his dream. Fortunately, she realised her error before it did irreparable damage to their relationship. In trying to keep hold of him she was actually pushing him away. What was the old adage? If you loved something, set it free…

If Pietro wanted a real future with her, involving the commitment she craved, it had to come from his free will. Had to be his suggestion. And all her years at the Foundation had taught her to respect herself enough not to settle for something which was not what she wanted. She wanted him—but she also wanted and deserved real commitment.

'It is very warm in here, Signora Fairclough, shall we get some air on the terrace?' Her partner stared seductively up her arm as he kissed the back of her gloved hand and she wanted to swat him away like a fly. Ingrained English politeness had her smiling instead.

'No, thank you—but you may escort me to the refreshment table.'

He held out his arm and she took it, pretending she couldn't see Pietro prowling around the edge of the dance floor to intercept them. 'Some champagne, *signora*?' Her eager young buck showed no signs of leaving as he handed her a chilled glass with more flourish than was required. He was reaching for a glass for himself, while simultaneously ogling her body, when Pietro's suddenly looming presence at his shoulder made him glance up.

'Basta! Vada via!'

The young man's eyes widened at the chilling tone and widened more when Pietro came to stand behind Lilian like her personal bodyguard, his face like thunder. His eyes glared at the poor chap with much more menace then was required, then appeared smugly pleased when he muttered a hasty *'buona sera'* and scurried off.

'I am not sure that was entirely necessary.'

'It was *entirely* necessary.' His voice dropped to a whisper. 'What do you think you are doing? Parading yourself around, dancing with strangers? Did you not realise that man was only dancing with you so he could seduce you?' Then his scandalised gaze dropped to her cleavage. 'And for the love of God, where has your shawl gone? That dress leaves nothing to the imagination!' He took her elbow and steered her into the alcove behind them.

'Do you not like it? Everyone else has been very complimentary...'

'That is because everyone else is imagining taking you to their bed and ravishing you!'

'Even the many ladies who have complimented me, Pietro?' She shook her head, ridiculously flattered at his possessive reaction. 'Anyone would think you were jealous.'

'And what if I am?'

'Then I think it serves you right for your silly behaviour over the last few days and for breaking your solemn pledge to never keep me in the dark about your whereabouts. I told you I was much too old for games, Pietro.'

'I didn't think... I had urgent business.'

'You ran for the hills because you were scared of your own feelings.'

He glared, ready to shamelessly lie to her, then huffed out a sigh. 'I did that as well.'

'I suppose we need to talk then, don't we?'

'I suppose we do. But not here. Come, I'll take you home and...'

It was her turn to huff out a sigh. How typically male. 'It can wait, Pietro. Just because you are now ready to talk doesn't mean I must jump to attention right at this moment. It will all keep well enough until later. Besides, I have been looking forward to this ball all week. I've also been looking forward to wearing this dress. For you—you idiot!'

'You wore it for me?'

'No... I wore it for that silly boy who was just flirting with me. The one no older than my son. Who could not seem to unlatch his eyes from my cleavage.'

'He is only human...' She watched the corners of his mouth begin to curve upwards as he looked her up and down appreciatively. 'It is a beautiful dress. Much more daring than your usual outfits.'

'I was going for more siren than matron.'

'Then you succeeded, *cara*. I haven't been able to take my eyes off you.' His gaze heated as it reached her eyes. 'Dance with me.'

'I promised the next dance to the Conte della...' She scrabbled for the card on her wrist to read the name, only to have it snatched from the thin ribbon which secured it. Then she watched, a little stunned and the bigger part of her thrilled, as Pietro tore the thing decisively into confetti and tossed the shredded remains over his shoulder. His cocky smile of victory was accompanied by a courtly, very Italian bow.

'Would you do me the great honour of dancing the next dance with me, Lilian?'

'I suppose... As you've asked so nicely...'

* * *

Pietro's disregard for etiquette continued for a good half an hour as he entirely monopolised her on the dance floor, refusing point blank to relinquish her even when a couple of the intrepid young bucks from her dance card bravely attempted to claim her. As much as she feigned exasperation with his possessiveness, she also delighted in it. She much preferred dancing with him and was quietly grateful she did not have to suffer the unwanted attentions of another over-zealous young buck on the lookout for a new conquest. They were all very silly to her mind, much too young and not the slightest bit interesting.

However, half an hour dancing with Pietro did have its drawbacks. Twirling around in his arms and staring longingly up into his hypnotic and seductive dark eyes was playing havoc with her body. Desire sat heavy in her womb and her breasts were desperate for his touch, and she was so warm. Unbelievably warm, in fact, and in grave danger of glowing crimson with a flush which had little to do with the heat of the glittering chandeliers above her and everything to do with him. Something the wretch knew.

'Come outside with me, *cara*… The gardens are quite lovely.'

His breath whispered close to her ear, causing goose pimples to appear on goose pimples. He briefly pulled her scandalously close, ensuring she felt the evidence of his own desire against her hip.

'There is a pretty little secluded bench… Just us and the stars… Would you like that, Lilian?'

Excited perspiration dewed her face and neck as fresh heat suffused her at the thought. Was she wanton enough to allow him to make love to her in Mrs Wayfair's garden? In the middle of a ball? While at least a hundred people were dancing and chatting close by? Apparently, she was.

'Yes.' But first she needed to splash some water on her skin and banish all evidence of the annoying perspiration. In a dress this lovely, she wanted to feel perfect. 'I shall be back in a moment.'

'I shall be waiting.' Again she felt his arousal press insistently against her. 'In complete agony. I missed you…'

Feeling decidedly off kilter and deliciously naughty, she hurried to the retiring room. Thankfully, it was empty when she arrived, allowing her to soak a towel in cool water and take that and a fresh dry towel unseen behind the privacy of the curtain, where she patted it on her chest, neck and cheeks, amused at herself.

What an unexpected turn up for the books this whole adventure had been. A few months ago, she had been very much the matriarch of the family, the centre. Burdened with responsibilities and dedicating every waking hour to others. She had thought at the time she loved it. It was her vocation. Her entire identity. She was a mother and the driving force behind Henry's Foundation. Yet a month in Rome and the pull of all that responsibility no longer drew her as it once had. Her family would always be a part of her life, but they had their own households, their own lives now, and, while she would always be part of that, she was no longer the glue which held it all together.

Rome had made Lilian realise she was still too young to become nought but a spectator on their lives and much too young to be content to take a step back from the busy lifestyle she had always led. Perhaps that was because she was learning to be just herself once again. Just Lilian. The sensual woman who loved art and had a life of her own to lead, standing poised at the crossroads, no longer fearful, but excited because she had dreams of her own to follow. A new man in her life to love and forge a future with.

And now she was running away with herself when she and Pietro were yet to talk…

Beyond the curtain she heard the door of the retiring room burst open. 'Ugh! I paid twelve *scudi* for this gown and all anyone can talk about is that dreadful Fairclough woman! I am furious at the *modista* for selling it to her! Especially when she promised me nobody would ever wear the same gown as me!' She recognised the voice instantly. Sofia—the Marchesa di Gariello. Apparently, now her arch-nemesis.

'Nobody would realise they are of the same design, Sofia.' The placating American tones of Mrs Ida Wayfair, their hostess. 'Hers is green, yours is red and you have such different figures the cut looks entirely different on you both.'

'You think she wears it better?'

'I think she looks lovely in her gown and I think you look equally as lovely in yours.'

'But Pietro follows her around with his tongue hanging out and hasn't bothered glancing in my direction.'

'Why would he? It is obvious she is his current lover.'

Current lover?

'He is normally much more discreet about his latest trollop.'

Trollop!

'Why would you care?'

'Because I have my heart set on being his *Duchessa*. I've waited quite long enough for him to stop his gallivanting and realise it is time to settle down with someone of equal stature…'

Ida chuckled. 'Darling, Pietro isn't the settling-down type.'

'What we had was special. It was more than an affair.'

'Really? How so?'

'He was so attentive, so devoted. He took me to the top of the Gianicolo hill to make love to me…' Ida's bark of laughter covered Lilian's sharp intake of breath at the revelation.

'Oh, darling, he takes us all there.'

Us?

'In fact, I think I've enjoyed one of Pietro's special picnics on top of that damned hill at least three times in the four years we've been lovers and I am not stupid enough to think I am the only woman who has enjoyed him on that particular spot. In fact, I know it. He's certainly taken Fabrizia there, and Edvige, as we have compared notes. Then there was that French widow last summer. The one with the huge breasts. She was most indiscreet about their nocturnal activities—but then she truly was a trollop.'

Lilian felt her stomach roil with queasiness.

'What you shared with him on that hill was no more special than all the rest of his numerous peccadillos. It's a wonder he hasn't worn a hole in the blanket or the grass out from under it. Although, if I was inclined to be the jealous type, like you, I would be spitting feathers, too, at the thought of him rolling around on it with Mrs Fairclough. Pietro is a splendid lover. One of the best.'

'But you are not jealous? Do you not want more?'

'Good heavens, no! Our relationship is based entirely upon lust and that is the way the pair of us like it and probably why he still warmed my bed last month and hasn't set a foot near yours in over a decade, darling.' Lilian heard the curtain swish open and the tinkling sounds of somebody washing their hands.

'As I keep telling you: forget Pietro. He's not marriage material. There are plenty more fish in the sea, Sofia, and a great many of them are here tonight. Can I recommend the Conte

della Montemerano? He doesn't have as good
a physique as Pietro, but he is equally talented
in the bedchamber. Or, if you have your heart
set on being a duchessa, I hear the Duca della
Bevagna is on the market for a wife now that he
is out of mourning and, because he much prefers boys, he will have absolutely no problem
with you taking on a legion of young, nubile
lovers…as long as you are prepared to share
them, of course.'

'The Duca della Bevagna is out of mourning?'

'He is…and still reassuringly and hideously
rich…'

The ladies left and Lilian stood like a statue
inside the small velvet-lined cocoon as she tried
to take it all in. She had been used. Allowed
herself to be used by a man who had clearly
shared a bed with most of the willing women in
Rome, if that overheard and enlightening conversation was to be believed. Sofia, Ida…the
trollop with the large breasts. She stared down
at hers spilling out of her dress and wanted to
cry. No wonder he knew the layout of their
hostess's garden so well and the exact location
of that discreet little bench. Like his dratted
well-worn blanket, he had doubtless seduced
more than one woman there, too!

What a fool! What a stupid, stupid, gullible fool! None of what she had shared with Pietro was special. It was all sullied now. Tarnished. Reduced to its basest elements. She felt dirty. Ashamed. Betrayed. And only when the tears came and her chest hurt did she realise she was also thoroughly heartbroken as well.

Chapter Fifteen

His first inkling something was very wrong was not when she sailed past him to go back into the ballroom, or even when she immediately danced with another man. He had been put out, of course, but amused, assuming she was teasing him on purpose because of his absence and to prolong the anticipation. A little theatre to pique his interest. But when one dance turned into five while she treated him as invisible, he started to feel uneasy. The clincher, the realisation, came when he finally caught up with her at the refreshment table among a little crowd and she responded to his subtle flirting with complete indifference. Then he had taken her hand and asked her to dance, felt her fingers stiffen before she snatched them away as if his touch was abhorrent and he had seen the emotion in her eyes—anger and disgust. There had been no disguising either and she made no attempt to try.

She had avoided him then and, despite there now being two Venturi carriages waiting to take their party home, made it plain she had no intention of being alone with him in one of them. Instead, he had climbed in with all of them, made polite, brittle conversation with his sister and Alexandra as it was quite apparent to all Lilian wanted none of him. The atmosphere inside that coach on the short journey home had been one of the most tense and horrific he had ever experienced, causing him to feel actual fear long before they finally rattled into the courtyard.

Both his sister and Alexandra bade them a hasty goodnight as Lilian stormed into the *salotto*, clearly having decided she finally had things to say.

To him alone.

Despite knowing he had done nothing between their waltz and her prolonged visit to the retiring room which could conceivably have raised her ire to the extent it had clearly been, the innate sense of utter dread at the impending conversation made his heart race and his throat constrict.

Something was very wrong.

He entered the room on reluctant feet to find her standing by the fireplace, shoulders thrown back proudly, hands neatly held in front of her. Yet despite her stillness, he could see her rage shimmering off her in waves. Ridiculously, he felt like one of the lost souls in Michelangelo's *Last Judgement* as he approached her, wanting to cower as he awaited his fate, sensing this couldn't and wouldn't end well despite not knowing what the hell he had done.

'What is wrong, *cara*?' He reached out a hand and she recoiled, staring at it as if it were the hissing head of a cobra. It was obvious she didn't want him to touch her or even come too close, so he planted his feet a little way from hers and quietly took a deep breath as he waited for her to speak. She stared at him for the longest time, then tilted up her chin.

'How many women have you made love to on a blanket on top of the Gianicolo hill?'

His blood ran cold. 'What sort of question is that?'

'A very pertinent one, I think, after what I've just overheard.'

'I have never denied having a past.'

'But you have never once been open about it either, have you?'

'It is the past. It has no bearing on the here and now.'

'I knew you'd had other lovers over the years. I am not stupid. But not a string of them! A legion of them.' She twirled her finger in the air. 'A fresh one in as the old one leaves. Like a factory. One after the other, after the other. And even then, those past women are not what bothers me about it all. It is your methodical, mercenary approach to it. You are shameless in your lies.'

'I have never lied to you!'

'A lie by omission is as much of a lie as one said outright to the face, Pietro! Because you led me to believe you had arranged a romantic picnic for us so I could see the best view of Rome. You had the servants pack a feast, too. Strawberries...champagne. A spontaneous gesture conjured in the heat of the moment. Entirely for me.' Her hand raised and for a moment he thought she was going to slap him before she clenched it into a fist, her pretty features contorted, loathing radiating out of her stormy green eyes. 'You allowed me to think it so touching and so charming. Told me how much you adored the sunset. Told me it how it brought the copper out in my hair as you unpinned it. Fed me strawberries. Yet now I realise it was more habit than spontaneous. A practised, perfected and perfunctory ritual you had off pat. For aside from me, there has been Mrs Wayfair, Fabrizia, Edvige...'

She counted them off on her fingers. Women who had meant nothing. Women he had bedded and forgotten. Women who didn't hold a candle to the wonderful woman who currently hated him. 'The French widow last summer with the huge breasts. Mrs Wayfair again... because according to her you last warmed her sheets a month ago.'

'More than a month ago.' Why was he clarifying that, when in so doing he merely condemned himself further?

'And let us not forget the Marchesa di Gariello. Who according to you was the biggest mistake of your life! Yet still you took me to that same spot where your biggest mistake happened, whispered sweet nothings in my ear and seduced me. You made me feel special that day, on purpose! Admit it! You arranged that picnic with the sole intention of getting me to lift my skirts and spread my legs for you like... like...a trollop!'

As guilty as he was of all the things she had charged him with, he hated her reducing what they had done to something so sordid, yet recognised he had carelessly made it so. 'It wasn't like that with you... I swear.' Because it hadn't been. It had been special. Even that day on the hill had been special. He might have taken his own meaningless pleasure there so many times, although never at sunset, but it had never felt as it had with Lilian. He had never spent the night there. Certainly never woken up with a women in his arms there. Because he never woke up with a woman in his arms. It was an unbreakable rule he always adhered to. Except with her, apparently. She had been the only one he had ever welcomed the morning in with.

'Was it not?'

'No...it was special. Surely you know that? It is always special with us... Surely you can feel it, too?'

'Thanks to you, I no longer trust my feelings!'

'We have a unique connection. One I want to continue when you return to England. I could open a gallery there... I could visit more frequently...'

'You mean continue exactly as we are.' Her features became flat, as if his suggestion was more a nail in their coffin rather than a lifeline for a future.

'Yes... No...' She shook her head and he could see he was losing her. 'All I know is that I don't want to say goodbye to you, Lilian. I cannot bear the thought of us having so little time left to be together.' The honest truth. Each time he had tried to contemplate her departure in the past few days and the demise of all they had, a gnarly, tight and painful knot had formed in his chest. It was there now, twisting violently as it grew unchecked, malignant and destructive and terrifying. Worse than the restlessness which had always plagued him. Worse even than the guilt he carried about Isabetta. 'Please, *cara*...sit. Allow me to explain. Let us talk honestly.' Something he dreaded despite knowing it was all he had left.

'You dare ask for honesty, yet you still haven't answered my question, Pietro. Where was that honesty when I asked for it a moment ago? How many women have you made love to on a blanket on top of the Gianicolo hill?'

He looked down at his feet, wondering what had possessed him to take her to one of his usual spots when nothing else about his relationship with her had been usual. If anything, he had taken her there to try to prove to himself this was a run-of-the-mill affair when he had known deep down it was nothing of the sort. What a fool!

'Ah… I see. Your silence speaks volumes.' She went to walk out and he caught her arm, realising if he let her go it would be catastrophic for him. For them. The entire world.

'*Cara*…we need to talk.'

'No, Pietro, we really don't. Because there is nothing that can be said to excuse it… And I am all done with this affair.'

'Done?' He couldn't seem to drag enough air in his lungs. 'You don't mean that…allow me to explain about the hill… There is so much more you need to know… Please, *cara*…let us discuss my stupid mistake like adults…'

'Mistake?' She ripped her arm out of his hand. 'This whole thing was a mistake! The biggest of my life. One I shall regret till my dying day.' As he reeled from her vitriol, he found himself staring at her pointed finger as she cast her final judgement. 'But because I am an adult who doesn't run away from my past and my feelings like a child when things get difficult or some pathetic old fool trying to reclaim his lost youth by behaving like Casanova, chasing every piece of available skirt he sees, I shall behave cordially towards you whenever I am forced to endure your presence.'

She glided to the door and paused in the door-frame. 'In case you are in any doubt about what that means, you may talk to me about art or the weather or the price of fish...'

'But what about us?' He was pleading when he never begged. Had never begged for a damn thing in his entire life. 'We *have* to talk about us.'

'There is no "us", Pietro. It turns out there never was. You make me feel sick, ashamed and furious with myself for ever allowing you into my body. So let us never speak of *it* again!'

He heard her slippers dash across the marble floor. Heard them take the stairs at speed. He made no attempt to follow her. Even if he had wanted to, his legs did not have the strength to walk. They crumpled beneath him as he staggered to a chair and for the longest time he simply sat with his head in his hands. The gnarly, malignant growth in his chest squeezed against his organs and screamed in his head.

She was done.

It was over.

She did not want to continue their affair beyond tonight and certainly not across the miles which would soon separate them.

He knew that was for the best. Exactly what he had wanted.

Knew he couldn't make promises or relinquish his freedom completely. Knew all of that went against his own rigid rules concerning emotional attachments and his hard-fought autonomy to live his life by his rules, not another's. Knew things had gone too far, too fast and too personal for his liking and couldn't fathom why he wasn't even a tiny bit relieved she had made the decision for him.

But he would respect it.

He had no choice. Nor any reason to fight against it because he was better on his own. And then, once the acute pain was gone, he would learn from it. Reinforce his rigid rules. Direct his course firmly back to his solitary path where it belonged. Guard his independence fiercely. No complications. No messy emotions. Be more discerning about his choices going forward. Actively avoid any and all women who interested him beyond the physical or spoke to his heart or his mind or loved art or life or friendship or conversation…

Who was he trying to fool?

There would be no other women. There wasn't a woman alive who would ever call to his soul as Lilian did. What a mess. An unfixable mess wholly of his own making. Suddenly he felt like the flayed skin in the painting—ripped apart. Torn into. An empty husk with nothing left.

Condemned to feel restless for ever.

Chapter Sixteen

Insufferable man!

Lilian shoved her feet into her slippers and stuffed her arms unceremoniously into her silk robe, annoyed that the wretched garment always reminded her of the many times he had peeled her out of it. Three days after having her heart torn from her chest and stamped on, she had decided to channel all the hurt into anger instead, hoping that would be more cathartic than throwing herself into sightseeing which hadn't worked at all.

Lilian had seriously considered cutting her trip short and fleeing home, but knew if she did it would only hurt her family. They had paid for her to come here and would be devastated to learn she had not had a good time. Once she acknowledged she was stuck here for the entire duration, stubborn pride dictated that while he had destroyed her self-respect along with her heart, she would not give him the satisfaction of spoiling Rome. Except it had. Even Rome and all its many treasures couldn't alleviate the grief—because it felt like a death and she mourned him. Everywhere she went reminded her of Pietro. Every sculpture or painting she saw she still wanted to discuss with him. Hear his insights. Share her thoughts.

She steeled herself every night to see him at dinner, but Pietro had gone to ground and was burying himself in work—or for all she knew to the hilt inside Mrs Wayfair—and she forced herself not to care about the ridiculously long hours he was keeping. Because of her insomnia, and the inconvenient location of his bedchamber next door, she knew only too well how ridiculous those hours were. He crept in well after midnight and crept out again at dawn. Her stupid ears refused to stop listening for him and her foolish heart couldn't stop caring even though she was determined to hate him.

That was the trouble. Lilian had always been more nurturing than vengeful. A rescuer at heart. Always trying to see the good in people and to make allowances for their bad choices or questionable behaviour to redeem them. Too many years of rescuing fallen women at the

Foundation had left its mark. There was always a reason why. Always at least one wound in the person's past which drove them to behave as they did and experience told her that once the festering was treated and healed, they were able to move on. Make amends. Change. In her head, she couldn't dismiss the belief the roots of Pietro's serial and shallow womanising lay with his dead wife. The woman he had not been able to stand being in the same room with. The one who had taken her own life and died all alone to leave him with all the guilt of it for all eternity. Nor was she able to banish the image of him when she had told him she was done. His eyes, the windows into everyone's soul, had revealed devastation. She still had the power to hurt him…which had to mean he cared…

Ugh! Idiot! There truly was no fool like an old fool.

Tonight, or rather this morning, it was past two and he had still not returned and she was beyond tired of listening out for him. Beyond frustrated at worrying about him. What difference did it make if he didn't come home at all? There were apparently plenty of willing women who would welcome him to their beds with open arms and doubtless Pietro had willingly gone to one of them now that her bed-chamber door remained firmly locked. Those women were welcome to him.

Good riddance to him.

She wouldn't allow it to hurt.

Except it did. She missed him. His company. His voice. His big, solid body next to hers in bed.

Ruthlessly, she quashed the mutinous thought. She was going to be angry. Furious with him, in fact. All this self-pity and introspection was unhealthy. Seeing as she was wide awake, she might as well do something with the time—like read the dull book she had discarded earlier in the *salotto*. At least that might stop her mind from whirring and finally send her blessedly into the arms of Morpheus and the soothing vac-uum of sleep. A little dullness might be exactly what the doctor ordered. Especially as the lamps on the stairs still burned low while they awaited their master's return. More proof if proof were indeed needed that he clearly wasn't suffering anything like she was if he had the inclination to burn the candle at both ends.

Insufferable man!

She pushed the door of the *salotto* open and marched inside, then stopped dead as he stared at her, stunned.

'Lilian!' He was sat in a big chair, nursing a glass of what she already knew would be cognac.

'Pietro.' She regulated her breathing and continued towards the dratted book she had discarded, not wanting to notice the dark shadows under his eyes or the troubled depths within them. When she had picked it up, she clutched it to her chest and turned around. 'Goodnight.'

'Ah…yes. *Buona notte…cara.*' He looked entirely bereft. Convincingly so as he stared down into his glass. She wouldn't care. Wouldn't be fooled. He was a liar. A big, fat liar who was a master at manipulating her feelings to satisfy his unslaked lust. She strode to the door, then paused, turning around to peek at him in silhouette. His big shoulders were slumped. He looked tired. Exhausted, in fact.

'Is work keeping you busy?' *Grr…* Sometimes she hated the weak and charitable side of herself. Hated her big, soft and clearly foolish heart.

'Not busy enough, I fear… Is Rome keeping you busy?' His eyes lifted from the cognac. Sorrowful. Hopeful. She wanted to poke her thumbs in them hard and kick him in the shins.

'I've been following the trail of Bernini. Inspired by the Fontana dei Quattro Fiumi in the

Piazza Navona. He is a great sculptor.' It was safe to talk about art, surely. Rigid English politeness was all he deserved now. No histrionics. No window into how he had made her truly feel. No clue she had stupidly fallen in love with him when for him it was just another affair.

'Then you should visit the Villa Borghese Pinciana. They have two of Bernini's finest sculptures. I could ask the family...'

'We went today. Carlotta knows the family, too. Obviously.' She watched his face fall and tried to muster triumph at the petty victory.

'Yes...of course.'

'It was most impressive.' *Stop swapping inane pleasantries with a man you are rightfully livid with. You want to hate him! Do not engage. Do not linger! Go to bed.* Determined to listen to the insistent voice in her head, she turned.

'Which did you prefer? David or Apollo?'

'Apollo.'

'Why?'

She found herself leaning on the doorframe, contemplating his question when she really didn't want to, when she should spit in his handsome, sorrowful, irritating face. 'I know I am supposed to prefer David as that is considered his seminal work, but...the depiction of

Apollo and Daphne is so tragic and beautiful at the same time. I love how Bernini has captured her in the midst of turning into a tree to escape him, the way the delicate leaves sprout from her fingers and the bark wraps around her legs.'

'I knew you would prefer that one.'

'How?'

'Because I do, too.' Too personal. Too much a reminder of the kinship she had felt between them before the truth destroyed it. Before he had smothered her love with the same blanket he climbed the Gianicolo hill with.

'Has the Botticelli arrived?'

'Tomorrow… Would you still like to see it?' He watched her hesitation, then sighed, for the first time looking all of his forty-eight years when he usually seemed a good decade younger. That called to the rescuer inside her—the idiot who always tried to see the best in people. The woman whose foolish heart still beat for him. 'I know what I did was wrong, *cara*. I know you can never forgive me for it and I have made my peace with the fact I cannot ask you to. But we did promise to remain friends no matter what for the duration and I should like to be your friend for the final days of your visit. I miss you, Lilian. I miss talking to you.'

She wouldn't tell him she missed him, too. Instead, she looked down her nose. 'I would not feel comfortable coming to your gallery.' Like his bedchamber, it would only remind her of the passion they shared. The love she felt. The gaping rip in her heart.

'I could bring it here.'

'Then I should like to see it.' She gripped the book tighter like a shield. 'Goodnight, Pietro. Don't stay up too late. You look tired.'

True to his word, he brought the *tondo* to the *palazzo* the following evening. But, not wishing to appear too eager to either see it or be in his company, she dallied over her hair in her bedchamber until dinner was almost ready despite being told by her maid he was waiting for her downstairs. Dinner was a little awkward, but they both put on a good front while Carlotta and Alexandra took responsibility for the bulk of the conversation, and after the meal the four of them retired to the *salotto* where there was no sign of the painting. Something which made her nervous, so like a coward she did not bring it up.

Carlotta did.

'What did you think of the Botticelli, Lilian?'

'I haven't seen it yet.'

'Oh, then go now! It is stunning. Isn't it, Alexandra?'

Oh, dear. They had both already seen it. Perhaps delaying her arrival to dinner to avoid being alone with him had not been the best plan. Especially as Pietro had already stood to escort her to wherever it was he had put it.

'Indeed it is. Exactly your cup of tea, Cousin.' Neither woman seemed keen to budge.

'Aren't you coming?' She gave Alexandra a pointed look. She had confessed to her Pietro had grievously hurt her after being directly asked two days previously, and, despite being scant on the gory details, had made it plain she never wanted to be left alone with the man again.

'I am too full. That will teach me to eat so much dessert.' Alexandra looked back at her accusing stare with blank innocence. 'Besides, I'm not the rabid art lover, dearest. You are. Go…'

'Yes, go,' added Carlotta with an imperious flap of her hand. 'The pair of you become very dull when you discuss paintings. There is only so much artistic adoration I can take and, like your dear cousin, I ate far too much of that dessert. I really must compliment the chef on that cake. The meringue…so light…'

'Sublime, darling.' Alexandra leaned towards her friend conspiratorially as if Lilian and the man who had callously stomped on her heart no longer existed. 'Do you think he would give me the recipe?'

'I doubt it. Giuseppe is notoriously temperamental…'

Pietro was waiting patiently beside her chair. She could smell his cologne. Sense the warm heat of his skin and his tension as he awaited her decision, yet seemed determined and resigned to accept her refusal if it came. 'Shall we?'

'Of course.' She was going to strangle Alexandra later—the Judas. Both she and his sister were in cahoots and were obviously conspiring to get the pair of them together again. He offered his arm and she pretended she hadn't seen it. 'Where have you hidden it?'

'In the Gran Salon. There is another little Botticelli in there…or at least I have always suspected it to be from his hand. I would appreciate your thoughts on it now that we have a genuine example to finally compare it with.'

Chapter Three

Chapter Seventeen

She was at least talking to him. The conversation was stilted, excruciatingly awkward and confined solely to art—but at least she was talking. After the hell of the past few days, it was a lifeline he was glad to cling on to for all he was worth.

Lord, he had missed her. He had never experienced anything like it before in his life. It was almost like a death, the grief and mourning was so intense. Not that he had ever lost anyone who had literally made his heart ache from it. His mother had died while he was too young to understand loss. He had felt unburdened when his wife had died and annoyance when his father had passed. But then dear Papà had left him with such a huge mess to clean up, one so much larger than he could have imagined in his worst nightmares, so that was hardly surprising.

Yet something about the loss of Lilian had cut him to the quick. He couldn't eat. Couldn't sleep. Couldn't think straight most of the time. He had spent nearly all the last four days sitting at his desk in the gallery, staring at the walls. This afternoon, to complete his misery, his head had started to pound relentlessly, making every movement an effort.

'You covered it in a cloth?' She stared at the round panel he had draped in purple velvet.

'You know me. I like a little theatre.'

He gestured for her to step back a little, making sure she was positioned directly in front of it, then whipped the cloth off. Watching her features as she saw it for the first time. Her eyes widened. Danced. Then she gave her only genuine smile of the interminably painful evening.

'Oh, Pietro…it is lovely. The colours…they are still so vibrant.' Testament to the number of hours he had spent today, fighting the lethargy and gently dabbing off centuries of dirt with diluted lemon juice so she would see it at its best. A task he normally entrusted to a subordinate, but something he had needed to do to keep his mind from racing. And to prevent him from seriously contemplating some of the crazed ideas he was conjuring out of desperation to keep her with him. Nonsense like begging her to stay and give them a chance, when he knew he had never sought for ever. Except for ever with Lilian didn't sound so bad any more, no matter how many times he tried to caution himself against the idea each time it relentlessly appeared in his aching head.

He went to stand next to her, folding his arms to prevent himself from giving in to the urge to touch her, knowing if he did she would bolt. 'It is not his best work.' The artist had needed to put food on his table, so religious commissions like this were his bread and butter rather than his passion. 'Nor his best *tondo* of the Madonna. But I like it.'

'But you don't love it?'

He shook his head, trying not to wince from the pain the movement suddenly caused or allow her to see what a state he had got himself into. 'There are several better examples in Florence. When you have seen his haunting *Madonna del Magnificat* or the perfection of his altarpiece from the church of San Barnaba, for instance, this one feels less...'

'Personal?'

'*Sì*...as if he had no true emotional attachment to the commission. He painted it because he had to.'

'The man had to make a living.'

'Don't we all? I have no attachment to the picture either, but I know it will bring an excellent price and sell quickly. Hopefully to someone who does love it.'

'And where is your suspected Botticelli?' She scanned the crowded walls of paintings. Most of those in frames he had bought and paid for himself to replace the treasures his father had thoughtlessly sold. Just as he would have sold the beautiful ceiling fresco had it not been an integral part of the structure of the *palazzo* and thus difficult to remove. Others were family portraits by unnamed and uncelebrated artists. Pictures nobody else would want—apart from the English new money who flocked to his gallery for such things. Yet they were images he was intrinsically attached to. This was his family's history and no matter how unworthy some of those ancestors were, they still belonged here in the *palazzo*.

'Here.' He pointed to the portrait of the woman he had bought years before from an impoverished visconte. 'There is something about her face, the expression, which reminds me of his work.' There had been a serenity about the woman which had called to him. A calmness which counteracted his restlessness, drawing him like a port in a storm. Odd, really, as it was those same qualities in Lilian which he now missed the most. She had apparently become his anchor in such a short space of time and losing her made him feel adrift.

He watched her lovely eyes flick back and forth from the portrait to the *tondo*, saying nothing until she had come to her own conclusions. 'I can see similarities.'

'And I can see you are not convinced.'

She shrugged in apology, her gaze briefly locking with his before moving away. 'I just do not get that sense of rightness I felt keenly when I first saw your Michelangelo sketches.' Sense of rightness... Something he now understood completely. She felt right. He felt right with her. Good Lord, he was tired if his brain was conjuring such nonsense. 'I am sorry.'

'There is no need to apologise. Art is subjective and all about gut feeling above all else. You have good instincts, Lilian. Now that I see them side by side, I am not convinced they came from the same hand either. Therefore, I must conclude my bargain find all those years ago is not a Botticelli... More's the pity.'

'That said—I think it's a lovely picture... I actually prefer it to the *tondo*.'

'So do I.'

She smiled. 'We always did have such similar taste in art.' A statement which seemed to bother her. She covered it by staring at the family portraits surrounding it. 'Every time I come into this room, my eyes are immediately drawn to the fresco. I've never really taken the time to look at all the paintings. Who are these people?'

'Venturis—past and present.' He tapped a picture which always made him smile. 'This chubby little fellow sat on his mother's lap is me around the time of my first birthday. I suit lace, don't you think?' The frothy, feminine concoction his mother had dressed him in combined with his big, soulful brown eyes made him look like an angelic little girl.

'There is so much of it. But it does suit you. You were a pretty child.' She blinked, uncomfortable again. Perhaps she would be so for the precious few days they had left. A depressing thought, but after he had hurt her, he had no choice but to take whatever scraps she was prepared to offer from her table. Anything was better than not seeing her. 'Is that a good likeness of your mother?'

'I don't know. I do not remember her. She died shortly after my sister was born.' He pointed to the picture beside it. 'But this is an excellent likeness of my father. The artist has captured his sour expression perfectly, I think.'

'You did not get on with him at all then?'

'He was a hard man to like. Very disagreeable. Very...oh, what is the word...? *Dittatoriale.*'

'Dictatorial?'

'Yes, exactly. His word was law and we all had to bend to his will. On everything.'

'Like your choice of bride.' What had made her bring that up? 'Is she here?' She gestured to the portraits, her gaze searching.

In the spirit of their new and fragile truce, he pointed to the only one of the many pictures Isabetta had had painted of herself that he had not consigned to the cellar. The least flamboyant and self-indulgent, but still to his eye obviously vain. Even after all these years, just the sight of her irritated him. 'This is Isabetta.'

'You really disliked her, didn't you?'

'What makes you say that?'

'Your reaction just then. Your eyes changed. Your jaw clenched.' And there he thought he always hid it well. Not even his sister, who had always been very vocal about her own dislike of Pietro's flighty arranged bride, knew he had entirely loathed her by the end because he still always publicly defended her. She was his wife, so he always felt he had to, and it went without saying, a proud man did not wash his dirty linen in public. Yet Lilian knew him too well because for some reason around her his guard kept slipping. But how to explain his obviously visceral reaction to his long-dead wife without seeming callous when she already thought him calculated and shallow?

'She and I were a bad match.'

'Is honesty really that hard for you, Pietro?' There it was again. The sharpness. The accusation and disappointment in her eyes as if he owed her the truth about his past, when it was his past and therefore nothing to do with now. This wasn't the Gianicolo hill. She wasn't affected by it or unwittingly embroiled in it. This was intensely private. 'You should be a politician. You have such a flare for sidestepping questions and skirting around the truth.'

Sometimes she was exasperating. Here he was trying to make amends and repair the tattered remains of their friendship and there she was, determined to be terminally disappointed in him. No matter what. Even when he had done nothing wrong. Or at least not recently. 'What do you want me to say? If I tell you the truth, you will hate me and if I lie you will know I am lying and hate me for that, too.'

She waited, the pregnant pause clearly a cue for him to continue with his anticipated confession. When he didn't, she shook her head. 'I am close to hating you already so what difference will it make, Pietro? At least it would be honest.' She picked up her skirts and regally began to sail towards the door with all the righteous indignation he would expect from a woman who had spent her life doing good deeds and being loved for them, making him feel unworthy for not being as intrinsically selfless. The archetypal pious saint and the sinner. Although in this instance, how dare she judge? The flash of temper made his head pound harder.

'You married for love, didn't you, Lilian?' Her step slowed, but she didn't turn around. So pious. Suddenly so irritating. 'What a luxury for you! To have a soulmate. The love of your life. A person to talk to. One always on your side. One who adores you unconditionally. One to weather the bad times side by side and to celebrate success with. Let me guess— no matter how hard life got for you, no matter how many obstacles life threw in your path, you always had Henry beside you. You always had his love and his strength. You could always rely on it, couldn't you?' She finally turned, her expression inscrutable. 'Well, I didn't! I married a woman I had met twice before my wedding night. The bride of my father's choosing. One chosen not for her charms or her qualities— but simply because she came from an equally noble family as mine and she came with a ready dowry. I was seventeen, Lilian! More boy than man and she was twenty.'

All at once he was that boy again. Confused, scared, entirely inexperienced, terrified and totally out of his depth. 'I begged my father not to force me to wed her. Begged him to at least slow the process down. Give us both time to see if we suited. Get to know one another. But no!'

He clenched his fists, fighting for control, when all he wanted to do was rant and rave and gesticulate like the most affronted Italian who ever walked the earth. 'Once the marriage had been brokered between her father and mine, mine wanted the fat dowry he had been promised immediately so I was sent down the aisle like a lamb to the slaughter. I went to the marriage bed a virgin, Lilian, expecting my new wife to be the same, yet I forgave her when I discovered she wasn't because I knew she had as much say in the match as I and both of us were cruel victims of circumstance.' Oh, how he had hated that night. The fumbling. The sense of expectation. The brevity. The ultimate disappointment of it all.

'I tried to be a good husband, especially in those early weeks. Lord knows I tried! But she was spoiled and selfish and flew into an irrational temper whenever she did not get her own way. I had never met such an unreasonable person. So volatile she made my father seem reasonable by comparison! I also soon learned why her father was in such a mad hurry to have her married off. She came to me pregnant.' He had never confessed that to another living soul. 'I never asked who the father was, but agreed to pretend the child was mine—for the sake of our families.' He stared up at his father's portrait and allowed the buried rage to build. He still did not know if his *papà* had known about the baby. He had always suspected he had, because Isabetta's dowry had been much bigger than her impoverished father could afford and the wedding fast. Too fast. And his father had prayed for a girl! Why else do that unless you didn't want another man's bastard to inherit the Venturi debts?

'What happened?' Pietro jumped at her whisper. While lost in all the painful memories, she had come to stand behind him. Close, but not touching. He willed her to reach out.

To hold him. To make it better. To forgive him for not being the saint she deserved.

'We had been married perhaps two months… In view of her condition and at her insistence, we kept to separate rooms after the painfully awkward and wholly contrived wedding night.' He had never gone to her bed again. Something they argued constantly about when she realised she had lost him and wanted to manipulate him. 'Therefore I wasn't privy to the argument which set her off—although by then I had already come to realise it never took much. There was a disagreement with her maid about a gown. Something inane and pointless. Entirely unnecessary. Isabetta stormed off, had a horse saddled and rode away angry. She was thrown from the saddle about a mile away from here. Broke her pelvis. Lost the baby…' The child everyone had assumed had been his. The only person he had truly felt sorry for in the whole miserable debacle. 'The physicians said she might heal in time. Be able to have more children, but…' He felt Lilian's hand come to rest on his shoulder as he stared up at the face of his wife. Finally felt the overwhelming comfort of that soothing touch. Felt oddly unburdened at saying it all out loud for the first time.

'They gave her laudanum for the pain. She

became addicted. Would never give it up. When I banned the physicians from giving her more and tried to wean her off it, she bought opium from unscrupulous dealers out of my sight and beyond my control. Six years later, it killed her... That was my marriage, *cara*. A living hell. So, yes, I disliked her and, yes, I actively avoided her because I couldn't stand to be in her presence—as a result she ultimately died all alone.'

He might as well tell her every sordid detail of the story.

'And when I heard of her death, I never mourned her. I never have. Not for a single second. I was just so thoroughly relieved to be free at last.'

Chapter Eighteen

Dratted man!

It was all his fault she couldn't sleep. Pietro's tragic story had haunted her all night and all day. He wouldn't elaborate. Wouldn't be drawn into what the glossed-over six years of marriage to an opium addict was like. He simply shrugged at the end of his story, then closed tight like a clam shell, briskly returning her to the others and bidding them all a goodnight. It was all done, he had said, the past. Like time, he had moved on. Except in many ways she was now entirely convinced he hadn't.

Not that it changed anything of course, but at least she felt she understood him a little more. Forgave him a little bit. It was hardly a surprise he was wedded to his bachelorhood and shied away from complicated emotions when his marriage had been so awful. And while it hinted at the reasons he kept his attachments shallow and transient, Lilian knew there had to be more to it to fully explain his serial philandering properly. Those six years must have been horrendous and it made her sad to think the residual guilt of it was keeping him from entrusting anyone with his heart.

Although she had to face facts, with only ten days left, him so guarded about his emotions, her heart still broken and the atmosphere between them still understandably tense, she sincerely doubted she would ever get to the bottom of it.

Probably for the best.

It was the past. His past. And it had absolutely nothing to do with her or her future. He had killed all the hope she had once felt of a future for them stone dead—years before they met on a well-used blanket on the Gianicolo hill. It was beyond vexing to both want to hate a man and to not quite be able to because he was so damned likeable.

She lifted her candle and stared up at the tiny portrait of Isabetta, into her eyes, in an attempt to see into the soul of the woman to fill in the many blanks she had about Pietro's marriage. All to no avail. All she saw was what her emotions told her to see. Selfishness. Weakness. For ultimately, if an addict could not find the inner strength to save themselves, experience told her they were doomed.

Much like any hope of sleep tonight until the dratted man came home. He had left before breakfast and had failed to return for the late dinner. As much as she hated her own weakness for it, Lilian found it impossible to relax until she heard the sound of his feet in the hallway outside her door and knew he was home safe. Clearly the stubborn man had gone to ground again after his revelations last night. Something he seemed to do whenever his own emotions rattled him. Dratted man! She needed to stop caring. Her continued concern for him after all he had done was irritating in the extreme.

Determined to go to bed and jolly well sleep seeing as it was well past midnight yet again, she was halfway upstairs when she heard a sound coming from the *salotto*. A muffled groan. She knew instinctively it was him, she could sense him, which also irritated her. She decided to ignore it, then heard a second mumbled curse—terse, sharp—almost as if he were in pain. It made her uneasy. Unless he had heard her and was purposely trying to manipulate her emotions…

But if he genuinely was in pain...

Ugh! Why couldn't she just hate him with impunity and not give a damn?

Hardening herself from being manipulated into sympathy, she turned around and stomped back down the stairs. She would poke her head in, assure herself he hadn't had an accident or been shot and was bleeding to death in agony, then bid him goodnight. Her preoccupation with Pietro was as pointless as it was unhealthy. The man really didn't deserve her sympathy. Not when he could get it just as easily from Ida Wayfair or the French trollop.

She marched into the darkened room, expecting to see him sat in the chair he usually reserved for himself, only to find it empty.

'Pietro?' Movement from the sofa made her go there and she watched him partially sit up and shield his eyes as if the dim light of her single candle caused him agony. 'Is everything all right?'

'I have a headache... Damn thing will not go.'

She took in the blanket he was swathed in. The tension around his scrunched eyes. The pallor of his normally tanned skin. The beaded perspiration on his brow and upper lip. Without thinking, she rushed to him and touched her hand to his forehead. It was clammy. Beneath her fingers she could feel him shivering. 'I think it is more than a headache.' Hadn't she warned him if he continued to burn his dratted candle at both ends, he would be ill? 'You have a fever, Pietro.'

'Impossible. I never get fevers.' He struggled to sit fully and winced, gripping his ribs. 'I've strained myself. That is all.'

'Strained yourself?' She couldn't stop herself from helping him to sit. Couldn't stop herself from caring he was in pain.

'I have lifted something incorrectly...that stupid Botticelli... I've had pains in my muscles since yesterday. And this head.' With his elbows now on his knees he buried his face in his hands. 'I thought some cognac might help, but just the smell of it turns my stomach.'

Nausea, fever, headaches...all the symptoms of a nasty chill. Or worse. 'Let's get you tucked up in bed and I shall summon the physician.'

'No!' He shrugged off her hand like a lion with a thorn in its paw. Wincing again and lurching sideways. 'I don't need a physician, woman, I just need sleep.' Then he tried to stand and the obvious pain winded him. *'Buon Dio! Le mie costole...'* She assumed he meant ribs because he gripped them. 'They are on fire!'

He was glaring at her warily as if she had caused him the pain.

'Can I look?'

Without waiting for an answer she deposited her candle on the side table and gently removed his waistcoat and lifted up his shirt. The angry band of red bumps slashing along the bottom of his ribs was unmistakable. She had seen it many times before. 'You have shingles.'

'Impossible! Only old people get shingles!'

'All people get shingles, Pietro. Especially people who are at a low ebb, who push their bodies to their limits as you do and keep unreasonable and unhealthy hours.' She couldn't resist the dig, despite knowing he couldn't possibly have been off philandering with shingles.

'You are no doctor! Who are you to make a diagnosis…?' How typical he would be a bad patient. 'All I need is sleep and I shall be back to my normal robust self by the morning.' He stood then, grunting as he winced, then turning a worrying shade of green as he tried to walk, holding his abdomen now. 'I've eaten something bad!'

Despite his grumbling, he made no complaint when she took his arm and he leaned heavily on her as she led him to the stairs, moaning the entire time. The noise roused the night footman, a man who spoke absolutely no English whatsoever. 'Can you summon the physician?'

At his blank stare, Lilian racked her brains for the Italian word and when nothing came resorted to the Latin she had learned in the schoolroom, praying it sounded similar. *'Medicus?'*

'Medico?'

'Sì... Medico...per il duca.' In case she was speaking absolute nonsense, she gestured to Pietro and mimed being sick.

'No doctor! I forbid it! I have a slight headache, is all…'

'What is going on?' Carlotto's dark head appeared over the banister. 'What is all the noise? Is my brother drunk?'

Before he roared and did himself a mischief at the accusation, Lilian interceded. 'He is unwell. Shingles, I think, but we need to summon the physician to be sure.' Thankfully, Carlotta responded by issuing a stream of rapid instructions to the footman, closely followed by a very Italian argument between brother and sister in which he no doubt reiterated his belief this was nought but a headache and his sister told him off for being so stubborn. The passionate *idiota!* which kept punctuating her tirade was the only word Lilian understood. And heartily agreed with. He was an idiot and a baby.

Between them they got a very belligerent Pietro up the stairs and into his bedchamber. Carlotta ordered him to undress and get into bed, then sailed out to see what was keeping the physician, leaving Lilian alone with him as he struggled with his shirt. When she attempted to help he became even more belligerent.

'I can undress myself!'

No, he couldn't. 'You never used to mind me undressing you.' In his current state, there seemed little point in beating around the bush.

'That was different! I am not a child!'

'Then stop behaving like one. And for pity's sake sit down before you fall down, Pietro. Do you want to vomit all over the floor?'

That quite feasible reality seemed to bring him up short and he lowered his body to the mattress. 'Your behaviour is ridiculous and counterproductive. You are ill. Obviously ill. I have never seen you so pale or so drawn. All this shouting and carrying on isn't going to help you get better.' Seeing that he was finally quiet, she took it as permission to help him and began to ease his shirt gently from his body. Reluctantly he lifted his arms to allow her to remove it, then turned his face to one side as she unbuttoned his falls, clearly ashamed to have to be treated like an invalid, but also clearly as weak as a kitten.

'How can you be sure it is shingles?' He held up one leg as she tugged off his boot, the effort of that one simple movement etched on his face.

'Because I have seen it many times before at the Foundation.' She paused to tug off the second. 'And my father had it once, too. The rash on your torso is a classic symptom. So are the headache and feelings of malaise and nausea. In a day or two, those bumps around your ribs will blister and weep.'

'It gets worse?' This seemed to alarm him. *'Buon Dio!'*

She couldn't help but smile at his horrified expression. Anger was giving way to the urge to feel sorry for himself. He was going to be a truly awful patient. 'You won't die, Pietro—although if you continue to behave like an unreasonable bear with a sore head, we might all wish it.' She smiled to soften her words and he looked adorably contrite. She helped him to stand so he could dispense with his undone trousers himself. 'But you won't be yourself for at least a few days.' She foolishly watched him step out of them and, in that second, she was forced to acknowledge the sight of him naked still had the power to quicken her pulse. Even ill, he was gorgeous.

'I don't want to go to bed for a few days. I have things to do. A gallery to run. Clients…'

'Then you run the risk of the symptoms lasting weeks. Without proper rest and adequate time to recuperate, I've seen shingles last months.'

'Months?' He was still standing entirely naked before her. A state of affairs which could not continue as it was playing havoc with her nerves, despite his weakened state and the wholly inappropriate nature of her errant thoughts.

'So perhaps you need to listen to me and rest?' He grunted—it was neither a yes nor a no. 'Lie down and I will tuck you in.'

He complied, looking thoroughly miserable as she covered him with the blankets. 'I am going to see what is keeping the doctor.'

His hand caught hers. His dark eyes pleading. So sad. A tad pathetic. Exactly like her son Silas used to be whenever he was unwell as a boy. 'No…stay, *cara*. Please… Don't leave me alone.' Lilian sat on the mattress and brushed her hand over his hair, watching his tired eyes flutter closed at the contact. 'I shall go quite mad if I am stuck in bed for days.'

'We will all visit you and keep you company.'

'Do you promise?' Now that he had stopped fighting it, his deep voice was slurred with sleep. The poor man was exhausted and, knowing Pietro as well as she did, she knew he had doggedly battled the tiredness and the illness rather than submit to it. Made things worse, *idiota*.

'Yes. I promise.'

Eyes still closed, his mouth curved into a pathetic approximation of a smile as he drifted off. *'Non so cosa farei senza di te nella mia vita... Amore mio.'*

'What does that mean?'

He was quiet for so long, she thought he might have slipped into sleep. But then he sighed and frowned as if he were suddenly bothered by something. Perhaps his own words.

'Just that I have missed you.' He turned his head away. 'That is all.'

Chapter Nineteen

Because clearly he had not suffered enough, Lilian was annoyingly correct in her diagnosis of shingles which meant Pietro had been sentenced to bed rest for at least three days. Being noble, he had refused her offer to stay with him and had insisted she visit the Via Appia with Alexandra as she had planned, knowing she would adore walking along the exact same cobbles, the exact same footprints, of the Ancient Romans of yore.

Several hours on from his grand and noble gesture, and with Carlotta at the gallery in his stead, Pietro thoroughly resented everyone's absence. Perhaps he wasn't in danger of imminent death, but leaving him all alone in bed with only the servants for company, a pounding head and a burning rash around his torso was just plain cruel. He had tried reading.

He had tried sleeping. And now he was left to stare helplessly at his ceiling and mull his own thoughts while life carried on around him.

And the biggest thing he was mulling over was what he had inadvertently said to Lilian last night when everything had seemed too much for him.

'Non so cosa farei senza di te nella mia vita...' That he would be lost without her in his life.

He had certainly felt lost for days. Lost and miserable and lonely. With no work to distract him, those feelings swamped him. Tormented him. But he certainly should not have said them out loud.

Especially as she seemed to have moved on and was intent on enjoying her little holiday as fully as possible. Not even sparing a day for him when he was so obviously in need of company... His ears pricked up at the distant sound of a carriage coming into the courtyard and he willed it to be her. A few minutes later and he could hear the tinkling sound of her laugh as she chatted to Alexandra and he willed her to come up the stairs to see him. But she didn't.

For ten whole minutes she made him wait before he finally heard her on the stairs. It was then that pride and vanity kicked in. He hastily ran his fingers through his hair, wishing he had had the foresight to attend to his appearance over the painful, long hours of staring. Then, on the off chance she might come directly to his bedchamber rather than go to hers to freshen up after her interminably long and selfish day of sightseeing, he picked up the book he had barely read a sentence of, opened it at a random page and pretended to be engrossed in it. He even bit his lip to stop from cheering hallelujah when she lightly tapped on the door.

'Come in.'

'I wasn't sure if you would be asleep.' She looked lovely. Windswept. Her hairstyle had collapsed and one fat, wavy tendril bounced near her cheek. Fresh little freckles dotted her nose thanks to the sunshine. Such an English thing, freckles, yet on her so utterly charming. 'How are you feeling?'

'Itchy.' Bored senseless. Aggrieved he couldn't have been there to see her face when she walked the Appian Way. Annoyed she had left him, even though he had told her to. 'My head is still spinning. That physician is clearly a quack as none of his medicines have worked.'

'Still in fine spirits, then.' She was laughing at him, or would be if she gave in to the twitching lips which plagued her. That galled.

'Shingles is no laughing matter.'

'No. It isn't.' He watched her bite her lip.

'Then why are you laughing?'

'Because you are not taking it well.'

'Would you? Stuck in bed while the sun shines outside and everyone else is enjoying the day as if you do not exist?' For some reason he seemed to want to fight, despite being ridiculously pleased to see her and never wanting her to leave his bedside again. Or at least for the duration of his inconvenient illness. He watched her eyes take in the crumpled nightshirt he had tossed in the corner an hour ago in a fit of pique because he could not stand the touch of the material against his rash, cursing his sister who had made him don the damn thing in the first place simply to look decent. He was the Duca della Torizia! This was his house and if he wanted to he would damn well stride around nude in it!

Lilian smiled, as if she completely understood why he had violently discarded it, and waved a small tied box at him. 'I bought you a present. It took for ever to track it down. But I finally found it in the Via del Corsa, else I would have been back sooner.'

He so wanted to be belligerent, but tried his damnedest to be magnanimous. Gifts were nice. Gifts were thoughtful. And if nothing else it did mean she had spared him a passing thought while she swanned down the Via Appia, having a high old time while he suffered all alone. 'What is it?'

'Calamine lotion. For the itching. And some emergency chocolate. For the crotchetiness… Which would you like first?'

He found his own mouth twitching at her obvious amusement. 'The itching potion. I swear, if I had some birch twigs, I would flay my own skin off at this point.'

'The itching is the worst. I remember when I caught chickenpox at the age of ten… I just sat in bed and cried.' Pathetically, Pietro had also shed a few tears this morning when he was all alone and forgotten. As much as they shamed him now, at the time, they had seemed appropriate.

She took out the little bottle and shook it vigorously, then hesitated. 'Would you like me to apply it…or do it yourself?'

'You.' He pouted naturally, then exaggerated it in the hope she might think he was doing it on purpose to be witty and self-effacing, when in actuality he had never felt more sorry for himself in his life. So sorry for himself he might well indulge in another little weep as soon as she left him. 'It hurts when I bend.'

He had to turn on the side not facing her, which was just as well, because he was pouting again for real. What a pathetic creature he had become in the last few days. Moody, childish, self-pitying, heartbroken...

Heartbroken?

Was he? If he was, it was another depressing thought in a day filled with them. He had hoped once she left Rome, it would be out of sight, out of mind. That his uncharacteristic emotional attachment to Lilian would wane swiftly with her departure. But if his heart really was engaged, then... *Buon Dio!* Best not to indulge that particular train of thought. It would pass because it had to. Their affair was over. He had promised her never to visit her in England. Vowed never to bind himself to a woman for all eternity ever again.

Air hissed through his teeth as she gently applied the cold lotion to his skin. 'I'm sorry... I'll be as quick as I can. Then in a few minutes it will feel better, I promise.'

He needed something to take his mind off it. 'How was your day?'

'Good...' She didn't sound too enthusiastic. 'The old road was fascinating...'

'I sense a but…'

He could hear the wistful smile in her voice, picture the faraway look she always got in her eyes when her mind was elsewhere. 'But I was preoccupied… With you, actually.'

The best news he had heard all day. 'I knew you would feel bad for leaving me to my own devices.' The soothing lotion was working its magic, so much so, he was enjoying the brush of her fingers against the bits of skin surrounding the hideous rash that weren't on fire. Not enough to feel desire, but still pleasant. As if she cared.

'I did. It's no fun being ill all alone.' Her palm came around his middle to pat the lotion on the last part of the rash which clipped his abdomen. It felt like a hug. One he desperately needed. 'And…if I'm honest, I've been distracted because… Well… I've been thinking about what you told me about Isabetta and the opium…'

Oh, no! Not that again. Was he not suffering enough?

'And thinking how awful it must have been for you to watch her decline. Feeling powerless… Your story has been preying on my mind, Pietro. Making me second-guess myself and the decisions I made long ago.' He felt the mattress give as she sat on it and when he rolled on to his back again saw she was deeply troubled.

'Long ago?' Which suggested before him. Before he had ruined everything with one thoughtless picnic on a hill he would now pay a thousand labourers good money to remove from the horizon.

'We had a few women like that at the Foundation. Three, in fact, in that first year when we still loftily believed we could save everyone simply by caring. They didn't faze Henry and, typically, he welcomed them with open arms intent on rescuing them. Neither of us had any experience of opium before and had no concept of what it could do to the mind of the addict. We learned very quickly we were out of our depth. The drug had such a hold on them and made them impossible to deal with. We tried to help them…of course we did…but they craved the oblivion more than they wished for a cure. It made their moods turbulent and dangerously erratic. It also made two of the women quite violent, unpredictably so, and in both cases— for the safety of all the other women in our care—we had to move them. Had to rely on the charity of others. But in moving them, and despite all our best intentions, it became harder to control their addictions from a distance. We did not have enough staff to watch them around the clock and the good people who took them in for us were ill prepared for the way the drug twisted and manipulated those in the grip of it—and the women used that to their advantage. Within two days, they had escaped and disappeared into the city. Your story has dredged all that up and now I cannot stop wondering what became of them or if I should have done more.'

She felt guilty. He could hear it in her tone. 'You didn't abandon them as anyone else would have done. You did all you reasonably could to keep them safe. You should not feel bad for doing what was necessary.'

'Then why do you?' Neatly hoisted by his own petard.

'She wasn't a waif or stray from the streets. Isabetta was my responsibility. My wife. I promised to look after her before God… In church… In sickness and in health.'

'It's funny, isn't it, that we both must have said similar wedding vows, made similar promises to our spouses in a church, yet I said mine freely while you were forced. It seems hardly fair in that case they should be as binding. Especially as love was not involved at all.' She was holding out an olive branch and in doing so caused the truth to tumble from his lips willingly this time. Bizarrely, knowing she could empathise, this made him want to talk to her. Make her see he wasn't all bad and perhaps help to prove that same thing to himself in the process.

'I adhered to all my other vows, Lilian...' the truth '...except the one to love. I was faithful...which meant I was celibate for six years.' Better that than go to her bed. 'But I never loved her.'

'Love has to grow from somewhere. It needs roots to anchor it and, like a plant, it needs sunshine and feeding. You cannot make yourself love a person any more than you can stop yourself from doing it.' Her eyes flicked to him for a second, making him wonder what that might mean, before she shrugged and he realised he was trying to manifest his emotions on to her. 'Perhaps you should not feel bad for doing what was necessary either? Unless you didn't try to help her...'

'For three years I tried everything. Then, to my shame, I gave up seeking a cure for her and simply concentrated on controlling her behaviour because...well...life was different.'

'In what way?'

'My father died. The family finances were a mess. I had to do something to stop everything crumbling around my feet.'

'You had bigger fish to fry.'

'What does that mean?' As good as he was with her language, sometimes he missed the subtle nuances because he translated things too literally.

'It is an old saying we have in England. It means you had more pressing problems which needed to be dealt with. To be frank, if you had tried everything for three years and Isabetta was neither engaged in the process or no better...' She had been worse. So much worse. 'Then it was extremely unlikely she would suddenly respond when she hadn't before.'

'Once she replaced the laudanum with opium, there was no reasoning with her or appealing to her better nature, because it destroyed her better nature.' Not that he had ever witnessed there being much in those early weeks before her accident. 'I hired nurses to keep watch on her, she was constantly supervised, I ensured she had no money to buy it, but...' He sighed, remembering all the frustration from so long ago. The arguments. The violence. The way all the fruitless repetition wore him down and made him hate her.

'Don't tell me…she managed to escape anyway? Stole things to trade for the drug? Found the oblivion regardless.' He nodded, a little choked that Lilian really did understand how unspeakably awful it had been. 'And this happened for six years! No wonder you felt relieved when she passed.' He felt her fingers brush his hair. 'But why do you think she killed herself on purpose?'

'Because it is what she used to threaten when I thwarted all her attempts at getting what she wanted. Before I left for that ill-fated business trip, I had bars fitted to her bedchamber window. I hated doing that, but, thanks to the opium, she could climb like a monkey, not caring how high she was from the ground or what dangers lay beneath. Unsurprisingly, she was not happy about it.' An understatement. Isabetta had come at him like a savage, claws bared. He had worn the marks of her nails like a brand on his cheek at her funeral. 'Her last words to me were she would take her own life the second I left her alone if I refused to have them removed. She attacked her nurse that night, stole her keys and fled into the city barefoot with two silver candlesticks to sell. They found her in an alley in the morning.

She had been dead for many hours. I always assumed she'd carried out her threat.'

'Probably more out of accident than design. With the oblivion, I noticed, also came a sense of infallibility. Certainly the opium addicts I have had dealings with, when under the spell of the drug, did not have the wherewithal to deny themselves more than they could take. I think you need to put your guilt to one side now. It is self-destructive and undeserved. You did all you could, but you must accept it was not enough. Nothing would have been enough. She had taken a path and refused to be swayed from it.' Pietro saw nothing but sympathy in her lovely eyes and all of it for him. Something as humbling as it was welcome. She understood. All of it. And while she might hate him for what he had done to her, she did not hate him for the mess he had made of his marriage or the way he had failed Isabetta. 'And it was easier to blame you, or the world, for the state she was in rather than face up to her own failings or her own part in her downfall. Once she was too far down that path, there was no turning back. Her death was probably as much of a relief to her as it was you.'

'Perhaps.' It was tempting to allow himself to accept her reasoning over the guilt. Especially now he had Lilian's permission to put it to one side. Something he was surprised to realise he had needed. Just as he apparently also needed to talk about it. 'I try not to think about it.' Before she made him dig deeper, he directed the conversation away from his part in the whole sorry mess of his marriage. 'You said there were three… At the Foundation. If you only moved two of them out, what happened to the third?'

'The same thing that happened to Isabetta. Eerily the same, in fact. Henry locked her in a room to allow it to pass through her system, but the symptoms of withdrawal were too strong. Dreadful to watch.'

'It looks like agony. Hell.' By the end, Isabetta resembled more animal than woman. Incoherent, rambling. Dangerously unpredictable.

'Yes, it does. Hell is a good word. She was in hell and exhausted and resistant to any and all attempts to help her. When we stupidly assumed she was finally asleep after days of ranting, she broke the window to escape. We didn't hear it. Nobody did. Henry went to check on her in the small hours and she was gone. We searched…but London is a big city and the dubious parts of it a warren of dark alleyways. I still have no idea how she found the money to

pay for the opium which killed her. There was
nothing worth stealing at the Foundation. I suspect she sold herself on the street, as so many
desperate women do. They found her body in
a yard near the docks the next morning. Poor
thing. She was only twenty-five.'

'Isabetta was twenty-six.'

'And you were just twenty-three.' She took
his hand, her eyes sad. 'Oh, Pietro… It is you
I feel the most sorry for.'

Chapter Twenty

'*Buongiorno!*'

He seemed to sense her watching him from the shade of the porch across the courtyard and gestured for her to come with him before she could dart back inside. But, caught red-handed, she had no choice. While he would always have her heart, he was worming his way back into her affections and she seemed powerless to stop it. Although this time around, it was his honesty rather than his charm which drew her.

After his frank answers to her questions, Pietro now seemed keen to talk about his past. She had spent hours at his bedside just talking. About their spouses, their lives, the formative experiences which shaped them, their hopes and dreams for the future, her idea for a gallery and the million other things that filled a lifetime. When they weren't talking, he insisted she make the most of her last precious days in Rome. Pietro seemed content to live vicariously through her, suggesting obscure new places to visit and then eagerly awaiting her opinions on the treasures he had directed her to find. She had enjoyed those conversations, looked forward to them even, perhaps more than she should as they reminded her of all the reasons beyond the physical why she had initially been drawn to him. Pietro was easy to talk to, their interests, humour and thoughts often so synchronised she couldn't help herself from becoming his friend again. However, now she felt she knew him, really knew him, inexplicably she only loved him more. Which hurt.

'What are your plans today, *cara*?'

'Packing.' Her overbright smile felt forced. 'I have been putting it off for too long and we leave tomorrow. After excessive procrastination, Alexandra has forbidden me to leave the *palazzo* today till it's done.'

His returning smile was equally as forced. They were both putting a brave face on things in their own over-polite way. Hardly a surprise when the ending was unsatisfactory for both of them, but both had to follow the path which was right for them—even if it made them initially unhappy.

It was as impossible to hate him as it was not to love him and her heart refused to be swayed or hurt at the way things had gone. Neither of them ever mentioned their affair, preferring to pretend it hadn't happened rather than bring the hovering veil of awkwardness back down around them. With just under two days left of one another's company, it seemed churlish and unnecessary to spoil things.

And what would be the point anyway? She wanted all of him, for ever, and the best he had offered out of desperation was to continue their affair on the infrequent occasions he visited London.

She was coming to understand why he ruthlessly guarded his heart. Six dreadful years trapped in a horrendous marriage was surely enough to put anyone off marriage for life. Pietro was a noble man who refused to make promises he didn't mean. He never had and she admired that about him. He was also finally facing up to his past and coming to terms with it—although he was a long way off healed because Isabetta had left deep scars.

She had considered telling him she would wait for him, wait for him to be ready for more because she was. But if her intense and painful reaction to Ida Wayfair and the French trollop was any gauge, she would go mad with wondering what he was up to in the interim. She was not built for affairs. She had failed miserably in keeping her body and her heart separate. Once her heart had become engaged, anything less than for ever was unsatisfactory. Making do. Therefore, it was all or nothing. No half-measures, no loose arrangements, no other lovers. No interminable waiting when no promises and no declarations had been made.

Therefore, the clean break they had originally agreed upon when she left Rome was really the only course forward and perhaps, with time, her heart would heal again as it had finally after losing Henry. However, at least now they were friends again, she would always be able to look back at her time with Pietro fondly. She wouldn't regret him. Thanks to him she was no longer lost. That pesky crossroads was behind her and a potential new path beckoned.

'With the right incentive, how quickly can you get it done?'

'Now there is a leading question. Why?'

'Because I want to take you somewhere special.' The forced smile gave way to a dazzling one filled with mischief.

'In that case, it will take all day as you are under doctor's orders not to leave the *palazzo* either. You know that, Pietro. Total rest and recuperation.'

After a couple of days of complete bed rest, the physician declared him well enough to convalesce downstairs and prescribed him plenty of fresh air. Hence he was now sat in the courtyard, reading the message which had just been delivered and looking more like his old self than the sick man he had been days before. As his health improved, so too did his mood. Which meant he veered between being a horrendous patient with no tolerance for anything and a supremely reluctant one who required constant entertaining.

'Even if the place I want to take you is not taxing at all because I can sit down for the duration? Even though I have arranged the carriage already and it will be here in an hour? And...' he waved the note which had arrived a few minutes beforehand '...even if it is so special, so secret, so difficult to get into, few in Rome ever get to see it?'

'Pietro...?' Lilian put her hands on her hips and shook her head. 'You are supposed to be resting.'

'Very well.' He folded the note and slipped it in a pocket. 'I shall apologise to the Cardinal for his vociferous petition of my behalf and tell him Mrs Fairclough no longer wishes to see the Archivio Segreto Vaticano…'

'The Vatican Archives?'

'*Sì…*' He grinned, clearly very pleased with himself.

'You have permission to take *me* into the Vatican Archives?'

'I do! But, alas, only to view the collection pertaining to Michelangelo. Not even the Duca della Torizia is allowed free rein in the entire Archives. The Vatican is very protective… It took a great deal to persuade them to allow a non-Catholic woman into the building…but if you have to pack and cannot…'

'Oh, my goodness!' Lilian giggled like a little girl, giddy with sudden excitement and more than a little incredulous. 'Give me an hour!'

'An hour. No more. And do not tell Carlotta!' He was laughing as she dashed away at speed. 'She will only chain me to the bed again and they will not allow you in without me.'

The packing, the painful chore she had been putting off because it all seemed too final, was done in record time because Lilian did something she never did in her haste to get in the carriage—she delegated. In fact, once she had rallied three willing maids and directed them to the items she needed left out, there was nothing left for her to do than get ready for her outing. She picked a conservative dress with long sleeves and a high neck, rationalising that she couldn't be too conservative and wondering if the pale green colour was indeed too flashy for such a profoundly religious place, despite having nothing plainer in her new, fashionable wardrobe. In honour of the occasion, she also put on gloves and a sensible hat, two things she had not bothered with once in all her time in Rome, and secured her hair in the same sort of austere and tight chignon as she used to wear at the Foundation.

The Lilian who stared back at her in the mirror looked not dissimilar to the old Lilian—except she wasn't the old Lilian any more. This place and that man had changed her. She no longer felt a spare wheel whose life was done and would return home no longer lost and feeling superfluous, but imbued with fresh ambition and a zest for life which had been missing for a decade. Her old passion—art—had become her new passion. The Foundation was in her past, an intrinsic part of who she was, but not everything any longer. She had fallen in lust, then love, then had her heart broken. Three things she had never expected to happen in a million years. Yet in doing that, she had finally let Henry go. The time for grieving was over and it was time to live again. For ten years, she had been frozen in a bubble—existing, doing what was right for everyone but herself, but not living. For several weeks now she had lived a whole different lifetime and wanted more of the same. And whatever life threw at her, she was determined to embrace it. Just as today, she was going to grasp the opportunity to visit the Archives.

Without telling either Alexandra, busy in the bedchamber next door, or Carlotta, who was reading in the *salotto*, she dashed back into the courtyard just as the carriage was pulling into it, grinning from ear to ear. They were escaping. Running away together to have an adventure. How positively marvellous and entirely frivolous was that?

Pietro had just helped her in when they heard his sister shout, 'What the hell do you think you are doing?'

He blew her a cheeky kiss, then threw himself in next to Lilian, both of them laughing as the carriage lurched away at speed before his sister could stop them and the big gates closed securely behind them.

* * *

The journey alone took almost an hour because this late in the morning the streets were alive and filled with people. While he told her about the Archives, she tried not to be too excited as part of her believed they would be turned away at the door as soon as the guards at the Vatican took one look at her—yet miraculously they didn't. They were escorted to the library, and then through the long library and to a heavy locked door under an arch. A Swiss Guard scrutinised Pietro's letter for a full minute before the door was unlocked and they were shown into an anteroom containing a dark table and several sturdy chairs. Where they waited. And waited.

Eventually, three priests came in, carrying huge cream files emblazoned with the symbol of the Papal crossed keys and one slim, but large, wooden box. They spoke directly to Pietro as if she did not exist, the Italian so quick she could scarce make out a single word. Then they left them, leaving a guard outside the open door to keep an eye on them.

'We have just two hours, *cara*…so we had best get started.'

As she knew he had seen this before, she allowed him to choose the wooden box first and gasped as she saw the piles of sketches within it, instantly recognising the one on the top as part of one of the preliminary drawings for the ceiling of the Sistine Chapel. Together, they marvelled at each sketch—some very basic in the form of lines and circles to map out the shape of a composition, some close-up detail of something recognisable, others entire miniature replicas of his work here at the Vatican. Seeing them, so many things drawn by his hand at close quarters was magical.

Pietro caught her frowning at one sketch of the bottom half of a man seated, particularly curious because as well as the skin and muscle, the artist had also sketched in detail the bones beneath the skin. 'Like Da Vinci before him, Michelangelo had watched the dissection of many bodies, both human and animal, to see what lay beneath the skin. Some say he performed numerous dissections himself, too. That is why his anatomical details are so accurate in all his paintings and sculptures. He knew the shape of every muscle, the position of every bone. Knew how the skin would sit over them.'

'I thought the church had banned dissection?'

'For centuries beforehand that was certainly

the case…however, Pope Sixtus IV—the same Pope who coincidentally commissioned the ceiling of the Sistine Chapel—issued a Papal Bull which allowed the corpses of those executed to be donated to physicians and *artists* to dissect with impunity as the condemned were damned for all eternity anyway.' He smiled at her horrified face. 'Although I suspect it was no coincidence he issued this edict…he wanted the ceiling, and all the other art he commissioned for the Vatican, to be perfect after all.'

'It is hard to imagine the hand which created this also hacked up bodies.'

'I doubt he hacked, *cara*…and this was another time, remember. The Renaissance was all about challenging old thinking and learning new things. People still do it now. For medical science to march forward, physicians need to cut up someone. And it is not as if they could feel it…they *were* dead.'

'I see you have made your peace with it.'

'Of course. It was for art, Lilian! I would forgive almost anything for art.'

With all the sketches laid out on the table, they went through his papers. Those written in Latin she could read well enough. Or at least as well as her schoolroom Latin would allow her. Pietro could fill in any gaps as he apparently read Latin as well as he read and spoke English. Those written in old Italian were another matter entirely and she gave up trying, happy to allow him to read and translate them in his lovely, deep, accentuated voice, finding it fascinating to listen to Michelangelo's letters because within them she could hear his voice, if not the actual sound of it, but his views and ideas.

She wasn't surprised to learn the man was a perfectionist who frequently fought his own corner in his complaints—especially those involving the escalating cost of his masterpieces. In his later missives, when he had practically given up painting in favour of architecture, he complained about the Pope's penny pinching. In one, he even went as far as telling the office off for failing to pay the guards at St Peter's for three months, warning the Pope they would walk unless he paid them immediately.

Il divino had been a closet revolutionary at heart, an intriguing little detail they both enjoyed immensely.

When the sour-faced priests returned to reclaim their treasures, there was still an entire folder they hadn't opened, but despite all Pietro's cajoling, they flatly refused to allow them as much as a minute more.

It didn't matter.

Those two hours had been a privilege. A dream come true. One she doubted she would forget until her dying day. As he helped her back into the carriage, she couldn't help beaming at him. 'Thank you. That was wonderful.' She adored she had got to share it with him.

'I wanted to do something special for you...' His face clouded. 'To go some way towards making amends for hurting you...and to thank you for everything you have done for me. I wanted us to part as friends.'

'We are friends, Pietro.' He smiled, looking tired as he settled back in the seat, reminding her he was nowhere near fully recovered and was supposed to be resting. 'We should get you home... I don't want to overtax you so soon after...'

'Not yet. Spare me a few hours more, *cara*.' His big hand engulfed hers and tugged it into his lap. A simple touch which, as always, played havoc with her pulse. 'Just a few more hours...please? I am not ready to say goodbye to you yet. Not when the day is still young and the sun is shining. You can see I feel better... I feel better and I am all done with playing the invalid. I have decided it doesn't suit me.'

'It really doesn't. You are the worst patient I

have ever encountered.' Something, bizarrely, she also rather liked about him. What a hopeless fool she truly was if she even loved his faults.

'Then you agree—I am better out than driving you all mad with my unreasonable behaviour. In many ways, you are performing an act of charity on my household by sparing them my presence this afternoon. Besides, we have the carriage already. Why don't we tour the sights one last time from the comfort of it? I cannot overtax myself sat in here.'

Lilian stared down at where their fingers were now intertwined and nodded. She wasn't ready to say goodbye to him either. Not when they still had all day. And perhaps, one sinfully selfish last night. Although there was no perhaps about it. She had already decided she wanted that night.

Chapter Twenty-One

'I never tire of this view.'

Her gaze seemed fixed on the foamy chaos of the river rapids, her expression wistful. She had indulged him all afternoon, seemingly content to see it all again. The Colosseum, the ancient ruins, the Pantheon, the Fontana di Trevi and finally, as they watched the sun go down for the last time together, even the Ponte Rotto—the place where it had all started. The place where he had discovered he loved to talk to her and simply be with her. That they had so much in common. That he could be more honest with her than he ever had with anyone. Lilian was one for complete honesty. He owed her one last piece.

'I need to explain to you about the hill…'

'You really don't.' She stared resolutely at the broken bridge, her fingers suddenly tense beneath his. 'We made no promises, Pietro. And it was unreasonable of me to expect you had no past. After Isabetta, those six years of celibacy, I appreciate that...' He placed his finger over her lips and stared deeply into her eyes.

'I have spent a quarter of a century avoiding complications, *cara*, fiercely guarding my independence and my freedom with rigid rules I never broke. Not once. But when you came along, things got complicated very quickly regardless.' He could not resist tracing the pad of his finger over her cheek, consigning the shape and feel of it to memory. 'I broke so many of my rules with you, Lilian. And gladly. Allowed you to know more of me than anyone before and...the pathetic truth is I panicked. I took you to the hill to prove to myself ours was just another affair...when it was not just another affair. Not from the moment I first met you last winter or from the second I collided with you searching for your soap in my hallway. You were always special, Lilian. Unique. I knew it then as I know it now. Yet I tried to prove to myself otherwise, tried to deny the effect you had on my emotions and for that I am truly sorry. If it is any consolation, while the sentiment that day was well worn and practised, with you it was unique and beautiful. When I said I had never slept under the stars I meant it. Nor had I ever watched the sunset or the sunrise with another and never once in all our time together did I ever think of any other woman when I was with you. On the hill…in my bed. In fact, you are the only woman I ever allowed myself to make love to in my house. The only woman I have ever allowed in my bedchamber and the only one I have ever woken next to. I have never shared a single morning with any other woman except you, Lilian…and I never will.'

He watched unfathomable emotions dance across her features. 'Those were unbreakable rules before you came into my life. Nor have I ever allowed myself to become so accustomed to another. Nobody else knows me like you. Certainly nobody else knows the entire truth about my marriage or my feelings or my fears. I have confided things to you I have never told a living soul. This time with you has changed me. Our love affair has changed me. With you I embraced all the complications and allowed myself to feel emotions which I normally run from. Yet all that, while terrifying and confusing, has enriched what we have shared. I beg of you not to regret our night under the stars because I never will. That wonderful night was the best of my life. And before you think it was all about my lust—I can assure you nothing can be further from the truth.' Alien and frightening words hovered in his throat. Words of commitment and feelings. He swallowed past them. 'You are the first woman I have wanted to make love to with my heart as well as my body, Lilian.'

It was as much of a declaration as he was comfortable with, although he was coming to suspect his feelings for her had more to do with deep affection than lust. A petrifying state of affairs. 'In fact, you have spoiled me for all women now, *cara*. I shall miss you when you are gone.'

'And I shall miss you.' Something had made the light dim in her eyes and he mourned it even though he did not know what it might have meant. This couldn't be the end. He couldn't bear it.

'I have to be in London in July… I could help you set up your little gallery…' He was thinking out loud, scrabbling for some hope. 'You could show me your favourite sights in your city…' This time it was she who placed her finger over his lips, her eyes sad and awash with unshed tears.

'No, Pietro. You promised never to seek me out when I return home and for the sake of my sanity… I beg you not to do so. As much as it hurts, as much as I am tempted, I really do not have the constitution for affairs—even with you. I cannot play games. I cannot keep secrets. I cannot separate my heart from my body. It plays on my mind…too much and that makes me miserable.' Miserable? He made her miserable? 'I need a clean break in order to move forward—and so do you. Goodbye *must* mean goodbye. We promised…'

He wanted to argue, wanted to suddenly make promises of the sort he had vehemently sworn against, but she didn't give him the opportunity. Instead, she kissed him. And because he suddenly found his own eyes awash with tears, he kissed her back, cursing fate for throwing her in his path and making him question everything he believed.

It wasn't a long kiss or a particularly passionate one by their usual standards. But it was the most heartfelt and poignant interaction with another human being he had experienced in his life. He poured all of himself into it, hoping she could feel his regret and indecision. Hoping she would offer some hope. A bargain. Even a demand for more. Anything which might force him to agree to the things his heart kept screaming for.

But of course she didn't. She simply sighed and held his hand, neither of them saying a single word on the short journey home.

He was staring at his bedchamber ceiling, flat on his back on his mattress, when the clock in the hallway chimed midnight. Tonight he accepted he would not sleep. How could he when both his body and his heart yearned for the woman in the room next door? The one who had been subdued throughout dinner and who had simply smiled sadly at him when she bade him goodnight. The one who wanted a clean break and a final goodbye when she sailed away tomorrow. Even the wretched pain of the shingles rash hurt less than the awful knot in his stomach and ache in his chest.

He already knew it would take more than a week to heal from this sickness. Hoped it would be weeks, suspected it would be months and dreaded the prospect of years lamenting her loss. Perhaps he should go to her now and tell her that? Beg her to let him visit her in London in the summer to see if the unfamiliar feelings he felt so keenly were not transient. That

he would still feel as intensely in two months...
twenty months...a thousand.

For ever.

It was that which terrified him. After just six
weeks, albeit the best weeks of his life, was he
ready to risk for ever?

The door clicked open and suddenly there
she was, rendering further contemplation impossible because his breath caught in his throat
at her beauty. Bathed in the soft light of the
hallway, hair loose and her lush body wrapped
tightly in her silk robe, she closed the door and
walked towards his bed. Pietro sat, tried to say
the millions of things he was feeling, but all of
them dried in his throat because her fingers had
found the knot in her belt. Undid it. Then the
robe cascaded from her shoulders and pooled
to the floor around her feet.

'A wise man once told me all affairs deserve a proper goodbye.' The moonlight cast
shadows on her nakedness, illuminating her
skin in an ethereal glow. 'Are you still too sick
to say goodbye to me properly, Pietro?' Now
inches from his stunned face, she reached out
her hand, brushed her fingers through his hair,
then along his jaw.

'I am as fit as a fiddle.' He tried to mimic
her accent, his eyes drinking in the sight of her.

'That is good news…' Her warm breath whispered across his lips a second before she touched her mouth to his, her kiss this time most definitely carnal. She took both his hands and brought them to her breasts as she pushed him backwards on to the pillow, then broke their contact to slowly drag the sheet from him, her eyes caressing his naked body from top to bottom before finally returning to settle on his arousal. 'Were you waiting for me?'

'I was hoping.' Not even the real wall between their rooms or the invisible wall of heartbreak had ever stopped him from wanting her. 'Praying…'

Her hand traced the shape of his chest. 'Then your prayers have been answered.' She smoothed her palm across the now taut muscles of his abdomen until her fingers grazed the root of his hardness. 'What would you like me to do to you?'

'Touch me.' She smiled and with excruciating gentleness ran the pad of her index finger along the length of him, her gaze locking on his as he sucked in a sharp breath as she circled the tip before his eyes closed. She kissed him then, wrapping her hand around him as he sighed into her mouth. He lay passive as she caressed him, revelling at the feel of her lips trailing down his body and then moaning when he watched her kiss him there, her eyes locked on his as she quickly took him to the edge.

Then, simply to torture him she stopped, arranging herself to sit astride him, cruelly denying his insistent manhood anywhere near where it desperately wanted to be. He didn't mind. If he could make the now last for ever he would happily exist here in this moment with her for all eternity. Even if it killed him. Something which was entirely possible.

She offered him her breasts and he gratefully received them, sucking her sensitive nipples into his mouth and tormenting her this time with his tongue and his teeth until he felt her hips writhing against his stomach. Both of them loving the anticipation and keen to stretch the agonising ecstasy out for as long as possible.

With the hooded eyes of a true temptress, she rolled off him, allowing her legs to fall open in blatant invitation. 'Kiss me now.' He loved her sensuality. Loved the fact she revelled in their lovemaking as much as he and wasn't timid about taking her pleasure. And simply to torture them both, he took his time exploring her body everywhere with his mouth before he brought it to the place she most wanted it to be.

He knew her body so well, instinctively, yet never tired of it. Knew if he kissed her a certain way, she would explode almost instantly in a euphoric cry. Knew, too, if he loved her slowly, everywhere, her passion would be slow to build and when it did, she would be a writhing, wanton puddle of nerve endings and her eventual climax would render her boneless for hours. Then she would curl up in his arms smiling, her hand resting over his heart, and fall asleep. He wanted that tonight. The truth of intimacy. To hold her and touch her and kiss her. Thoroughly worship her. Wanted them to part on that memory. Wondering that if they did, then perhaps she would be more open to his visiting her in London. Something he was fairly sure he was going to do anyway and be damned. Because tonight could not be goodbye. He wouldn't allow it.

As she called his name and shuddered beneath him, he moved his big body to cover hers, join with hers, but at the last moment she turned him on his back. Instead of him slowly inching inside her body, she lowered herself on him as if they had all the time in the world and tilted her pale hips to receive him fully. Then, neck arched, breasts thrusting proudly, she undulated her body gently to pleasure them both.

Her lovely eyes locked on his as she watched the devastating effect it had on him.

Pietro had never experienced anything like it. Perhaps because her presence here was so unexpected. She had come when all the pain was raw, his confused emotions too close to the surface, and because of that, the usual guards he kept around his heart weren't there and for once, his pragmatic and wary head wasn't screaming at him to reinstate them. Instead he wanted the cosy and intensely personal intimacy with her tonight, offering himself stripped bare and vulnerable—yet he didn't feel vulnerable.

He felt humbled and grateful as well as completely floored all at the same time. All the passion, all the excitement and building anticipation was the same—yet more intensely personal and so much better for it. Bodies, heads and hearts intertwined and he felt adored. He wanted to show exactly how he felt. Honouring her with his body as the ancient wedding vow dictated. Odd that he had never fully understood exactly what that had meant before tonight. But this was an homage. A pilgrimage. A benediction. As necessary as breathing and as beautiful as a sunrise.

Because he loved her.

Suddenly he had to say it.

'Ti amo...'

Part of him—the fearful part—hoped she didn't understand. The other part, the part that never wanted to let her go, wanted to hear it back.

He felt the silken walls of her body convulse around him, her eyes on his. Her hands in his hair. The warm comfort of the emotional bonds which bound them, bonds which felt nothing like the oppressive chains of his marriage.

'Ti amo tanto...'

Head thrown back, she moaned her pleasure and something odd happened. Something peculiar. As his passion exploded in the bright white light of a thousand stars and before he plunged headlong with her into oblivion, he realised exactly what it was he wanted. What he had always striven for. The root cause of all his restlessness and the source of his dissatisfaction. The thing which had always been missing from his life was her. And he wasn't frightened any longer.

'Voglio invecchiare con te!'

He wanted to grow old with her.

Chapter Twenty-Two

When Alexandra had received the message informing them their sailing had been brought forward to catch the afternoon tide as they had been dressing for dinner, Lilian had sworn her cousin to secrecy, arguing it would only spoil their last meal in Rome if they told their hosts they would be leaving first thing rather than in the afternoon as planned. She lamented how she hated long, drawn-out goodbyes and that it would be better if they did it in the morning. Less messy, less upsetting and creating less upheaval for their generous hosts who would be able to spend the rest of the day at their leisure once they were gone.

Using his health as leverage, she even went as far as saying their trip to the Vatican had worn Pietro out and the last thing she wanted was for him to jeopardise his recovery by his insisting on taking the dreadful road to Civitavecchia with them to wave them off, only to have to spend further hours on it on the trip back. He was such a stubborn and proud man, after all, not at all comfortable with his current weakness, so really they were doing him a service.

Lilian must have been convincing because Alexandra eventually agreed. After all, what difference did a few hours make when the bulk of their luggage was already with the grooms ready to be loaded? And as poor Pietro was still not over his bout of illness, it was a kinder way to assuage his noble male pride then attempt to argue with him as he was about to climb in the carriage. Carlotta wouldn't mind. Not when she was spending the entire summer at Alexandra's country estate as she did every year now she was widowed, to escape the oppressive Roman heat.

Like the perfect hand of cards, her lies worked a treat, when the truth was, for the sake of her own sanity, Lilian needed to escape. She wasn't brave enough to say goodbye to his face. Did not trust herself not to cry and by default make him feel beholden to her. People had to follow their own path. Listen to their own heart. If the calls from his weren't loud enough, then that was that.

After they had made love and he had fallen into the exhausted sleep of a man fully satisfied, she had tiptoed out. She would not wake him before leaving because she had written him a letter. A surprisingly calm and objective missive considering she had penned it with tears streaming down her face, thanking him for everything, wishing him well and acknowledging she would never forget him despite goodbye most definitely meaning goodbye—knowing it wouldn't take much to get her to agree to carry on their affair indefinitely if he asked again.

It was better this way.

That was the mantra she had repeated over and over as the tears failed to stop through the night. With no parting words, neither of them would feel compelled to say things they didn't mean or accept things they didn't want.

As soon as the last trunk was loaded, she had pretended to wake Pietro while Alexandra woke his sister, then joined her cousin in Carlotta's bedchamber to kiss her goodbye, citing his tiredness from the day before as his excuse for his absence and passing on his good wishes to her companion, and they set off.

They had left Rome far behind by the time the sun came up and with each passing mile she tried not to picture his face as he reached across the mattress to snuggle against her and realised she wasn't there. She hoped he wouldn't rush to get downstairs or discover her letter on his washstand too soon. As far as he was concerned, her carriage would leave at noon and by the time he realised otherwise she would be long gone, walking up the gangplank and on the cusp of setting sail.

Unless he came after her and intercepted her. In which case, she would pathetically fall into his arms and likely agree to whatever he wanted. Which wasn't at all what she wanted. Not that she had told him explicitly what she wanted. She had hinted and he had been set on simply continuing their affair. But it was too late for regrets now. Again, it was probably better this way. No marriage should begin solely because the bride had pressured the husband into it. Pietro had been a reluctant bridegroom before and after Henry, there was no way she was prepared to settle for significantly less than the open and honest union they had shared.

'I still think it was awfully rude of him not to have said goodbye.' Alexandra had alternated between frowning and sighing since they had left the *palazzo*. 'I know he was besotted with you—but we have been friends for years. It is most unlike him. Most impolite. Something I shall be sure to tell him when he comes to stay in the summer.'

Lilian said nothing.

'Are you looking forward to his visit in the summer?'

'I won't be seeing him.'

'Why ever not?' Although she had not confided in Alexandra that she had indulged in an affair, Lilian knew she suspected. How could she not? With hindsight, they hadn't been that discreet. 'I thought the pair of you would have made plans. I was rather looking forward to another wedding…'

'If that is what all your matchmaking was intended for, then I am afraid it was in vain. Pietro never had plans to walk up the aisle again.'

'Then he never should have dallied with you, the scoundrel! I am outraged on your behalf.'

'Don't be. I knew it and accepted it. He has always made that perfectly clear from the outset.'

'All men think that at the outset, dearest. If we all took heed of what they said at the outset of anything, nothing in this world would ever get done.' She shook her head, exasperated. 'It is a crying shame you are not younger, Lilian. There is nothing like the risk of pregnancy to speed up a wedding.'

'For the tenth time, there will be no wedding! And I will thank you to keep your opinions on the matter silent once we get home. I do not want the children to know I...' it was on the tip of her tongue to say *I fell in love* '...had a scandalous affair in Rome.'

'Heaven forbid they should discover their mother is not a saint or serves any other purpose beyond selflessly serving others.' Alexandra harrumphed loudly. 'Although I dare say your girls would have something to say on the matter.'

'I absolutely forbid you to tell the girls!'

'Why? Because you know Lottie and Millie will only encourage you to listen to your heart? Or do you stupidly believe they expect you to grieve for their father every day until they lower your shrivelled old bones into the ground? They are both grown women. They both have *needs*...'

'Oh, for goodness sake, not this again! I

have no desire to contemplate the *needs* of my daughters any more than I dare say they would want to consider mine! When I am home, I do not want to hear Pietro's name as much as mentioned! Do you hear me?' Just saying it left her bereft and weepy. She still felt like a part of her had been cut away and the thought of never seeing him again cut like a blade. 'I want to carry on as if he never existed. What happens in Rome...'

'Oh, Lilian...' It was the sudden sympathy that did it, unleashing all the ugly, noisy, hopeless tears she had held in all morning. 'You fell in love with him, didn't you?'

Her nose now engulfed by her cousin's bosom, Lilian nodded. 'I tried not to. Really, I did. But I am not made for affairs it turns out.'

'Your heart is too big.'

'It is! And now it's broken. It's been broken since the Wayfair ball and I can't seem to stop it hurting.' She took the proffered handkerchief wafting in front of her face and cried into it noisily. 'What sort of an idiot falls in love with a man who is so adamantly opposed to emotional complications he has spent his entire life avoiding them?'

'I still cannot believe he wanted to sever all ties.'

'I severed them. I had to! The only future he ever saw for us was to pick up the affair where we left off whenever he travelled to London... But what am I supposed to do for the rest of the time? I would rather have none of him than spend my life pining away for his next visit and wondering whose sheets he is warming in the interim.'

'Are you certain he doesn't want more?'

'Quite. He reiterated his proposition just yesterday afternoon. He never asked me to stay. Never asked me to wait. Never even promised fidelity in the meantime—just that he would miss me but would be in London in July...two whole months away!'

'The scoundrel!'

'He's not a scoundrel.' That was perhaps the hardest part. 'He is honourable and decent and has a very good reason never to be tied down again.' Her words came out in a hiccupping staccato in between sobs. 'This really isn't Pietro's fault. It's all mine. I thought I could cope with an affair, but I am just not made for affairs.'

'There, there, dearest...'

'What am I going to do?'

'Cry. Curl into a ball. Let it all out. Then when there are no tears left, you will do what all good women have done for centuries. You strap on your brave face and move onwards and upwards.' Alexandra stroked her hair. 'And per-haps…given time…you will allow yourself to love someone new. Your heart really is too big to be alone for ever, dearest. There are more fish in the sea than your stupid, near-sighted and stubborn Italian.'

'I don't want any other fish.'

'You will, Lilian. Now that you have dipped your toe in the water. Time heals all wounds.'

'It took me ten years to get over Henry. I cannot bear the thought of spending ten years grieving for Pietro.' Who would probably be wondering exactly where she was right about now.

'All the more reason to replace him swiftly.' A terrifying prospect which felt entirely all wrong. 'As soon as we get back to town, I shall redouble my efforts to find you a suitable man. I am only sorry I actively thrust you in front of that one! I have a good mind to ride back to Rome and give him a piece of my mind.'

'I just want to go home, Alexandra. And please, I beg of you, no more matchmaking.' There was not a chance in hell she would ever dip her toe in those dangerous, murky waters again.

* * *

The house was oddly quiet when he awoke, the space beside him in bed stone cold. Yet initially, he wasn't unduly worried as he was too preoccupied with all he suddenly had to do to give it much thought.

He was in love.

That was a momentous thing in itself. Huge, in fact. Entirely unprecedented. And while it panicked him, it didn't suffocate him as he had always feared it might. It did not feel like the prison of his marriage. Lilian wasn't Isabetta.

Lilian was selfless and inquisitive. Generous of heart. She cared about people and things. Looked after them—even when they didn't deserve it. Just as she had him. She was passionate and alluring. Which certainly helped sweeten the pot, but it wasn't so much that which drew him as her essence. She was, for want of a better word, his soulmate. The other half of him which had always been missing. His lover and his friend and he had never enjoyed a better example of either.

With fresh clarity brought about by both acknowledging and accepting his feelings, he had fallen asleep properly pondering her reasons for wanting a clean break.

She wanted it for her sanity…because she could not separate her heart from her body. Which suggested her heart was having feelings which extended beyond the physical. That it was engaged. That she cared deeply. He hoped with all he had her feelings mirrored his. The evidence certainly pointed in that direction. Why would she have been so devastated about his past lovers if she only wanted him for passion? She had admitted leaving him would hurt and that she was tempted to agree to his proposition they continue the affair, but she could not play games or keep secrets.

Honesty again. Lilian sought that above all else.

So he would be honest and face his fears. If Lilian was absolutely nothing like Isabetta, it stood to reason marriage to her would be the complete opposite, too. Love would conquer all, just as she said it could. He had to believe that and trust it.

He would need to procure a ring, of course. The Venturi jewels had disappeared long before their paintings, so he had no heirloom to put on her finger. Buying new also did not sit right, not when Lilian loved the stories behind the objects more than the objects themselves. It would have to be an antique. Something as special and unique as she was, and things like that did not grow on trees. That meant she would have to wait for the ring, but a piece of jewellery shouldn't be the sole reason he delayed his proposal. Especially with her leaving today.

Which meant he really did have a great deal to do before he climbed in the carriage beside her. Propose. Pack. Make all the urgent preparations to ensure his staff were able to continue in his unanticipated absence. And all that was assuming there was even space for him on the ship she was booked on. He would cross that bridge when he came to it, but it was imperative he returned with her to England to meet her family and talk to her son. As the head of the Fairclough family, correct protocol dictated he ask the fellow for his mother's hand even if the asking was just a formality at their age.

So much to do and none of which he could do lying on his back. He grinned and threw off the covers, excited now instead of nervous, and padded to his dressing room, rubbing the bristles on his chin. A shave was the first order of the day. He couldn't propose looking unkempt. He was about to splash water into the bowl when he saw the letter. Read it. Felt the rage burn, then kicked his washstand over.

Goodbye. I'll never forget you.

So much for her belief that love could conquer all. The blasted woman was sending him mad!

Chapter Twenty-Three

'Is everything all right, Mama? Only you do not seem quite yourself.'

Lottie peered at her through her spectacles over the rim of her teacup, causing Millie and Mary to scrutinise her, too. The ladies were all gathered in one parlour while the men pored over Silas's plans to extend his American railway line in the other. It felt odd, them all being on top of one another again in the small confines of her modest house—especially as she had apparently become much too used to rattling around a huge *palazzo*.

'Still a little fatigued, perhaps, from the long journey, but otherwise quite well.' She smiled before hiding behind her own teacup, just in case they probed further. Because she wasn't all right. She was broken and lost all over again. Losing Pietro was exactly like losing Henry. It cut that deep. Hurt that badly. Felt that desolate.

She had thought home would soothe her, when instead it only served to heighten her misery. She was surrounded by young couples in love. Contented pairs while she was all alone. The blue skies of Rome were now replaced with the slate-grey skies of London. As if in sympathy with her mood, the rain had fallen relentlessly since her first glimpse of the white cliffs of Dover a week ago, pummelling the railway carriage mercilessly all the way home and the windowpanes of her bedchamber every night since as sleep evaded her.

'Aunt Alexandra said you had a brutal crossing. Said she had never been so seasick.' Her daughter-in-law was unconsciously rubbing her belly, her pregnancy showing now after the three months Lilian had been gone. 'I am so relieved Silas and I shan't be returning to America until after the baby is born. I cannot recall such a dismal month in all my life. It feels more like November out there.'

Oh, how Lilian hated the winter!

'I am just so bored with being stuck inside.' Always the most restless of her daughters, Lottie heaved a dramatic sigh. 'I feel as if I haven't had an ounce of fresh air in days.'

'Me either.' Her eldest, Millie, was more pragmatic. 'But looking at it positively—at least we are altogether again. Now that we are all married and spread out, we must solemnly promise to gather together at least once a year. As much as I love my new life in the country, I miss this. The comforting familiarity of home.'

That familiarity should have comforted Lilian, but didn't. She had attempted to slot back into her old life within hours of her homecoming, busying herself to avoid wallowing in the self-pity which had consumed her every single interminable day for the entire long and seemingly never-ending journey back across the Continent. She had visited the Foundation to catch up on things and had taught four embroidery lessons in the week since. But now that Lottie and Jasper were at the helm, there really wasn't much else for her to do and she didn't want to interfere. The tasks she had regularly done before Italy—like the bookkeeping or the food ordering—had been regularly done by someone else now for three whole months, reminding her she wasn't indispensable.

That realisation made her torture herself by wondering if he had already replaced her, too. Or was he miserable? Full of regret?

And why was she so intent on punishing herself by wondering?

If he'd had felt the same intensity of emotion as she, he would have come after her. Been hours behind her. A day at most. But three weeks on from that fateful last day, there had been nothing and she needed to accept that. Goodbye had meant goodbye. Her express stipulation. She was unreasonably furious at him for honouring her wishes.

Twice, she had given herself a stern talking to and attempted to put pen to paper to work out some plans for her gallery idea and twice nothing at all had been achieved. Then she had given up, realising she was still grieving and acknowledging she probably needed to do that thoroughly before she attempted to move forward. Except grieving when you were trying to pretend to be perfectly content with life for the sake of your family was proving to be a challenge. One which left her feeling exhausted as well as heartbroken and lonely beyond belief. Especially now that Alexandra had gone home, too, and she had nobody to confide in. A shock to her system when she had had a soulmate again for just six much-too-quick weeks and the void he had left in her heart was proving impossible to fill and impossible to ignore. It hurt too much.

'Will you excuse me for a minute?' To all intents and purposes, she now visited the retiring room a great deal, too, when in reality she had used it as an excuse to flee each and every time the tears threatened. But as she had only just used that excuse, she had to think of another lie in case one of her daughters worried about the state of her bladder and summoned the physician.

'I must fetch a shawl. I am a little chilly.' Impossible when the fire was roaring in the grate despite the fact that spring was knocking on summer's door. 'I think my body has become too acclimatised to the heat of Rome.' And the comforting warmth of Pietro beside her. 'As Mary said, it feels more like November...' Embellishing the lie probably made it less convincing, but with the sting of imminent tears pricking her eyes, it was all she could think of.

Lilian walked sedately from the cosy parlour and up the narrow staircase to her bedchamber, biting her lip to hold back the emotion. Only once she was inside it and the door firmly closed did she go to her wardrobe and reach for the ornate, flat, wooden box from the top of it and lay it lovingly on the mattress. She ran her fingers over the intricate Italian marquetry top before unclipping the latch and reverently opening the lid. A bit of theatre to build the anticipation…exactly like Pietro would do. Then she simply gazed at the sketch and his note as the tears fell.

To remember me by…

Not that she needed a Michelangelo to remember him.

Pietro was imprinted on her heart as indelibly as Henry was. Yet this selfless and overly generous parting gift was bittersweet. He hadn't mentioned it on their last night together—doubtless because he knew she would never accept it—and instead she had found it wrapped in a nightgown in her trunk on her first night of travel, the shores of Italy conveniently left behind. She had no way of returning it, knowing full well she would never entrust something as precious and priceless to a faceless messenger and knowing she would never return.

Finding it had cut deep as there was no mistaking what it was. His final goodbye to her and the final nail in any foolish hopes she might have he intended to come after her. Until that precise moment, and without her consent, a tiny part of her heart had secretly held out hope for a miracle. Now she knew there would be no miracle.

Goodbye really did mean goodbye.

Yet the precious gift also brought him closer. When she stared at it she could hear his voice as clearly as if he were whispering in her ear in bed. Each time she gazed upon it, it conjured the happy times. The wonderful memories. It was madness, but as the days since she had last seen him stretched to weeks, thanks to this little sketch and despite the endless miles she could sense him and she took comfort from that. Thanks to this little sketch he was never too far away.

The door cracked open and Millie's dark head slipped in before she had time to hide her box. 'I am worried about you.'

'There really is no need…' Briskly she closed the lid and was about to slide it under the bed when her eldest stared at it.

'What is that?'

'Just a present. From a friend.'

'Pietro?'

Hearing his name on her daughter's lips shocked her. Since her return she had only ever mentioned him in passing and always as the Duca della Torizia. 'Er…'

Her daughter sighed and held her gaze. 'I know all about him, Mama… Aunt Alexandra told me you had a little romance while you were gone.' Lilian was going to strangle her cousin when she next saw her. 'I am happy for you… You deserve a life of your own after all your years of work.'

'It was more a friendship than a romance, Millie. We had a great deal in common. Especially art.' She hoped she sounded matter of fact.

'Aunt Alexandra said you loved him and he broke your heart…'

'What nonsense!'

'Is it?' Millie's expression was full of sympathy and understanding. 'It would explain why you are so withdrawn and weepy.' So much for hiding her emotions under her stiff upper lip. 'You are not yourself, Mama. We are all worried about you.'

Did they all know about her indiscretion? The thought of them knowing and politely saying nothing mortified her because it was so… English and so humiliating. 'I suppose Alexandra has gossiped about me to the entire family behind my back.'

'No. Just me. She took me aside before she left and told me to look after you and I swear I have not told a soul. Not even my husband. But they all suspect something is amiss.' Her daughter came to sit beside her on the mattress. 'Is it true? Did you love him?'

'It is impossible to fall in love in just six weeks, Millie.' She wouldn't cry in front of her. Wouldn't allow Millie to see all the hurt and the pain and the hopelessness.

'I fell completely in love with Cassius in less.'

'Yes…but you are young and have your whole life ahead of you.'

'Is that how you see it? That I am young and you are an old crone in the twilight of her years? Because I don't. I should like to think I will be just as happy in two decades' time with my man as I am now. I know you loved Father. Don't you want that sort of closeness again with someone? A person to love and grow old with?'

'I have responsibilities. My family… The Foundation…'

'You once told me to live my life for me and not continually for others. You said I was too selfless and too generous of heart for my own good… That was good advice. Advice I shall now spin back to you. Because if I am selfless and too generous of heart, it is because I am exactly like you—so I know that there is room in your heart for another and nobody deserves happiness more than you. Your children and the Foundation are all coping perfectly well without you. You were an excellent mother. An excellent wife and the most dedicated and hard-working advocate of the Foundation—but it is your turn now. If you love this man, please don't allow your misguided loyalties to everyone else get in the way of your happiness. We sent you to Rome for that express purpose. If you go back there, we will all be nothing but happy for you.'

'I shan't be going back there. My relationship with Pietro is over. It was a mutual decision.' She brushed it aside as if it was no matter, while deep down the pain of it clawed mercilessly in her chest. 'I am sad, of course I am, perhaps even a little weepy thanks to fatigue—but life moves on. Besides... I do have some plans of my own. I have been thinking of opening a small shop selling art.'

She watched the indecision about how to proceed play on her daughter's expression and, like a coward, Lilian hoped she would choose that easier path rather than probe deeper into the cause of her heartbreak and thus make her lie through her teeth. 'You have always had a love of art.'

She suppressed the urge to sag in relief at the welcome change of topic. 'I have and Rome re-awakened it.' Alongside all sorts of other things which she had forgotten along the way. Like what it felt to love a man completely and feel loved in return—even if his love wasn't as deep as hers. The loss of him now felt like a void. A big, gaping, empty chasm which would take an eternity to heal over. 'There are plenty of gal-leries in the city selling the Great Masters, so I thought I would champion the new talents. Give them an outlet to show their work and help them find a clientele for it.' Lose herself in work just as he did in the hope it would dis-tract her from the sadness.

'Is that what the picture in the box is all about? Is it the work of a talented new artist you wish to champion?'

'Not exactly.'

'Can I see it—or is it intensely private to you and Pietro?' She saw the stubborn challenge in her daughter's pretty face and knew she could potentially hang herself with her response. If she was determined to act blasé about their affair, then she needed to show it in her deeds as well as her words.

'Of course you can see it.' The nonchalant smile felt awkward on her lips as she gestured to the box, the contents of which were intensely personal to her and Pietro. In a roundabout way, it had brought them together and it was all she had left of him now they were done. Watching Millie flip the small latch and lift the lid, then gaze at the figure of Christ from the centre of *The Last Judgement.* Trying not to recall how the first time she had seen it in Pietro's office, he had made mad, passionate love to her on his desk. 'It is a preliminary sketch for a piece of the fresco in the Sistine Chapel.'

'It is beautiful… Who is the artist?'

'Michelangelo.'

'Michel…' Millie's mouth hung slack. 'He gave you a Michelangelo?'

'Pietro is much too generous and he slipped it into my luggage without me knowing, else I never would have allowed him to part with such a precious thing.'

'I don't understand… And I do not wish to be insulting, Mama, but why would he part with something so…rare and valuable based on such a short acquaintance?'

How could she tell her daughter they had

been more than acquaintances without letting on they had indulged in an intensely physical, passionate and scandalous relationship? 'We visited the Sistine Chapel together to see the original...'

She was about to babble. To over-embellish as she watched her daughter's eyes fix on the note. Read the solitary fragment of text in his flamboyant, sloping handwriting.

Lilian felt her cheeks heat. 'He had four sketches in total. But this was the one I most admired, so this was the one he decided to give me.'

'To remember him by.'

'Yes.' Lilian pasted what she had intended to be an over-bright smile on her face, supremely conscious it was more of a grimace. 'Isn't it lovely?'

'A tourist's watercolour of Rome would be lovely. The beautiful box he put it in would be lovely. But I am fairly certain a Michelangelo is significant, Mama. He must love you very much.'

She waved that away, feeling choked by the tight bands of tension squeezing her throat at the painful reminder he simply did not love her enough. 'We had a mutual love of Renaissance art. That is all.' In the distance, the ominous sounds of thunder seemed eerily apt. The heavens knew she was a liar and were not afraid to call it. Her daughter undoubtedly knew it, too, but might allow her the charade regardless.

'He knew I loved Michelangelo above all others and, because he is a stubbornly generous man, he gifted me one. It is a lovely gesture.' Too lovely. Too intensely personal. Significant in the extreme. 'Although goodness only knows what I am going to do with it. I would be too nervous to hang it on the wall in this part of London and I really do not want to loan it to a museum.' Babble, babble. Trying to steer the conversation away from her foolish heart—just as Pietro had done with her so many times. 'It has been bothering me since I discovered it. That is probably why I haven't mentioned it.'

'Probably.' Millie reached out and squeezed her hand. 'Because it couldn't possibly mean that the sight of it reminds you too much of Pietro or you are determined to hide your feelings from us and carry on regardless as if nothing has happened in case we are scandalised by the thought of our mother in another man's arms.'

'That, too.' Lilian stared down at their joined

hands in defeat. 'It is ridiculous for a woman of my age to be pining for a man she cannot have.'

'Why can't you have him?'

'It was not meant to be. His life is there. Mine is here. All much too complicated.'

'But if you love each other...?'

Lilian shook her head and turned away so her clever daughter wouldn't see the truth, closing the ornate box decisively like a chapter in a book. A fitting analogy. It was a different story, incongruous with her character, which did not fit in the predetermined plot of her life. 'It wasn't meant to be, Millie. Let us leave it at that.'

She heard her sigh as more thunder rumbled. Closer this time. Like trouble brewing. 'I suppose we will have to if you refuse to confide in me. But if you should change your mind, I would like to listen.'

'I won't.' At least she hoped she wouldn't. As the mother, it was her job to be the rock. The shoulder to cry on. Not the weeping mess who was broken and lost and thoroughly defeated. 'And, Millie... I would prefer not to hear his name spoken again.'

Self-preservation.

Cowardice.

Reluctantly her daughter nodded, then stood. 'If that is what you truly want.'

'I do.'

'Mama?' Lottie's head suddenly appeared through the gap in the door. 'There is a man downstairs demanding an audience with you. A furious one. He says his name is Pietro...'

Chapter Twenty-Four

They kept him waiting in the hallway. Even though he had given them his calling card which had his illustrious and ancient title emblazoned upon it alongside the family crest and despite looking every inch the aristocratic gentleman he was in his fine clothes. Although he had never put much stock in his bloodline, it occurred to him as he stood there, dripping on the floor, that not once in all the years he had been the Duca della Torizia, or even before, had anyone ever made him wait by the front door like a common criminal. As angry as he was, Pietro quite admired that.

Especially as he had just seen what lay outside the Fairclough Foundation. Lilian did not live in the fashionable part of London. She lived on the very edge of the slums and those streets were dangerous. It made him feel better knowing she had people looking out for her.

Not that he was enjoying their hostile scrutiny. Neither could he return it with hostility or disdain. These three men were Lilian's family. The one currently stood glaring at him, arms folded, whose eyes eerily resembled his mother's, must be her son—Silas. One of the twins, he recalled. Brother to Millie, the only one of her family he had briefly seen at Lady Fentree's in December. As the head of the family Silas was flanked by two men he assumed were her sons-in-law. Both were as tall as he. One dark. One blond. Jasper and Cassius— husbands to Lottie and Millie respectively— although he had no idea which was which. In all their conversations about her family, Lilian had never discussed anything as mundane as hair colour. He knew one was a former soldier and one did something involving trains. Neither appeared to the sort to mess with—but mess with them he would if it came to it because he was in no mood to be trifled with. Three weeks of being royally furious and desperately lonely, combined with the hundreds of miles he had travelled to get here, had worn his patience scarily thin.

'What business do you have with my mother?'

He returned Silas's glare blandly despite wanting to bellow and gesticulate like a Roman market trader who had been short-changed. 'We have things to discuss.' It would do him no favours to alienate the fellow now. Not when he would need to get on with him later. 'Important things.'

Which was exactly when he expected things to get interesting. Because if she thought for one second she could send him packing, citing his promise never to contact her again or any nonsense about their affair being done, then she had another think coming. He had things to say. A great many things. And the only way he was leaving this house this afternoon was with *his* ring on *her* finger.

He heard a noise on the landing and felt a shift in the air, and there she was. Looking lovely. Shocked and a little pale. She looked tired, too, and the sight of those dark shadows under her eyes gave him hope. They wouldn't be there if she was sleeping well and if she wasn't sleeping, he sincerely prayed he was the reason—because neither had he. It turned out he had lost the ability to sleep soundly without her comforting body stretched out beside him.

'Pietro…?' Behind her, her two daughters flanked her like sentries. Her pregnant daughter-in-law seemed to have taken root in the doorway. Six strange pairs of eyes were staring at them both.

'Hello, Lilian. We need to talk, I think— and before you say we really don't, let me assure you we *really* do.' He stared at her levelly, knowing she knew him well enough to read between the lines. 'I would prefer to do that in private, *cara*.'

But if she refused, he was fully prepared to say it all here in front of their audience. If ritual humiliation was what it took, then so be it.

'Er… Yes… Of course.' Her foot stumbled on the stairs and she caught herself, although not before four pairs of male feet started forward, then stopped dead to look each other up and down.

'We can talk in my office.' She swallowed, remembering another office when she had been all alone with him, then gave a tremulous smile to her family. 'Perhaps you could all wait in the parlour?'

A request which seemed to anger her son. 'I do not…' His sister Millie grabbed his sleeve, the image of her mother, her eyes flicked to Pietro's briefly and he realised she knew about them. Was even, perhaps, on his side?

'They really do *need* to talk, Silas.'

Her brother frowned at the unspoken message in her gaze. 'As I suspect do we, Sister.' He turned to Pietro, his piercing gaze narrowed once more. 'I shall keep the door ajar, Mama. If you need me, just call.'

Lilian gestured down the hallway and the men parted to allow him through, and they walked in silence. Once inside the tiny little room, she closed the door and looked at him with such wariness, it frightened him. For the last three weeks he had been a man on a mission, so determined to propose he hadn't considered quite what he would do if she refused him. Her expression made him consider it now, as did the stark distance she had put between them in such a confined space. Both rendered him temporarily speechless.

'What are you doing here?'

'You left.' His voice cracked as emotion leaked. 'You never said goodbye.'

'I wrote a letter.'

'Don't I deserve more than a letter, Lilian? Don't we?'

She blinked. Glanced down at her feet. 'Saying goodbye would have hurt too much.'

'Waking up in an empty bed hurt more, I can assure you.'

'I am sorry… It was cowardly… I…'

'I love you, Lilian.'

'But...' He watched her swallow and blink.

His declaration surprised her... Yet it shouldn't have because he had said it before. That last night. He knew he had. He had told her he loved her and wanted to grow old with her...

In his mother tongue. A language she didn't understand.

Idiota!

'I told you exactly what I felt that night. Clearly badly, else you would know I wanted you to stay. But you left and my heart broke, so I am here. Because I cannot bear the thought of never seeing you again.' He reached out and took her hand, his heart breaking a little more when she tugged it away. She stared down at the floor again rather than look at him.

'I cannot be your occasional mistress, Pietro... I am not built for affairs...'

He tipped up her chin with his finger and forced her eyes to lock with his. 'Neither am I...any longer.'

'I don't understand...'

'Ti amo molto... Sei il grande amore della mia vita... Voglio invecchiare con te... Mi vuoi sposare?'

She shrugged, baffled, her lovely eyes swimming with tears. 'I am only fluent in the gestures, Pietro.'

He nodded. 'I believe the gesture for this is universal, *cara*.'

He dropped to his knee and rifled in his pocket for the ring. Tried not to panic or to say the words in a jumbled tumble as her mouth hung slack.

He repeated himself in English this time. Very slowly for both their sakes. 'I said I love you, Lilian. You are the love of my life and I want to grow old with you. Marry me, *cara*.'

Her silence made him rush on. 'I know I've been a fool. A nightmare, even…but I had it in my head that commitment meant I was trapped, when with you the opposite is true. I have spent my life feeling restless. Feeling like something was missing, but could never quite put my finger on what that something was. I filled the void with work and meaningless affairs, yet none of that chased the restlessness away. Then you came along and it went. I felt…content for the first time in my life. Complete. The moment I met you, it all slotted into place. But I denied the truth to myself over and over. I thought it was just about lust…but it wasn't. Thought it was simply art or friendship which bound us…but it wasn't that either. I tried not to fall in love with you, tried to let you go when you ended our affair and tried repeatedly to tell myself I would get over it once you left until it came to the time I had to say goodbye. Then I had an epiphany. I realised you were what was missing, Lilian. You were what was missing all along and I have simply spent my whole life waiting for you to come into it. *Ti amo, cara.*'

'You love me?'

'In a nutshell.' She laughed at his attempt at her accent and swiped a tear from her cheek. 'Do you love me?' He held his breath, feeling unsteady, then hopeful, then back to unsure again. 'I know I can never replace Henry... I know I am not the love of your life, but...'

'I do. You are.'

'I do not understand.'

'It turns out it *is* entirely possible to have more than one great love, Pietro. It's why I ran. I lost my heart to you somewhere in Rome and then couldn't bear the thought of not being everything to you—because you were already everything to me. I've been a mess without you.' Her fingers went to her chest as a solitary tear trickled down her cheek. 'You are my soulmate.'

Relief made him laugh, too. He felt drunk. Giddy. 'Then you will marry me?'

'I will.'

His hand shook a little as he held out his ring. The pretty antique had called to him and he had paid an absolute fortune for it without haggling for the first time in his life. Couldn't muster the enthusiasm to care because it was perfect.

'Because I know you love a bit of history, my darling, and mostly because my father pawned all the family jewels so I had no Venturi heirloom to give you, I had to find an appropriate engagement ring, else I would have been here sooner. A man only proposes once in his life and I wanted to do it properly. As soon as I saw this, I thought of you. I knew it was the one…' The glittering emerald cabochon had reminded him of her eyes. The diamonds surrounding it the stars they had gazed at before their first morning when he realised, now, he had fallen hopelessly in love. 'It's a puzzle ring… Called a gimmel ring, actually…and made in the Renaissance…obviously.' It was her favourite period, so no other would have done. 'And because you know I love a bit of theatre…' He clicked the ring apart and she gasped to see it was now two interlocking bands—the emerald on one and the diamonds on the other. 'The two separate rings symbolise two people—like us—both unique and free to do as they please, but locked together for ever to create the perfect whole—like us.' He pointed to the tiny secret hollow compartment beneath the emerald. 'Carved here are the clasped *fede* hands of ancient Rome—the symbol of betrothal which has survived through the ages.'

'From old Amedeo's fresco.'

He nodded, not being able to stop himself from kissing her hand before he twisted the rings back together. 'But this is my favourite part.' He laid it flat on his outstretched palm. 'Read the Latin inscription, *cara*.' It had been the inscription which had sold it to him. The inscription which would have made him part with every *scudi* in his purse if he'd had to.

'*Omnia vincit amor.*' Her voice was a whisper as she gazed down at him in awe.

'*Sì... Amore mio...*' He slipped the ring on to her finger next to her old wedding band which he would never ask her to remove, then kissed them both, accepting both her past and their future while marvelling at the lack of panic or fear he felt at the complicated, unbendable commitment it promised. 'Love conquers all.'

'It is perfect.'

'You are perfect and I am a fool for not realising it sooner or listening to my heart because my thick, stubborn head refused to hear it.'

He stood and pulled her into his arms. As he kissed her, for the first time since she'd left, the world seemed to suddenly spin on its correct axis again. The floor beneath his feet became steady. The path ahead miraculously straight and sure once more. Even the grey London sky and the storm outside the window seemed to become sunrise. One more beautiful than the sunrise of their first morning together because this one held the promise of many mornings. Every morning and he couldn't wait for all of them. He deepened the kiss and they staggered backwards, knocking something from her desk. Neither cared as it clattered to the floor. Neither noticed till the door flew open.

'What the hell is going on?'

All six of them spilled into the tiny space, filling it completely, some baffled, some smiling and one glaring because he was the head of the family and a strange man was embracing his mother with deliciously over-familiar impertinence.

Still smiling and clutching his lapel, Lilian held out her hand for them to see the ring. 'Quite unexpectedly, it appears I am engaged.' Then she beamed at all of her grown-up children's stunned faces and ran her palm lovingly over his. 'I suppose I should probably introduce you all to my handsome new fiancé... Everybody, this is Pietro.' She sighed as her lovely eyes locked with his. 'The second love of my life.'

Epilogue

Despite all her previous experience of parenthood and running the Foundation, her patience was taxed to its limit. 'Henry—give it back now!'

But her four-year-old grandson was intent on remaining selectively deaf in the absence of Silas and his mother, torturing the girls by swinging the pretty little rag dolls Lilian had bought for them this morning by their legs around his head. His sister, Anne, two years his junior, was shrieking in outrage at the top of her lungs, determined to alert the whole neighbourhood to the injustice, while her two-year-old cousin Lily—the mirror image of Millie at the same age—stumbled after him, arms outstretched like it was the best game in the world.

Because her grandchildren were not making her suffer enough, three-year-old George, the only child who actually lived in this madhouse and had the same rebellious and wilful nature as his mother, Lottie, had used the chaos to slip unsupervised into the kitchen and find the honey.

Or at least Lilian assumed the sticky mess daubed across his chubby face and in his hair was honey.

He had also let his puppy out of the dining room. She knew this because at least one of Millie's dratted cats was hissing and snarling at him as he whimpered terrified in the hallway. Although knowing those cats, they could all be ganging up on the poor thing. Circling him to torment him as they had done earlier. But she had to fight the fights she could win first. Which meant it was dolls first, dog second and sticky honey last of all because that was going to be the most problematic.

'Henry!' She lunged as the boy ran past and scooped him wriggling into her arms, reminding her so much of her own son at this age. Silas had always been a headstrong handful. 'I shall take those, young man.' She prised the first doll out of his clenched fist and held it out to his screaming sister, who miraculously stopped screaming to gloat at him as if she had won the battle without having to lift a finger.

'Send him to bed, Grandma!' Already Anne was a bossy little minx who had her father's quick, logical brain and used it with the warped logic which only a small child could.

'I've a good mind to send the lot of you to bed with no supper, young lady. What was all that carrying on about?' Lilian lowered her thwarted and frowning grandson to the ground before placing the second doll in her namesake's outstretched arms. Little Lily giggled and hugged the doll close, then hugged Henry, his behaviour already forgotten. She had her mother's generous and loving nature. Too good-hearted and even-tempered. Just like Millie.

'Go sit on the sofa, all of you, while I see to George.' Who absolutely had to be dunked in the bathtub first before his parents came home and saw what a mess she was making of looking after their house. Lottie and Jasper ran a tight ship. Not a chaotic one.

Not that she had imagined for one second she would be watching all four of her grandchildren, one puppy and six cats all on her own this evening when she had graciously volunteered her services while their parents went out. That would teach her for being such a selfless and generous soul. She would only have herself to blame if it were not for the inescapable fact she had foolishly assumed there would be two pairs of eyes watching the Fairclough menagerie this evening. But her soulmate had apparently disappeared over an hour ago without a word, the wretch, and she hadn't seen hide nor hair of him since.

No wonder he'd had a mischievous glint in his eyes. She was going to kill him when he finally decided to show his irritatingly handsome face.

She had scrubbed the worst of the mess from George as she heard the sounds of stamping feet outside the back door.

'It's snowing again.' Lottie bustled into the parlour carrying a pile of wrapped packages, fresh from her expedition to Bond Street for some last-minute Christmas shopping before they left for Alexandra's tomorrow. Behind her trailed a similarly laden Millie and Mary. Both her daughters and her beloved daughter-in-law had bright pink cheeks from the cold.

'Is it? I hadn't noticed.' Largely because she hadn't stopped in hours.

She watched the ladies shrug out of their coats. Millie scooped up little Lily and snuggled her in her lap while Lottie fetched one of the tangled towels Lilian had hastily discarded to deal with the riot leaving to fetch them in the first place had caused, waddling slightly as she approached the tub to assist with her son George.

Having had a set of them herself, and by the enormous size of her pregnant belly, she suspected her daughter was carrying twins, but hadn't mentioned it in case the prospect of twins turned her ever-efficient and terminally organised son-in-law Jasper into a sergeant major. He would drive everyone mad planning for the event, when she knew first hand there really was no planning with twins. With two babies, even the best-laid plans were doomed to fail. You did what you could and embraced the chaos the rest of the time. Something her impetuous daughter would take in her stride—and so would poor Jasper once it was a fait accompli. There seemed little point in panicking him on just a suspicion and kinder to everyone not to say it.

One thing was certain, whether it was twins

or not, another baby would certainly curb their travelling in the next few years. Since their marriage, and since Lilian had moved to Italy, she had relieved them of the Foundation once a year for two months so they could explore all the far-flung places they had always wanted to visit. Their recent trip to visit Silas and Mary in Baltimore would be the last one for a while. Travelling with three young children anywhere beyond Hyde Park would take more planning than even the diligent Jasper was capable of. But perhaps they would surprise her—as her family so often did. Nothing much fazed the Faircloughs.

She could pat herself on the back for that at least. She had raised a fine family alongside the Foundation. If Henry was looking down on them, she knew he would be proud of the people their three children had become and prouder still of the lives they had made for themselves. His beloved Foundation was flourishing in Lottie's capable hands.

It had been odd taking over at the helm of the Foundation again. As each year passed, and her old life was overtaken by her new, Lilian had forgotten how all-consuming it could be. But then, all vocations were all-consuming, whether they be charitable foundations or art galleries. Except juggling the Foundation and the new Venturi gallery in London as well as the original one in Rome from a distance was nowhere near as easy as she had first assumed it might be. But it was good to be busy and it was always nice in December when they all gathered together for Christmas. It was the only time in the whole year when all her family were under the same roof altogether. A tradition which they had happily all adhered to, no matter how busy they all were.

'Why is there honey all over the kitchen floor?' Jasper came in laden with still more packages and looking confused. Beside him was Silas, ineffectually trying to dab a lump of the stuff from the hem of his trousers with his handkerchief, then groaning when he started to sneeze and realised he no longer had a clean handkerchief to sneeze into.

'Did you have to bring those blasted cats, Millie?'

'Where we go, the cats go, Silas. They always come here when we visit Lottie—and she certainly has no problem with them. Just because you have made your annual pilgrimage across the Atlantic to grace us with your presence doesn't mean we have to change what we are all used to simply to accommodate you.'

And that was another problem with twins. In Lilian's experience, hers had bickered all the time. But then obviously Silas and Millie weren't identical and perhaps identical twins were more forgiving of one another. Hers were each other's fiercest critics and biggest champions. Always had been. She had given up trying to mediate a long time ago, as had both their spouses.

'Speaking of the cats…it might be prudent if you go rescue your dog, Jasper. The last I heard they were terrorising him in the hallway.'

Her son-in-law simply rolled his eyes, smiling, and strode away, his limp not quite as pronounced as it had once been. He had mellowed somewhat since he had married Lottie and he ran the Foundation alongside his own successful engineering business with a precision Lilian envied. Now that he was home from his holiday, having travelled back on the exact same Cunard steamship which had brought her son and his family back, too, doubtless he would have the place shipshape again in no time. With his talent for organising everyone and everything and Lottie's exuberant enthusiasm, they made a phenomenal team, complementing each other's characters despite being total opposites.

But as they were still hopelessly in love, their many differences had never seemed to matter.

'Come and help me clean up the honey.' Millie handed her toddling daughter to Lilian to bathe and threaded her hand through her brother's arm. Their disagreements never lasted long and, because they were now separated by thousands of miles, they both treasured their time together.

Her eldest daughter adored being mistress of Falconmore. She was a natural mother and had a great way with people. Now that her husband, Cassius, was heavily involved with Parliament, using his title and influence to bring about health reform, that useful characteristic had come into its own. After years of dogged campaigning, the government looked increasingly likely to pass the first ever public health act. The reluctant Lord Falconmore was one of the peers drafting the bill and he was relentless in his belief that people from whatever station in life should have access to clean water, cleaner streets and proper sanitation. The new legislation would make some concession to the cause, but nowhere near enough for Cassius. But as she and Millie often stated, it was a start, and just the start was momentous in itself. From little acorns…

That had certainly been the case with Silas.

The restlessness of his youth was now chan-
nelled into his extremely successful business
in the United States. The Baltimore Southern
Railway had made him a fortune—largely
due to the new steam engine it had developed.
Aside from being richer than any of them, Silas
and Mary were now the talk of Baltimore society. She was still shunned by her family here,
of course, but had come to terms with it since
having little Henry. Thankfully, she was still in
contact with her sister and would visit her this
Christmas just as she had for the last few years.

Cassius was the last to arrive, shaking the
snow off his coat and gratefully taking the
tea Millie handed him. All the children were
bathed now and Lottie and Mary were about
to put them to bed.

'Where is my husband?'

As everyone else was accounted for, she had
assumed hers had crept off to join his titled son-
in-law at his club. Cassius had gone there on
business—to garner more support for his lofty
reforms. Hers would claim he was also there
on business. The business of charming potential clients and selling the spectacular Raphael
he had just taken delivery of only yesterday.
Because many English aristocrats, it turned
out, were as impoverished as the Italian ones

and were increasingly eager to discreetly sell off their treasures in order to fix their leaking roofs.

However, she knew if he had sought out Cassius in his club, it would be to play billiards. The latest in a long line of simple pleasures he thoroughly immersed himself in.

'I haven't seen him. Not since this morning at any rate.'

'Then where is he?' Worry started to replace irritation. 'He left over an hour ago without saying a word.' And it was getting late. Very dark outside. Big flakes of snow were falling steadily beyond the window.

She had taken to pacing when he finally walked in grinning, clearly pleased with himself for something and entirely oblivious of the fact she had been worried sick.

'Nonno!' Henry barrelled into him first, closely followed by George and Anne, with little Lily pulling up the rear. He bounced each child vigorously, to each of their great delights, reminding Lilian it had been his bouncing which had created all the earlier chaos in the first place, before he had disappeared and left her to the cats and the honey.

'Stop bouncing them. They are about to go to bed.'

He met her warning glare with a typically Italian shrug. '*Bambini* need to be bounced. I am sure that is written in stone somewhere.' Then he directed them all to their parents and bent to kiss her on the cheek.

'Where have you been?'

'Did you miss me, *cara*?' He never squandered an opportunity to flirt.

'I was worried about you. One minute you were here and the next gone.'

'I was arranging a little surprise for you.'

Knowing Pietro, he probably was. As thoughtful as he was, she was still miffed. 'I would have preferred you here…to help with the children like we promised.'

'No, *cara*…you promised. The first I heard of it was this afternoon and, as I had already made plans, I had to slip out.' Then he grinned, his dark eyes dancing with mischief. 'Put your coat on, *cara*. I am taking you out.'

'Not tonight, Pietro… I am tired.' Exhausted, in fact. Running around after four boisterous children when you were half a century old was no mean feat. But while she currently felt every one of her fifty years this evening, her incorrigible husband never seemed to age a bit. Aside from the solitary flash of silver in his black hair—a flash of silver which only served to make him look more dashing, dratted man— he looked just as he had when she had first met him all those Christmases ago.

'But you have to come outside, Lilian. Your surprise is there.' He took her hand and tugged her smiling towards the door. 'Indulge me.'

Still a little annoyed and most definitely tired, she allowed him to help her on with her coat. Then, because he couldn't resist a bit of theatre, he covered her eyes as he led her out into the street.

The chilly night air caught her by surprise, the fresh snow crunching under her feet and melting as it fell on to her cheeks. 'Are you ready?'

'Yes…'

He removed his hands and she stared. 'It's a carriage.'

'But not just any carriage. Don't you recognise it, *cara*?'

She stared at it again and, not seeing any clue or livery, shook her head. 'No.'

He tutted, then opened the door with a flourish, solicitously helping her in before squeezing himself close on the seat next to her. The inside had been warmed. He wrapped a thick blanket over her legs and then knocked on the roof, smiling at her as it lurched forward.

'Where are we going?'

'Do you know what day it is?'

'It's Thursday.'

'And the date?'

'The eighth of December.'

'And what happened on the eighth of December?'

She shrugged again. 'I genuinely have no idea.'

'Then, seeing as you like a bit of history, I shall tell you. At around this time on the eighth of December, in the year 1842, the wickedly handsome Duca della Torizia found himself alone in this very carriage with a mysterious and very beautiful lady.'

'This very carriage?'

He smiled at her obvious surprise. 'I had it sent down from Alexandra's stable.'

'Even though we are going there tomorrow?'

'But tomorrow is not tonight and it is tonight that is significant. Therefore, tonight shall be just you, me, the quiet road and the carriage where it all started.' He kissed her hand, then rearranged her wedding rings to sit straight. 'I even made sure she sent it with the exact same driver. The devil, *amore mio*, is always in the detail. The snow is courtesy of God, though. I had no say in that, but I am grateful for his efforts none the less.'

'Do you intend to recreate our journey from Lady Fentree's to Alexandra's tonight? It will be dawn before we get there and it *is* snowing…' He placed a finger over her lips to silence her.

'Not every detail has to be exact. Especially, as I recall, we never paid much attention to the actual road during that fateful journey, thank goodness, therefore I have taken a few liberties with the location. I have a particularly quiet road in mind which leads to a particularly quiet and shockingly romantic inn.' He smiled, those dark eyes she adored with all her heart dancing with mischief and promise. 'But I digress… I was telling you a story about a handsome duke.'

'And his mystery lady.'

'Indeed… She intrigued him.'

'Did she?'

'He flirted.'

'Did he?' Lilian slipped her arm through his and snuggled against him. The most vexing part of her husband was that she could never stay mad at him for long. Or resist him when he was being so thoroughly charming and intent on seduction. 'I don't suppose you remember what he said to her that fateful night?' Because she knew he would and she wanted to hear the words again. His beautifully accented deep voice still had the power to thoroughly disarm her.

'Signora Venturi…you have such beautiful eyes…' He stared deeply into them, tracing the pad of one finger gently down her cheek and making her skin tingle again like the first time he had touched her half a decade ago. 'For some reason they have always called to me…'

Then his lips whispered over hers and everything—the carriage, the snow, all her myriad responsibilities, all the noise of her boisterous family, her tiredness, even the insignificant road which led to a particularly quiet and shockingly romantic inn—everything but him disappeared as she lost herself in his kiss all over again.

* * * * *

MILLS & BOON

Coming next month

STOLEN BY THE VIKING
Michelle Willingham

'I am Breanne Ó Callahan,' she answered. 'My foster father is King Feann MacPherson of Killcobar.'

'I know who he is.' He turned at that moment, and his gaze fixed upon her. 'I recognised you the moment I saw you. And you are worth more than a slave.'

'How could you possibly know me?' she demanded. 'I would have remembered you.' Heat flared in her cheeks when she realised what she'd said. But it was too late to take back the words. Breanne tightened her grip upon the drying cloth, and in that heated moment, she grew aware of his interest. He studied her face, his gaze drifting downward to linger upon her body. There was no denying that he wanted her.

But worse was her own response. She was caught up in his blue eyes and the dark hair that framed a strong, lean face. There was a slight scar on his chin, but it did nothing to diminish his looks. The *Lochlannach* warrior was tall and imposing, his physical strength evident. Only the slight limp revealed any weakness.

'What do you want from me? A ransom?'

He reached out and cupped the back of her neck. It was an act of possession, but instead of feeling furious, his sudden dominance made her flesh warm to the touch. His blue eyes stared into hers as if he desired her, and she was startled by the unbidden response. Though she tried to meet his gaze with resentment, her imagination conjured up the vision of his mouth descending upon hers in a kiss. This warrior would not be gentle…no, he would claim what he wanted from her. Heat roared through her, and she thought of his hands moving down to pull her hips against his.

That might be what he wanted from her, after all. She was well aware of how female slaves were used as concubines. The thought shamed her, but another part of her was intrigued by this man. She could not deny the forbidden attraction, and she had the strange sensation that his touch would not be unwelcome.

As if to make his point, Alarr stroked the nape of her neck before releasing her. 'You will remain with me at all times, obeying everything I ask. If you do this, then I will remove your bindings.'

'When?' she demanded.

'When you have earned my trust. Not before.'

Continue reading
STOLEN BY THE VIKING
Michelle Willingham

Available next month
www.millsandboon.co.uk

COMING SOON!

We really hope you enjoyed reading this book. If you're looking for more romance, be sure to head to the shops when new books are available on

Thursday 20th March

To see which titles are coming soon, please visit

millsandboon.co.uk/nextmonth

LET'S TALK

Romance

For exclusive extracts, competitions
and special offers, find us online:

facebook.com/millsandboon

@MillsandBoon

@MillsandBoonUK

Get in touch on 01413 063232